Praise for C

Married by Monday

"A really fantastic and brilliant read."
~ Romancing the Book

"Engaging tale of true love, danger, sacrifice, and happiness."
~ Reading Between the Wines, 5 Wine Glasses

"Heartwarming romance."
~ Harlequin Junkie Top Pick

Wife by Wednesday

#1 Amazon Bestseller
New York Times Bestseller
USA Today Bestseller
Wall Street Journal Bestseller

"An enchanting and titillating modern-day fairy tale romance that hooks the reader from page one and doesn't let go." ~ #1 Indie Reader Bestseller, 5 Stars

"You will find a fun and sizzling romance, great characters that trade verbal spars like fist punches..."
~ Sizzling Hot Book Reviews Read of the Month

"Catherine has a simply delicious, sexy sense of writing style and I am adding her to my list of future reads." ~ Romancing the Book, 5 Stars

"The story is full and the pacing is perfect, filled with ups and downs for this new couple."
~ I Just Wanna Sit Here and Read

"Ms. Bybee has brought to life two engaging characters, a conniving villain and a series of obstacles, which leave you turning the pages with eager anticipation to find out what happens next."
~ Happily Ever After Reviews, 4½ Stars

"The chemistry between Sam and Blake just oozes between every line." ~ Coffee Time Romance, 4 Cups

Binding Vows
"Such an amazing book...possibly the best I have read so far this year...so much fun..." ~ Bitten by Books

Silent Vows
"A fascinating time-travel tale of ancient Druids and modern heroes that pulls the reader in from the very first page."
~ Affaire de Coeur, 5 stars

Redeeming Vows
"As in the first two stories, the plot comes together with danger, suspense, romance, and the author's own blend of humor." ~ The Romance Studio, 5 Hearts

Before the Moon Rises
"*Before the Moon Rises* has earned the distinction of being one of the top e-books I've come across..."
~ Nights and Weekends

"A page-turning mix of fast cars, sexy shapeshifters, and paranormal suspense."
~ Caridad Pinero, *New York Times* bestselling author

Embracing the Wolf
"Richard and Kate's story was so intoxicating. I was so deliriously drunk on their instantaneous chemistry."
~ Romance in the Backseat

Married by Monday

Also by Catherine Bybee

Contemporary Romance

Weekday Bride Series

Wife by Wednesday

Married by Monday

Not Quite Series

Not Quite Dating

Paranormal Romance

MacCoinnich Time Travels

Binding Vows

Silent Vows

Redeeming Vows

Highland Shifter

The Ritter Werewolves Series

Before the Moon Rises

Embracing the Wolf

Novellas

Soul Mate

Possessive

Erotica

Kilt Worthy

Kilt-A-Licious

CATHERINE BYBEE

Married by Monday

Book Two in The Weekday Brides Series

Married by Monday

Contact Information: catherinebybee.com

Cover Art by Crystal Posey
Visit Catherine at www.catherinebybee.com

Publishing History:
First Edition published in 2011.
Second Edition published by Montlake Romance in 2013.

ISBN-13: 9781611099089
ISBN-10: 1611099080

This one is for my mom, who passed on to me her love of reading romance novels. I love you!

Chapter One

Getting married every single year was becoming a pain in the ass. Especially for the maid of honor.

"I really didn't think he was serious about a yearly wedding." Eliza Havens fiddled with the edges of the yellow chiffon bridesmaid dress, which had entirely too many yards of material. The damn thing belonged on a slow-talking Southern belle, complete with parasol and white ribbons, not on her as she stood up for her best friend—again.

"It's romantic," Gwen offered.

"It's stupid."

Samantha and Blake were going on two years of marriage and already had little Eddie. At first, when Blake announced he was going to marry Sam every year on their anniversary in a different state, Eliza had thought it was sweet. Now, after a full week of non-stop wedding planning, she and Gwen, Blake's sister, were sweating it out in San Antonio planning their big Texas-themed wedding. Except, Gwen was English and entirely misguided about Texas. Where there should be cowboy hats and Western-flavor attire, everything had turned South. Deep South. More like a scene from *Gone With the Wind* than *Dallas*.

"Don't fret, Eliza. They won't all be this grand." It had taken some time to get used to Gwen's British accent, but Eliza was used to it now.

"I'm not fretting. I'm *pissing* and *moaning*. Get it right! Do you have any idea how hot these dresses are going to be outside in the smoldering heat?"

Gwen displayed perfect teeth as she smiled. She pivoted in a circle, reached into a large bag from the bridal knickknack store they'd found the day before, and removed two white-and-gold folding lace fans. "I thought of that."

Well, at least it isn't a parasol.

Gwen handed her the fan and turned to the bag again. Out came two perfectly matched frilly umbrellas.

"Ugh! I spoke too soon."

"Excuse me?"

Eliza refrained from rolling her eyes as she reached for the parasol.

Why does it have to be yellow? Nobody wears yellow!

"You don't like them." Gwen's arms dropped, and her excited expression fell.

I hate 'em. "They're very…country." *In a Southern plantation kind of way.* But Eliza couldn't say that to Gwen. Pampered, rich, and completely naive, Gwen meant well. She executed poorly, but did it with a golden heart.

"Isn't that what we're going for—country?"

Eliza opened the sunny umbrella and forced a smile to her lips. "This does say country."

"Splendid. I think we have all we need, then." Oblivious to Eliza's unease, Gwen continued removing small trinkets from her bag—perfectly matching earrings, necklaces, and yes, even ribbons for their hair. Eliza started to think she'd look like a buttercup on top of the cake by the time Gwen was finished. "Oh, look at the time. We need to run," Gwen said.

"I thought we were done."

"We need to make another pass at the ranch and assure Neil that security won't be a problem." Neil, Sam and Blake's personal bodyguard, was built like a brick house, completely immovable if he wanted to stay in place. He smiled so seldom Eliza hadn't known he had teeth until after she'd known him for six months.

"Can't Neil check it out himself?" She was hoping for a cocktail in the hotel bar, followed by a hot bath in the penthouse suite. While in Texas, she was working on finding new clients for Alliance. Men and women. Samantha had founded the elite matchmaking firm and brought Eliza on as full partner after she married Blake. In the past two years, Eliza had recruited over a dozen women and matched three couples. Unlike other matchmaking companies, Alliance matched couples based on their life goals, not for love or a happily ever after. There were men out there who wanted a wife as a status symbol or needed a temporary partner to obtain a job or promotion. In Samantha's case, she and Blake had married because of a mandate in Blake's father's will. As it turned out, the two fell recklessly in love with each other and had Eddie before their first anniversary.

Eliza was always on the lookout for new clients. What better place than Texas, where the men were often rich and the women were perfectly polished and sometimes available.

"You know how difficult Neil can be. I'll need to convince him the paparazzi won't make it past the gates."

The taste of that cocktail was drifting farther away. Eliza reached into her purse and grasped a clip before piling her shoulder-length hair high on her head. The humidity had flattened it to nothing on their earlier excursion. No use pretending her hair would cooperate after more assaulting heat.

"OK, let's go. But I'm driving."

Gwen was used to having a hotel driver taking her wherever she wanted to go. She said she didn't like to drive in the States because of the cars being on the opposite side of the road. Eliza didn't care for the dependence on another driver to get her around, so she'd opted to rent a car.

Thirty minutes later, they were driving down a Texas highway in a compact rental car. The air conditioner running at full speed hardly made a dent in the oppressive heat. Eliza clutched her fist and hit the top of the dashboard. "I don't think the air is working right."

Gwen sat quietly in her seat, using the folding fan she'd bought for the wedding. "It's not far. We'll survive."

Yeah, but the heat was weighing on Eliza's nerves, not to mention her shirt was sticking to the back of the seat. Considering Gwen was from Europe, Eliza was surprised she wasn't full of complaints.

In fact, Gwen hadn't stopped smiling since they'd left the hotel.

Hmmm, she'd have to analyze that.

There was a guard gate on the property. When they approached and Eliza gave them their names, the attendant waved them through. "Mrs. Hawthorn is waiting for y'all," the cowboy said while tipping his hat.

"I love the Texan accent, don't you?" Gwen asked.

"It grows on you after a while."

"I think it's charming. Everyone seems so polite."

Eliza drove the car down the long tree-lined drive to the front of the sprawling ranch house. "Americans think everyone with a British accent is intelligent. We both know that isn't true. One night in a honky-tonk and you'd learn that not all cowboys are polite." For some reason, Eliza felt it was her duty to keep an eye on Gwen, much like an older, more experienced sister would.

"I'm not as naive as you think I am," Gwen chided.

"Hmmm." *Yeah, right.*

"I'm not."

Eliza glanced over and met Gwen's scowl. Her porcelain features and perfect makeup, along with the accent, added to the innocent poster child image.

"I may have gone to boarding school and lived most my life at Albany behind locked gates, but I've done some traveling on my own."

"Let me guess, with a bodyguard the size of Neil hanging around?"

"Hans isn't nearly as big as Neil."

Eliza rolled her eyes. "Hans? His name is Hans?"

"He's from Sweden. His specialty is in martial arts."

Eliza would have laughed if Gwen weren't so serious. "So where is Hans now?"

"At home. I didn't think he needed to accompany me here. I knew I'd be with you and could call on Samantha or Blake anytime. Besides, you don't seem to need anyone holding your hand to keep you safe."

That's because I know how to take care of myself. "You're not me."

"No, but I'm capable of staying out of trouble without a bodyguard."

Unaccredited confidence could lead to trouble. "You know I'm leaving the day after the wedding."

"I know."

Eliza put the car in park and kept it running to keep what cool air they could blowing on them as they talked. "When are you flying home?"

"I haven't decided. Mother wants me to fly home with her, but I think I might stay here for a while longer."

"I think you'd be better off going home with your mom."

"I'm not a child."

"Didn't say you were."

"I think you did."

Gwen's defenses were up. Eliza placed a hand over the other woman's. "How old are you—twenty-five?"

Gwen's jaw dropped. "I'm thirty-one."

Too old to be walking around with a babysitter. "I tell you what. Tonight we'll put on a pair of jeans, find a couple of hats, and look for that honky-tonk. Maybe I can give you a few tips so you can stay out of trouble." Not exactly the environment to recruit new customers, but leaving Gwen to her own defenses was kind of like leaving a kitten with a dozen pit bulls.

"What if I *want* to find some trouble?"

"Then it's best you have someone to keep you from getting hurt. Hence, you'll need someone like Hans."

"Fine, no trouble. I'd like to keep myself safe, have some fun, and leave unaccosted."

"Fine."

Gwen smiled and pushed the door open.

The sweltering heat sucked the energy from every pore of Eliza's body. Maybe a cool bar and a beer would help knock her out of her current funk.

Eliza hiked her purse over her shoulder and rounded the front of the car.

"Oh, Carter, how nice of you to come." Gwen's voice pierced the air with her greeting.

Eliza skidded to a stop. *Carter?*

Gwen reached the steps to the ranch house and greeted Carter in the classic European style, kissing both of his cheeks. Dressed in casual slacks and a cotton button-up shirt, Carter Billings tossed on his easy smile. As usual, he said exactly the right things at exactly the right times. "Don't you look lovely. You'd never know it's a thousand degrees out here."

Eliza's heart pounded in her chest. Here stood the real reason for her unease. Carter Billings was everything she'd ever wanted in a man, but completely out of her reach. Something inside her ignited every time she saw him. Sadly, that response usually ended up in a snarky remark or defensive battle. He walked with more confidence than a tomcat in a dark alley in Brooklyn, charmed everyone he met with only a smile, and oozed sex appeal like syrup dripping off a double stack of pancakes.

Carter ran his hand through his sandy-blond hair and caught her gaze when Gwen walked past him and into the house. Eliza watched his chest rise and fall with one deep breath before he started down the stairs to greet her.

"Hello, Eliza."

"Hey, Carter. What are you doing here?" Damn, that sounded snotty. The heat was frying her brain.

"I take it you're not happy to see me."

"Didn't say that. Wasn't expecting you is all." *Is all?* The local dialect was infiltrating her speech.

He crossed his arms over his chest, tucking his fingers under his arms. "Gwen asked Neil to come; Blake asked me to give a report on Gwen."

Eliza glanced over Carter's shoulder to the empty doorway. "Why doesn't Blake ask Neil about her?"

"Neil doesn't offer gossip, only facts. Blake would be more frustrated with a 'She's fine' response." Carter dipped his voice to mimic Neil's. Eliza couldn't help but smile.

"She *is* fine." How did one woman instill such a need for these men to coddle her?

"I'll be the judge of that."

Eliza shoved a lock of hair, which had managed to fall out of her loose bun, from her eyes. Carter watched the movement, his eyes wandering to the tip of her head. "Let the judge, judge, then."

"I'm not a judge any longer."

"No, you're a *politician*."

"You say that like it's a bad thing."

"Politicians are hated almost as much as lawyers." Which Carter was—or had been, anyway. At thirty-seven, he'd climbed more ladders and overturned more goals than a man twice his age. His sights were now on Sacramento, and according to the polls, his chances were good.

"Ouch."

"I call 'em as I see 'em."

He stood aside, his smile never falling from his full lips. "Well, why don't you call 'em inside? It's hard to judge my ward out here in the heat."

"She's not your ward," Eliza informed him as she walked by. Even in the heat, she managed to catch the scent of the musk rolling off his frame. She shivered, ignoring the pleasure his scent brought over her.

"She's not yours, either, but I didn't see her driving up here alone."

"Don't you have laws to pass or something?"

He chuckled as she passed him on the stairs. "I'm not the governor—yet."

"I'd think babysitting a grown woman was off your list of judicial duties." The cool interior of the house was welcome relief from the heat.

"Maybe my political ones, but not my friendship ones. You'd do the same for Sam, and don't even try and deny it."

He had her there. Not that she'd let him know her thoughts. "Whatever."

Carter followed the lucky bead of perspiration that traveled down Eliza's neck and disappeared down the V of her shirt. He shifted on his feet as he thought of where that tiny bit of moisture might have traveled. At five-seven, Eliza's sun-kissed skin and sultry brown eyes had a way of drawing him in.

As if sensing his attention, Eliza tilted her head to the side. Her movement forced his eyes from her breasts to her face. He didn't even have the decency to be embarrassed about being caught checking her out. He should have been, he knew. But he wasn't. Carter lowered his eyes to their hostess, who stood beside Gwen and Neil and pretended to listen.

Thirty minutes later, they stood on a vast lawn surrounded by split-rail fences a few hundred yards away. The smell of horses and heat filled the air.

"We own over five hundred acres," Mrs. Hawthorn was explaining.

"How do you keep out unwanted guests?" Neil asked.

"I'll have extra ranch hands available to head off any wandering spectators. They'll have to walk a long way to reach us here. And if they drive a car, we'll see them long before they have a chance to sneak in."

Mrs. Hawthorn strolled over to the large outdoor entertainment area, complete with fire pits and permanent tables. Bales of straw outlined the area, adding to the charming Texas setting.

Eliza walked away from Mrs. Hawthorn toward one of the ranch's employees. The cowboy wore tight blue jeans, boots, and a Stetson. The man smiled and tipped his hat when she strolled up. Carter walked a couple of steps her way but couldn't hear what she was saying. The young cowboy glanced over at Gwen and made a couple of hand gestures. Eliza seemed to thank the man and turned back to their tour.

Gwen directed her attention to Eliza. "Why don't you go on and show Carter the inside layout while I speak with the man in charge of security?"

"Don't have to ask me twice. It's hotter than sin out here." Eliza pivoted on her heel and beelined toward the house. "Coming?"

Carter picked up his pace to meet her at the door, holding it open while she walked inside.

"Mrs. Hawthorn has offered a half-dozen rooms for our use the night of the wedding—for guests who might have too much to drink or for those who come at the last minute without accommodations." Eliza walked past a back staircase and pointed. "There's a balcony overlooking the venue—one where Blake can post extra security who might be able to spot something in the distance or an uninvited guest."

Carter followed behind, watching the sway of her butt as she rounded the corner and walked down the long hall.

"You guys can stage in here while you're waiting on Sam."

She kept walking and talking. Carter barely heard a word. Much like most of the times he'd been in Eliza's presence, she numbed his brain to nothing, making it difficult to think. He'd always feel a sizzle when she walked in the room. If he had to guess, he'd say she was as attracted to him as he was to her. Yet neither of them ever acted on it.

Well...almost never.

Christmas the year before, while celebrating with Blake and Samantha and about fifty friends, there was their almost kiss under the mistletoe. They'd both been drinking, barely skimming the surface of sarcasm with each other the whole night. Eliza had worn a skintight red dress that was slit halfway up her thigh. She'd pulled back her dark hair, allowing only small bits of it to swing along her slender neck. Every time she'd passed him that night, her perfume caught hold of him. It was like she'd gripped his neck and squeezed.

Sucked in by her light, he'd noticed when she peeled away from the crowd, and followed her.

She'd turned unexpectedly, colliding into him. They stood there for a moment, appraising each other. Eliza broke eye contact and glanced at the ceiling. She'd mumbled something under her breath, and he'd looked up. *God bless mistletoe.* He placed a hand on the side of her face and fanned his fingers to the back of her neck. He remembered the need to kiss her slowly.

So much for that plan.

Just as he leaned in to taste, one of the party guests called his name from across the room. Eliza jumped back and out of his arms.

Neither of them ever spoke of it. In fact, they went on as if it had never happened.

He supposed it was because both of them were such good friends with Sam and Blake that neither of them wanted to screw that up.

Carter went on to date, or at least be seen with other women, and Eliza did whatever she did for the company she and Samantha ran.

"So what do you think?" Eliza was talking to him, but he didn't have a clue about what.

"Excuse me?"

"The house?"

"What?"

"You've not heard a word I've said."

"No. No, you told me about the room we'll be in, about the balcony."

She perched her hands on her hips and offered a haughty look. "I went over that fifteen minutes ago. I don't know why I bother," she said, turning away.

"I'm distracted," he admitted. "Lot of things on my mind."

"I have better things to do with my day too. Tell you what, why don't you just tell Neil you approve, and we'll be on our way?"

Carter smirked. "Trying to get rid of me?"

Her eyes shot to his faster than lightning strikes in a stormy sky. "Wanting you gone would imply I care that you're here."

She was trying hard to keep a disinterested look on her face, but she started to nibble on her fingernail and broke eye contact. *You care. You might not want to, but you do.*

"Ouch."

She glanced at her fingernails and fisted her palms. "Oh, forget it. Let's get out of here before I melt."

"Sounds good." Because standing here fantasizing about her wasn't doing anyone any good. Besides, last time Carter checked, he had a date for this wedding, and it wasn't with the woman in front of him.

Eliza strolled off, and he followed way behind. He really should be thinking about the Texas millionaires attending this "renewal of vows" ceremony and not about the maid of honor.

"I've thought of everything, Neil. You can tell my brother he's perfectly safe and the only media pictures being taken will be from the one reporter he's invited to attend." Gwen waved Carter's way. "Be a love and appease him, will you?"

Carter eyed Neil and shrugged.

"Thank you again for your time, Mrs. Hawthorn. We'll see you in a few days."

Mrs. Hawthorn allowed Gwen to kiss both her cheeks and waved as the other two women climbed into the car. "Have fun, girls."

Carter stood beside Neil and Mrs. Hawthorn while Eliza and Gwen drove away. Eliza didn't even glance in her rearview mirror as she drove away.

"They were in a hurry to leave," Neil announced.

"I noticed that too."

Mrs. Hawthorn placed a hand on one hip. "Wedding planning isn't easy. They've been working hard. It's a good thing they can get away for a night of fun before the festivities."

"Night of fun?" Neil asked.

Carter followed the dust down the road.

"According to Billy, Eliza asked about a local watering hole where the two of them could kick back and relax for a few hours. Dance a little and blow off some steam."

Carter rolled his eyes. "Watering hole?"

"I can't see Miss Gwen in a Texas bar," Neil exclaimed.

Eliza, maybe. But Gwen? "Looks like you're not flying home tonight," Carter told Neil. Passing up the opportunity of spying on Eliza and Gwen was out of the question.

Chapter Two

The hotel gift shop provided the perfect pair of skintight jeans, cowboy boots, and cowgirl hats. Gwen wasn't about to go into a Texas bar dressed as the daughter of a duke. Unlike shopping for the yellow bridesmaid dresses, Eliza actually enjoyed their brief walk on the country side of the store.

Loud music, with just the right amount of twang and lyrics about lost love, filled the bar. Several couples crowded the dance floor. Their bodies were glued together and moved as if they were one unit.

Eliza took the lead and walked through the crowd to a couple of empty seats at the bar. The two of them turned a few heads and received a couple of smiles before they sat down.

"I can't believe how crowded it is," Gwen said over the noise.

"Makes it more interesting," Eliza told her.

The bartender placed a couple of napkins in front of them. "Ladies," he said, tipping his hat.

She lifted up two fingers. "Two beers."

Gwen scoffed. "But—"

"You can't drink wine in a beer bar, Gwen." Eliza knew where her friend was going with her haughty *but*. Surprisingly, Gwen didn't argue.

Gwen folded her hands in her lap on top of her purse. She sat ramrod straight with her big doe eyes wide open. Her fingers tapped to the music, and a smile played on her lips. What did Gwen see? For her, this night was about adventure and overcoming some of her social fears. Sure, there were people dancing and having a good time. From the looks of the crowd, there wasn't anyone completely wasted yet. Beer drinkers tended to get rowdy later in the evening.

"Here ya are, ma'am." The bartender sat the bottles down. Eliza reached into her purse to pay. "Already taken care of," he said, nodding to the end of the bar. There sat two single men with button-up Western shirts and Stetsons. Eliza made eye contact with the one sitting closest to her. His dark hair and finely manicured mustache outlined a ruggedly attractive face. She lifted her bottle with a tiny nod.

"Did they buy the drinks?" Gwen asked.

"Seems so."

"Should we go over and thank them?"

Eliza turned away from the men and brought the bottle to her lips. After a sip, she said, "No need. They'll be here in less than five minutes."

Gwen held her bottle and smiled over the bar to the cowboys. "How do you know that?"

"Because you're still staring at them, which they'll take as an invitation."

Gwen dropped her glance to the floor and swiveled in her seat.

"My God, you really don't get out much."

Gwen's cheeks turned red. "I'm pathetic."

"You've been sheltered. Not completely your fault."

Gwen sipped her beer. To her credit, she didn't frown at the taste. "Sheltered and pathetic."

Just how innocent are you? "Please tell me you've had boyfriends."

Gwen's jaw dropped. "I've had lovers. I'm not a virgin, if that's what you're implying."

"Why, that's a mighty fine piece of information, darlin'. I could swear you're as innocent as a newborn calf."

Eliza and Gwen both shot their eyes to the rugged cowboy who had made it to their side in less than two minutes.

Gwen's cheeks grew instantly red, and her eyes opened wide.

"Thanks for the drinks," Eliza said, trying to remove the attention from Gwen's outburst.

"My name is Rick. This here is Jimmy." Jimmy was an inch or so shorter than Rick and a good twenty pounds thinner. Both were easy on the eyes.

"Eliza," she said, "and my nonvirginal friend Gwen."

Gwen elbowed her in the side and Eliza laughed.

Rick and Jimmy were kind enough not to keep the joke going. "Mind if we join you?"

Eliza nodded to the empty seat on her right. Rick sat, and Jimmy said, "I'll keep an eye out for an open table."

Gwen moved a little closer to Eliza when Jimmy stepped closer to her. This was going to get awkward in a heartbeat. "Why don't I hold this"—Eliza reached for Gwen's beer, removed it from her fingers—"and you two dance?"

Gwen leaned over and tried to whisper. "I don't even know him."

Eliza smiled and nudged her out of her chair. "Go. We're here to have fun."

Jimmy was already reaching for Gwen's elbow.

"But I don't know how to dance like that."

Jimmy helped her to her feet. "Where are you from?"

"Outside of London." Gwen set her purse on the barstool.

Jimmy winked. "Well, English, I learned the two-step when I was five. I'm sure I can show you."

"You sure?"

"C'mon."

Eliza's eyes followed Gwen as her friend stepped on the dance floor. She stiffened when Jimmy wrapped his arms around her waist and pulled her close to his frame. After only a couple of missteps, Jimmy successfully had Gwen swinging to the music in what appeared to be complicated dance moves.

"Do you always watch your friend so closely?" Rick asked.

"It's in the handbook of girls. We go to the bathroom in pairs, tuck each other's tags in, and we watch out for each other."

"She doesn't seem to be watching you."

Eliza let her gaze drift to the cowboy on her right and smiled. "She's just trying to keep from breaking your friend's feet. Hard to do that and watch me at the same time." Rick was cute. His accent added to his smooth demeanor, but he wasn't doing a thing for her libido. Chemistry was a bitch that way. On the outside, two people might seem to be right for each other, but on the inside, they simply didn't fit. Or they exploded, much like her and Carter.

Rick must not have felt the same. He settled into his chair and kept the conversation going.

Carter elbowed Neil into the back of the bar, far away from Eliza and Gwen, and did his level best to slip into the shadows.

From the look of Gwen's faltering steps, the women had been in the bar for at least an hour, maybe two. Gwen's hair was falling out of place, and on occasion, her voice rose above the others. She'd danced with at least three different men in the short span of time he and Neil had been there. If it was any consolation, Eliza had dumped some of Gwen's drinks into forgotten glasses on the table.

Neil's white knuckles clutched the beer in his hands as he watched Gwen spin around the dance floor. "She's drunk," he muttered through clenched teeth.

"I'd say you're right." Carter took a pull on his beer, eyes glancing over at Eliza. She was talking with two men sitting at her table, where she'd spent most the night. One of them stood and offered her his hand. She hesitated, but then stood and let him lead her to the dance floor.

Her tight little ass wiggled in step with the music as if she were born for country-and-western dancing. Her partner kept his hands on her hip for about thirty seconds, and then they started to slip.

It's hard to hold the glass when my fingers want to crush it. Another couple blocked Carter's view. He shifted in his seat but still couldn't find Eliza in the crowd. When he caught up with her, she'd called the dance short and was sitting at her table again, this time talking with another guy. When cow-dick number two reached over to touch Eliza's shoulder, Carter couldn't take any more. "You watch Gwen."

"Don't worry, I am," Neil said.

The music shifted into something slower by the time he reached Eliza's table. Not too gently, he removed cow-dick's fingers from Eliza's back and grasped her elbow.

Her shocked expression met his, and the cowboy took to his feet. "Can I help you?"

A tattoo of a cross adorned the man's hand who was making time with Eliza. It was almost unnoticeable, but Carter knew its meaning. "You owe me a dance," Carter told her while ignoring the man.

Maybe she was too shocked to deny him, but she stumbled to her feet and let him pull her in his arms. Her heat socked him in the gut as his body grazed hers.

"What the hell are you doing here?"

Carter darted a glare at the men watching them from across the room. "Saving a woman from a bunch of yahoos planning on a night of fun."

He spun her around; she spun him back and glanced at the men. "They're harmless."

"Really?"

"They only look rowdy."

"So they've been buying you ladies drinks all night to test your limit for nothing?"

She stepped on his foot. He quickly recovered and kept them dancing. "How long have you been here…watching?"

Oh boy, he'd shoved his foot in far this time. "Long enough."

"How long, Carter?"

"Neil was worried about Gwen." Thinking of his best friend's sister, he lifted his gaze around the room to try to find her. He caught a glimpse of her blonde hair and petite frame as someone led her out the door. "Oh, damn."

Carter abruptly ended the dance and tugged Eliza alongside him.

Neil was already ahead of him.

The crush of sweaty bodies made it hard to cut across the bar. Carter knew at least one of the men at Eliza's table had followed.

"What are we doing?"

"C'mon," he told her. They finally reached the front door and emptied onto the parking lot just in time to see Neil grab the guy Gwen had been dancing with. Neil pinned him to the hood of a truck and pulled his fist back.

"Stop!" Gwen shrieked.

Neil hesitated, but only for a second before his fist flew.

The man across the hood of the truck was no match for Neil. The bodyguard let loose two blows and pulled back. "The *lady* said no."

"Where the hell did you come from?" one of the men from the bar yelled as he shoved his way into the mix.

More people poured out from the bar to watch the drama. Carter was sure at least one cell phone zeroed in on him. A bar fight in a parking lot in Texas was probably not the best way to get votes.

"It's all over, buddy. The big guy here is just protecting an innocent woman," Carter said, trying his best to defuse the situation.

"She looked willing to me," the guy yelled before the stranger's fist flew and connected with Carter's face.

He spun around and came up low, tackling his attacker around his waist and shoving him onto the nearest car.

Everything exploded around him. Carter took another blow to his torso before he returned punch for punch. Adrenaline ran through his veins like fire, fueling his swings. Muscle memory took action, and within twenty seconds, Carter had the man pinned to the car alongside his buddy. "No always means no!"

The man under him stopped struggling. Men from the bar broke through the crowd like linebackers at the fifty-yard line.

"Dammit, Jimmy, what are you two doing?" someone called.

Carter pushed away from the man he'd fought and stepped out of swing range. He stared at his enemy, waiting for him to flinch.

He didn't.

"Neil," Carter yelled, "why don't you take Lady Gwen back to her rooms? I'll ride with Eliza."

Eliza patted Gwen on the back. "I'll see you back at the hotel."

When Carter focused on Eliza, she had her arm looped through Gwen's, both of them staring at the crowd with unease.

Gwen nodded.

He motioned for Eliza to move to her car.

"My purse is in the bar," she told him.

Neil escorted both women away from the drunken men, and Carter went inside after her purse.

He picked up Gwen's designer bag and then Eliza's. When his hand landed on Eliza's bag, he felt something hauntingly familiar inside. Unable to stop himself, he opened the purse and found exactly what he thought he'd see.

Why was Eliza carrying a gun in her purse?

Chapter Three

Eliza grabbed her purse from Carter, removed the keys, and handed them to him.

She'd screwed up. Put Gwen in danger instead of helping her ward off unwanted advances from strange men. Gwen shook as Eliza and Neil led her to the town car that Neil drove. She said she was OK, but Eliza didn't believe her. She kept glaring at Neil with misguided anger.

Once they returned to the hotel, Eliza would have her answers. Until then, she had to deal with Carter.

Why were they in the bar to begin with? She should have been happy with his intervention, but all she could think was that if she hadn't been distracted with Carter showing up, she could have handled everything fine.

Carter drove in silence until they hit the interstate. All Eliza could focus on was his hard profile. Strong jaw and sexy mouth, with that slightly swollen lip.

She shuddered, thinking of the pain.

"Why?"

She sucked in a deep breath, let it out slow. There wasn't a need to ask what he was referring to. *Why* were they in that bar to begin with? *Why* had she taken Lady Gwen, a sheltered debutant from the ball, to a bar? "We wanted to blow off some steam."

"Doesn't the hotel have a bar?"

"Yes. Perfectly safe and boring," she told him. "Gwen wanted more."

"Gwen doesn't know what she wants. She could have been hurt."

Eliza glanced at her hands in her lap, covering her purse. "Gwen was starting to believe that all cowboys were gentlemen because they say 'ma'am' and pull out her chair. If she didn't go to that bar with me, she'd have gone alone."

"And you helped her, how?"

"If you hadn't shown up and distracted me, I'd have kept her from leaving with that guy." Her voice rose, and anger bubbled to the surface.

Carter huffed and signaled to leave the freeway.

"Why were you there, anyway?" she asked.

"To keep both of you from becoming part of tomorrow's headlines. Looks like Neil and I showed up just in time." Carter's hands clutched the steering wheel as he pulled into the hotel parking lot. He bypassed the valet and opted to self-park.

"It wasn't that bad."

"The guy with his hands all over you was a drug dealer. Did you know that?"

She knew about tattoos. Knew of their meaning. "Small town, at best." Not that she'd given any attention to the guy when he showed up at their table. In fact, when he sat down, Eliza was ordering coffee so she and Gwen could make their way out of there. She suspected the guys around her had realized none of them were going to get laid, and tension had started to fill the room. She was on the verge of making their excuses when Carter showed up and dragged her onto the dance floor.

"Small town—that's all you have to say on the matter?" Carter pissed wasn't a pleasant look. His jaw was so tight and his eyes narrowed to slits so small that stickpins would have bounced off him.

Instead of giving him more, Eliza shoved herself out of the car and slammed the door.

She had made it two yards from the car when Carter spun her around for the second time that night. "Admit you were wrong, and I'll let it go."

The hell!

They stood there facing each other, toe-to-toe, glaring.

She took a few breaths, refusing to give in. If he thought he could wait her out, he was going to be *so* sorry. No one did the silent treatment better than she did.

"God, you're stubborn."

"Don't forget it," she told him.

His grip loosened, and something in his eyes shifted. His voice softened. "You could have been hurt."

"You mean Gwen could have been hurt."

His gaze traveled from her eyes to her lips, and awareness ignited. "Her too," he all but whispered.

From the look in his eyes, Gwen hadn't been his concern.

His fingers ran up her arm, and sparks flared from his touch. His switch from anger to fear sucked the air from her lungs and left her light-headed. His lips moved, as if he were saying something to himself, as he started to close the space between them. She knew he was going to kiss her. A colossal mistake, to be sure, but she couldn't stop him, didn't want to. She held perfectly still and waited for his touch.

His cell phone rang from inside his pocket and cracked the tension like an ice cube hitting hot water. "Dammit," he uttered.

Eliza backed away and shook her head as he reached for his pocket.

"What?" he barked into the phone. "Yes...No...Son of a bitch."

The color faded from Carter's face. He ran his free hand through his sandy-blond hair, making him look even sexier.

She really shouldn't be thinking of him as sexy.

"Yeah. You know what to do." He hung up his phone.

"What's wrong?"

"Apparently, tonight's little party is all over the social media. That was my campaign manager."

"Oh, no." That couldn't be good. Men were tossed out of elections on less.

"More than *oh, no*. C'mon, I need to get you inside so I can go do damage control."

Every step into the hotel was riddled with guilt. What happened to the walls she'd worked so hard to build? Eliza attempted to mask her feelings and hoped Carter couldn't see through her slipping facade.

He shoved her into the penthouse suite without a word. He took one look at Gwen, pointed at her, and said, "Next time you want to go out, take Neil." Then he pivoted on his heel and slammed the door behind him.

It's all my fault.

The door to the penthouse shut, and Gwen shot to her feet. "I've never had so much fun in my entire life."

Eliza stared at her, speechless. "What?"

"First, those cowboys. So cute. And the beer. I didn't think I'd like beer. My mother told me it tasted like dirty bathwater and that ladies didn't drink beer. And the dancing...My word, I've not danced that way, ever." Gwen paced the room, her voice rising at least an octave as she rushed her words, one on top of the other.

Eliza shook her head. "Are you crazy? Neil saved your not-so-virginal ass from that jerk in the parking lot."

"I noticed Neil an hour before he decided to walk into the spotlight. I was never in any *real* danger."

Eliza felt her mouth going dry. "What?"

"You didn't see Carter and Neil walk in? I can see how Carter might have entered unnoticed, but Neil? The man is built like one of those trucks on the interstate. Solid muscle." Gwen lifted her left eyebrow, and her glossy eyes from one too many beers glossed even more.

"You like Neil?"

"I didn't say that."

Not a denial. Interesting.

Eliza rubbed her hands over her face, smudging whatever makeup she had left. "Tonight was a huge mistake."

"I disagree."

"Carter is running for election, and he was just involved in a bar fight. Apparently, photos are already circulating." Eliza couldn't help but hope she wasn't in any of them.

"Oh…Oh!" It looked like Lady Gwen was finally getting a clear picture of the problem.

Eliza flopped on the couch, hands at her side. "It's all my fault."

Gwen sat beside her and placed a hand on her knee. "No. I'm just as guilty as you."

The responsibility lay squarely on Eliza's shoulders. Now the question was, how was she going to fix it?

With his head buried in his hands, Carter sat in front of his laptop, with his campaign manager, Jay, watching via Skype. "…and because Gwen Harrison was involved, you've even made the London papers and tabloids. We're screwed."

I need to fix this.

"Nobody wants a bar-brawling single man in office. They don't mind adultery and drug use, but fighting in the bar parking lot—not gonna work."

"There's got to be something we can do." He was planning to officially announce his candidacy in less than two weeks. One night of protecting a woman's honor and all his life plans were shot out of the stratosphere. "How soon should I do a press conference?"

"And tell the reporters what, exactly? That you were in a bar drinking—"

"I wasn't drinking."

"How long were you in the bar?"

"An hour."

"And you weren't drinking?" Jay's sarcastic tone laced his words.

"I nursed one drink." He'd sipped on one beer so he wouldn't appear to be spying on Eliza.

Jay huffed out a breath. "Like I said, you were in a bar drinking, picking up women—"

"I did not."

"The pictures I saw were with you standing next to a dark-haired sex-is-my-middle-name woman."

"That was Eliza. Samantha's best friend. After the fight, I drove her home. Neil drove Gwen," he defended.

"I don't think the papers are going to care whose friend she is. Listen, Carter, they're going to say you were there drinking, which isn't a lie; you picked up a chick, which isn't a lie; and you bloodied a man's face, which isn't a lie."

Carter was a hair away from saying, *But he started it.* How *high school* could he be?

"When is Blake's party?"

"Two days."

"Stay low and watch who you talk to. Maybe some of this will blow over, and we'll figure out how to handle it."

Carter rubbed the growing tension in the back of his neck. "Ignoring this isn't going to make it go away."

"No, but what choice do we have? Unless it's you walking down that aisle tomorrow, or within the next week, I'm not sure how we're going to turn you into a trusting family man ready to take office. The image of the bar brawl isn't going away. The best we can do is cover it up or make it out to be some kind of heroic gesture. Even then, it's going to be an uphill battle."

The image of Kathleen, his date for the wedding, swam in his mind.

Marriage? Not gonna happen.

"There has to be something we can do."

"I'll consult with some of my friends in DC. They deal with this kind of thing all the time."

"Call me."

"I will. Oh, and Carter?"

"Yeah?"

"Stay out of redneck bars."

Carter ended the call and tossed the phone on the bed.

He was so screwed.

Chapter Four

The dress was even hotter than she'd thought it would be. The yellow didn't add to Eliza's pasty complexion, the one she'd worn daily since the infamous bar brawl.

"You look…sweet," Sam said, her eyes shifting from Eliza to Gwen and back again.

"Like icing on a cake." Only, the inside of the cake was bitter and tart. The thought of facing Carter as they walked up the aisle left her nauseous. Where were her snarky attitude and her quick comebacks when she needed them?

"At least the temperature dropped," Gwen said, optimistic to the core.

"By what, five degrees?" Eliza swept open the silly fan and used it.

There was a knock on the door.

"Come in."

Mrs. Hawthorn poked her head in. "Oh, don't you girls look lovely."

Eliza refrained from snorting. Sam's dress was equally ridiculous, but at least it was white. Mrs. Hawthorn obviously needed her eyes examined. Only Gwen appeared to wear the gown, and the yellow, well.

"Are the men ready?"

"They are, they are. Can I tell them to play the music?"

"Please," Eliza pleaded. The sooner they started, the sooner it ended. Then maybe she could slip into the shadows. She'd yet to come up with a way to make up for her "party foul" with Carter. The news had jumped on his "bar brawl" and painted him as a volatile candidate. Carter didn't address the media, even though they camped out at the hotel in search of a quote.

Sam lifted her heavy dress to avoid stepping on it as she walked by.

Halfway down the stairs, Eliza spotted Carter and Neil, both decked out in tuxedos with yellow ties. Carter smirked at something Neil said before Neil's eyes found them.

Carter swiveled his head, and his smile fell as his gaze landed on her.

Eliza swallowed hard, attempting to ignore the building tension in her gut.

Carter took his place at the bottom of the stairs and waited. His eyes glanced over her before he stuck his arm out for her to take. He was stiff and unyielding.

This is going to be fun.

"Hey," she managed without stuttering.

He offered a *hey* back, but averted his gaze to Neil. "Let's get this moving."

Gwen's radiant smile beamed toward Neil, and she snuggled into his arm.

Neil pulled at his collar and nodded toward Carter.

The music outside started to play, and Eliza let Carter escort her down the hall.

As soon as she and Carter stepped into the aisle, his charming smile manifested, and he moved Eliza a little closer to him.

He finally allowed her a glance, but must have not liked what he saw. "You look lovely," he said.

"You must be blind," she whispered and smiled as she did.

Two photographers snapped pictures. One hired by Samantha, the other handpicked from the media. The camera seemed to focus an awful lot on the two of them.

Good thing Neil had the OK to delete any pictures he didn't deem appropriate.

"You look like Daisy Duke. Very Texas," he managed from the corner of his upturned mouth.

"Daisy Duke would be wearing cutoffs and showing her butt cheeks." Eliza nodded toward one of her and Sam's clients who was seated on her right.

Carter chuckled under his breath. More flashes of light arrested her senses.

He led her up to the front and held her hand briefly before letting go and taking his place beside Blake.

The ceremony was brief. A renewing of vows with a sprinkling of words of devotion spoken from both Sam and Blake.

And though the gown stuck to Eliza's skin by the time they were done, a tiny bit of emotion clogged her throat. Samantha and Blake were very much in love, and seeing them together gave Eliza a splattering of hope for humanity.

Eliza snagged a glass of champagne from a passing waiter, and Carter's palms grew damp as she let the sweet beverage trickle down her throat.

He licked his lips while a shot of desire wedged in his gut and wouldn't let go.

Kathleen nudged his arm. "Is that the girl from the pictures in the paper?"

Embarrassed he'd been caught staring at—and if he were honest, lusting after—a woman other than the one he'd arrived with,

Carter turned to his date. "The woman with the dark hair?" he asked, forging innocence.

Kathleen offered a wan smile. "I'm not a fool."

No, Kathleen wasn't that. "Yes, that's her."

His date took a moment to stare over her glass. "She's very beautiful, despite that awful dress."

He nearly laughed and twisted his head toward Eliza again. He thought of her comment about cutoffs and butt cheeks and felt some of the week's tension lift. "I suppose."

"Suppose? Please, Carter, you've hardly taken your eyes off her all night."

Damn. "I'm overloaded since the bar incident. Seeing her and Gwen again has my thoughts turned around." Which wasn't a lie. Only, it wasn't Gwen who fueled his apprehension.

Kathleen placed a hand on his forearm and managed a half smile. "I think it might be more than that."

He started to shake his head and she stopped him. "Tell me, do you think you have the same chances today as you did last week to win in November?"

"We'll start damage control tomorrow."

"But you're not as sure any longer?"

Kathleen's blue eyes met his.

"I'm not sure." He might have to wait another four years for the opportunity to clear his image.

She sighed and tilted her head. "You know what you need?"

"No, tell me."

"You need a new scandal to overshadow the old. Something noble. With an impact of a soldier coming home from war."

Perhaps.

The back of Carter's neck tickled with awareness. He twisted and noticed Eliza shift her eyes away suddenly.

When he turned back to Kathleen, she shook her head and lowered her eyes. “This isn’t working for me, Carter.”

He stared at her for a long moment, neither of them speaking. Memories of their short time together flashed and were finished in less than a minute. He wanted to feel something with her declaration, and he did. She was calling an end to their dating, and he was relieved.

“I’m sorry,” was all he could say.

Kathleen lifted her head high, leaned in, and kissed his cheek. “Good-bye, Carter.” She turned and walked away.

It wasn’t her business.

She didn’t care.

Eliza noticed Carter’s beautifully polished date slip away from his side. The woman was clingy. Not something Eliza thought he’d admire in a woman. Apparently, she was wrong.

Samantha waved a hand in front of her face. “Earth to Eliza.”

They’d been talking about something, but she couldn’t recall what. “I’m sorry. What did you say?”

“Are you sure it’s OK if Gwen stays with you for a while?”

That shook Eliza awake. “Stay with me?” Had she agreed to something while staring at Carter and his date?

“You’ve not heard a word I’ve said, have you?”

“No. Yes, I heard you say Gwen is staying in Malibu while you and Blake take another honeymoon. Which is the only thing about getting married every year that’s worth the effort, by the way. What’s this about Gwen staying with me?”

“We’re only going to be gone five days. Gwen will be with Eddie and our staff, but when we come home, she wants to stay with you. She said you were fine with it.”

I am?

"You're not fine with it," Samantha said.

"No, I'm just…We didn't discuss it."

Sam shrugged. "She thought it was OK." She rubbed the inside of her palms together, a sure sign she had something to say, but wasn't uttering a word.

"Out with it."

There were very few things the two of them kept from each other. No reason not to be blunt. "C'mon, Sam. You have something to say."

"Gwen wants to work for Alliance."

"Work? Has Gwen ever worked a day in her life?"

Sam squeezed her eyes together. "Technically, no. But—"

"It's a bad idea." One week with Gwen, and Carter was losing an election and Eliza's face was plastered on papers all over the world.

"Hear me out. I don't think Gwen is cut out for office work. But we could use her connections to find more women for our registry. Who knows, she might even be able to find men to match with the women."

Sam had a point.

"If you're that against it—"

"No. I'm not." Eliza took a deep breath. Ultimately, Samantha was the boss. Though she'd always respected Eliza's opinion, and they'd never taken on a client that rubbed one of them wrong. This was a different matter. And to top it off, Gwen was Sam's sister-in-law. Not something they could overlook. "I'm standing here wearing something the yellow tooth fairy threw up. All because Gwen is hard to say no to."

"Which is why she'd be great for recruiting."

Sam's pleading eyes said it all.

"OK, we give her a trial run. She'll probably hate living in the burbs after a week and want to go home anyway."

"Probably," Sam agreed with a smile. "Thanks."

Sam hugged her and left her side. Eliza attempted to peel away the material of her dress from her chest. She hated the heat. After flicking open her fan, she found some relief with the forced air against her damp skin.

"Are you ready for those cutoffs?"

Carter's voice caressed the back of her neck. The vision of him almost kissing her flooded her senses. She swallowed but didn't turn his way. "Do you have any?"

"I can arrange them." Why did his words sound so much like a seductive offer?

"Trying to get me out of this dress?"

"I've had worse thoughts."

She turned and saw his cocky smile. "Don't you have a date?"

"Yep."

"Then why are you standing here flirting with me?" Eliza was a good many things, but a poacher on another woman's guy, she wasn't. Even if Eliza had known Carter a lot longer than his arm candy, he didn't arrive with her, and that made him off limits.

"Is that what I'm doing?"

"That's what it feels like. And I have to tell ya, it's a bad idea."

"What's a bad idea?"

"You and me…flirting. We clash. Remember? Last Christmas we were shouting at each other over the Christmas pudding."

"We were arguing about a call between Green Bay and Carolina. The ref sided with me."

"The ref was blind." Her voice rose, and all thoughts of Carter flirting with her sailed away like a pesky mosquito running from Raid.

Carter smirked.

"What's so funny?"

"All you need is a big black stripe, and you'd look like an angry hornet in that dress."

She would have hurled an insult at him if he weren't so flippin' right. Instead, she huffed out a laugh, glanced down at her dress, and let her arms flop to the side. "God, it's awful. For the record, Gwen picked it out."

Carter turned around. "On Gwen, it isn't that bad. It's not good, but..."

"Something tells me Gwen would look good in whipped cream." She was that beautiful. Classic lines, the perfect height, and laughing eyes. Gorgeous. And currently surrounded by three guys.

"Whipped cream, huh?"

Eliza placed her focus on Carter and felt a simmering heat along her skin.

Whipped cream and a trickle of chocolate syrup down your thick chest. Eliza nibbled on her lower lip, and a flash of light sucked her out of her brief fantasy.

She and Carter both turned to glare at the photographer. Unfazed by their anger, the photographer was checking the digital display and nodding. "Man, it's hot tonight," was all he said before walking away.

"Should we allow that?"

Carter shrugged. "Better than a bar fight."

For a brief time, Eliza had completely forgotten the fight. "How's the campaign?"

He hesitated with his answer, then said, "Not good."

My fault.

"I feel responsible," she admitted.

"You do?"

"Well, yeah...If I hadn't taken Gwen there, you guys wouldn't have followed. One thing led to another and all that. If there's something I can do to help..."

Eliza considered repeating her words when Carter stood, staring at her. Somewhere in his head, he was thinking up something and struggling with the image it created.

"Carter? Are you OK?"

"Uh-huh. Just thinking if there is something you can do." His words came out slow and steady.

"Right. I was there. I know you didn't start the fight. I could tell a reporter."

"Uh-huh." He kept staring and mumbled, "I don't know."

"You don't know what?"

"Know what?" He repeated her question.

"You're not making any sense."

He snapped out of his thoughts. "When are you leaving tomorrow?"

"In the afternoon. I'm flying out with Sam and Blake."

"So you'll be in LA after that?"

"It's where I live, Hollywood. Not all of us have the funds to charter a private plane." Eliza used the nickname Samantha had given him when they met. His big-screen good looks were every producer's wet dream. Instead of searching for fame, he'd picked law. *Yawn!*

"Right," he said, with the smirk returning to his lips. "I have a press conference in two days at the Beverly Hilton. Can you be there?"

She swallowed and felt her palms dampen even more. "To explain what happened?"

"If need be."

What could she say? It was her fault he needed the press conference. She had to do something to make it right. "Yeah, I can be there."

Carter let loose a full smile, the one Hollywood would love to have.

"You should get back to your date. I'll bet she's looking for you."

Carter tore his eyes away from her and glanced around the room. Eliza noticed his date laughing at something another man was saying. "Looks like someone's moving in," she told him, nudging his arm.

"She cut me loose. They can move in all they want."

Eliza stared at him. "She dumped you?"

He nodded, but his expression didn't change. Kathleen obviously wasn't that important to him. Or maybe there was more to the dump.

"Wait, she didn't dump you because of the election, did she?"

He shrugged.

A strange weight fell on Eliza's chest. A mixture of relief that Carter wasn't attached, which was completely unwanted on her part, and a dose of what a rat Kathleen must be to dump a guy for such a shallow reason. If his date knew Carter at all, she'd knew that, beyond his often arrogant demeanor, he'd protect a woman despite how the media would take it. Guys like Carter didn't exist outside of books.

"She's not good enough for you anyway," Eliza mumbled.

"What was that?"

"If a woman is only with you to be the first lady of California, then you don't want her." Kathleen was leaning into a Texas cowboy in a five-hundred-dollar suit. *Probably has an oil field.*

"Is that so?" Carter asked.

"Yeah. That's so."

The music playing in the background stopped, and the emcee for the event picked up the microphone. "Well, folks, looks like we need to do a little cake cutting so we can let the hosts run off and start their third honeymoon."

Eliza glanced up to find Carter observing her. He smiled and offered his arm so the two of them could help at the cake table.

As Eliza slid her hand along his arm, an electric current fluttered in her chest and raised gooseflesh on her skin. Her already warm body heated with his simple touch and tightened in all the right places.

Chapter Five

"I need your help." Eliza stood in Samantha and Blake's living room pleading with Gwen.

"You need *my* help?" Gwen sat taller and lifted a manicured eyebrow high. She appeared just as surprised to hear Eliza's request as she was in giving it.

"Shocking, I know. But you have experience with this kind of thing, and I'm clueless." Eliza didn't like asking for advice, but she didn't have a choice.

"What experience?"

Eliza lifted her hand to her mouth and nibbled on a fingernail. "Carter asked me to join him at a press conference tomorrow. I don't know what to wear—don't know what to say. I don't want to come off as some hick. Lord knows those pictures of us in the parking lot were less than flattering."

"I thought they were splendid," Gwen said.

"For a jeans and beer ad, maybe. This is a big deal for Carter. I should look…I don't know…dignified. I'm good at evening gowns. I can do casual. But a press conference? Not a clue."

Gwen placed a hand on her chest. "I'm proud you came to me."

Oh, good. "So you can help?"

"If there is one thing my mother taught me, it was how to handle the media." Gwen stood and stuck out her hand. "Come. Let's start with the perfect clothes."

Thirty minutes later, they were standing in a designer dress store Gwen had obviously scoped out on one of her visits. The owner greeted them the moment they crossed the threshold.

Someone pressed a glass of wine into Eliza's hand while Gwen explained to Nadine, the owner, what they were looking for.

Drinking the wine kept Eliza from biting her nails.

She half listened while the other women walked around the room. Gwen removed a couple of skirt-and-blouse combinations from the rack. "I think dark colors will bring out her complexion and photograph well."

"Right. But not black. You're not attending a funeral," Nadine announced.

Eliza laughed, not able to shake the feeling that standing in front of a bunch of cameras might actually feel like a funeral. She'd spent most of her adult life hiding from cameras. Now she was going to be center stage.

"What about a hat?" Gwen asked. "I realize it's English of me, but a hat adds mystery and can hide some of your nerves."

Eliza snapped her attention to Gwen. "I like that idea."

Nadine left the clothes she had in her arms on a sofa. She then stepped to the back of the store and returned with a few hatboxes, removing each hat carefully. "We want mystery, not a statement. Nothing small or with feathers."

"But I like feathers," Gwen announced.

"Well, maybe a small one on the brim," Nadine agreed.

One at a time, the hats met with Eliza's head, briefly. Other than a baseball cap to hide her hair on bad hair days, Eliza didn't wear hats. The large brims felt awkward. After seeing her reflection, she couldn't help but admire how they transformed her face.

"I like the second one," Gwen said.

The brim covered Eliza's face enough to where she could dip her head maybe an inch and hide her identity. "I like it too."

"Super. Now, on to the dress. Clean-cut, nothing too low. It will be warm, so short sleeves on the jacket, and it needs to be silk. You'll feel confident despite your heart pounding in your chest. Never let them see your nerves," Gwen said.

As she spoke, Nadine removed different dresses and placed them behind a screen.

There was some debate of color, but they decided on a deep navy, matching the hat. The shoes were practical two-inch heels, and if Eliza were honest, more comfortable than her six-month-old running shoes. Amazing what a pricey shop could provide.

Thinking about the price of the ensemble shocked her back into reality. Although Lady Gwen and Samantha could tap into a duke's wealth, Eliza could not.

As they bagged the dress and the hat made its way into a large round box, Nadine handed Eliza the bill.

She drew in a quick breath. Three grand was a hard pill.

"You take credit cards?"

"Of course."

"Let me," Gwen offered.

"When I asked for your help, I didn't mean financially." Eliza removed plastic from her purse and pushed it toward Nadine.

"I'll be living with you by next week. I owe you something for that."

Although Eliza couldn't afford the dress, she wasn't about to let the other woman pay for it. "When you move in, we'll arrange something."

Gwen must have seen the determination in Eliza's eyes and dropped the debate.

The doorbell rang to the Tarzana house Eliza had shared with Sam before her marriage. Carter was five minutes early.

"Coming," she yelled down the stairs, not sure he could hear her. She slid on her heels and checked her appearance one last time. She wasn't sure where Eliza Havens had gone. The woman in her reflection was a stranger. A mysterious—and yeah, slightly beautiful—stranger. "You can do this," she said to herself, desperate to calm her nerves. The entire ruse would crumble if she started biting her nails and fidgeting.

Gwen's pointers had gone long into the night.

Stand still. Shoulders back, chin high. Not too high. Now tilt your head to the side and let your lips lift a fraction. Not a smile, not a smirk. Perfect.

The tips went on and on.

Gwen had done the impossible. Turned Eliza into a sophisticated lady overnight. *Maybe not impossible.*

The bell rang again, and Eliza blew out a deep breath. "Here we go."

She straightened her skirt one last time before opening the door to greet Carter.

It wasn't Carter.

"Ms. Havens?" The short man wore a three-piece suit and a smile. In her driveway was a town car and a driver standing at the passenger door.

"I am."

The man removed his glasses and did a quick scan of her body. Nothing sleazy, just a short appraisal. His lips spread into a large grin like a man with a secret. "I'm Jay Lieberman, Carter's campaign manager. Sorry for the inconvenience, but he has to meet you at the hotel."

Disappointment punched her gut. "Oh."

"It's OK. I'll go over what to expect and what you need to say to the reporters."

Eliza nodded, took a deep breath, and stepped through the door. After securing the dead bolt, she turned to the car and let Jay lead the way.

Twice, she caught herself lifting her fingers to her lips. She reduced herself to pinching her hands to keep them in her lap. Of late, the nail-biting was becoming an issue. Normally, her nerves were steady. She patted her purse at her side and remembered the small pistol she kept there.

It was a security blanket. One she probably didn't need any longer, but she couldn't be too careful.

Jay explained that Carter would do most of the talking. She was to nod, smile, and tell the media that if it weren't for Carter's intervention, she and Gwen would have been in danger.

"They'll ask personal questions. Don't answer them," Jay told her. "Let Carter do the sidestepping. He is the politician, after all."

Right! And everyone in office masters the art of doublespeak their first week on the campaign trail.

The driver maneuvered them around the front of the hotel, where news vans from every local station were parked. The driver didn't stop in front; instead, he took a side entrance, parked, and opened the door for the two of them.

She was thankful for a few minutes out of the spotlight. Jay and the driver flanked her sides as they walked her into the hotel. A few employees glanced up as they walked through an obvious staff entrance, but no one stopped them.

The brim of your hat will hide your unease. Use it, Gwen's voice echoed in Eliza's mind, and she tilted her head.

The hard floors shifted to lush burgundy carpet as they passed a doorway. The cool, dry air inside the hotel circulated the smell of whatever cleaning agents the staff used. She kept her gaze low, barely noticing where they were walking.

Jay held open another door and Eliza passed through.

"Jay, what's going on? Where's…?" Carter's voice trailed off when Eliza lifted her eyes to meet his.

His jaw dropped, and his words dried up. Shock, admiration, and desire flashed in his eyes. "Eliza." Carter's voice was breathy.

A wave of feminine power tugged at her pride as he stood there speechless.

"Hey, Carter," she said.

"Wow."

Her cheeks warmed. The others in the room grew silent.

"You approve? The hat isn't over-the-top, is it?" Not that she was taking it off. She felt safe under it, which was silly, but she did.

"Perfect. Everything is perfect."

Behind Carter, someone cleared his throat. He turned and the half dozen men in the room returned to whatever it was they were doing. "Ten minutes," a kid, maybe in his twenties, said, waving a phone in the air.

Carter managed two steps in her direction and grasped her hand. He led her to a second door in the suite, where there was a king-size bed, perfectly made, with a garment bag draped over the frame.

"Sorry I had to send Jay to pick you up. Something came up."

"You're a busy man."

His hand rested on her arm after he'd pulled her through the door. He didn't remove it.

"You look…amazing."

She expelled a nervous laugh. "Are you trying to make me nervous?"

"No. I'm just...I mean, you've always been beautiful, but this"—he waved his hand in the air—"this is perfect. It's as if you had a political coordinator telling you what to wear."

He thinks I'm beautiful? Really? "Gwen," she said, still stuck on his compliment.

"Gwen what?"

Shaking out of the daze, she gave him a better answer. "I knew Gwen would know what I should wear. If you need a political coordinator, she's your girl." *Maybe it's the dress and hat he thinks are beautiful.*

Carter squeezed her arm. "Are you nervous?"

"No," she lied. "Yes...a little. Jay briefed me in the car. *Nod, smile, and say very little.*"

"Right. Let me do the talking."

She chuckled. "Jay called it sidestepping."

A knock from the other side of the door interrupted them. "Time to go, Mr. Billings."

Carter let his hand drop to hers. "You ready?"

"As much as I can be."

His hand squeezed hers. He paused. "Eliza, do you trust me—outside of football plays, that is?"

She remembered their conflict at Christmas and laughed. "I think you're an honest man." For good measure, she added, "I'll vote for you."

"But do you *trust* me?"

Would she call him in an emergency and expect him to drop everything to be there? "Yeah, I trust you."

He bobbed his head. "OK...OK. That's good."

He was having a short conversation with himself, she mused.

Someone knocked on the door a second time. "Mr. Billings?"

"We're coming," he called and directed them through the door.

—

He felt the moment her palm went damp. Double doors opened and the two of them, surrounded by his manager, one bodyguard Neil had insisted on, and three of his staff, escorted them onto a raised platform.

The last thing Carter wanted to do was let go of her hand, but when he reached the podium, he didn't have a choice.

He gave her a reassuring smile, squeezed her hand, and let go. She held tight to her purse but otherwise appeared unaffected by the constant flashing of lights set off by the photographers in the room.

"Mr. Billings?"

"Carter?"

"Mr. Billings?"

Reporters called his name repeatedly. He lifted his hands and waited for all of them to calm.

"Thank you for coming," he began. "Everyone has been patient. I hope to ease your curiosity today. Thanks to YouTube, many of you witnessed an interesting video last weekend. As many of you know, myself and Miss Havens"—he glanced at Eliza, who smiled and nodded—"stood up for our very close friends Lord and Lady Harrison, the duke and duchess of Albany, as they renewed their wedding vows in Texas—"

"Don't they do that every year?" someone from the mash of reporters called out. A few reporters laughed.

Carter smiled. "Yes, they do. Love makes people do things like that."

"Give 'em five years. That'll stop."

Carter lifted his hands again. Sticking with his speech, Carter told the reporters he'd been in the bar briefly when he and Blake's bodyguard noticed a couple of unsavory characters giving unwanted attention to Eliza and Lady Gwen. He purposely used Blake and Gwen's titles to add a sense of class to the situation. Earlier today,

Blake suggested he use their titles as much as he needed if it would help the situation.

Blake didn't know that the press conference was only one phase of Carter's plan.

The reporters would figure out the bar was sleazy, and after a couple of interviews, it would be discovered that Gwen and Eliza weren't completely uncomfortable up until the fists started flying.

"It's unfortunate that my intervention was needed. Let it be understood that I will not stand by and watch a crime unfold in front of me without intervening." Several reporters dipped their heads and frantically wrote down his well-practiced and thought-out words.

Carter glanced over his shoulder and reached a hand to Eliza.

On the outside, she looked the picture of composure. But he sensed the frantic rate of her heartbeat when he touched her wrist. He noticed her chest rise and fall a little too fast.

She held his hand almost like a lifeline.

"Miss Havens?" a recognizable network reporter called out. "Can you tell us what happened?"

Carter met her gaze, and she allowed a half smile to reach her lips. "Of course," she said, standing next to him as she leaned into the microphones. "Lady Gwen and I weren't familiar with the area. We'd been in San Antonio for a few days preparing for the wedding. We thought it would be nice to hear some country music. It *was* Texas, after all," she offered.

Carter's shoulders started to relax as a few of the reporters laughed. Even Eliza seemed more at ease as she spoke.

"Like Carter said, a man led my friend outside, and if it weren't for Lord Harrison's personal bodyguard and Carter, I can't imagine what might have happened."

"Who threw the first punch?"

Eliza swallowed. "One of the men from the bar struck Carter first." She glanced at him. "I, for one, am proud to know we have the opportunity to vote for such an honorable man."

More pictures flashed.

A warmth filled Carter's stomach.

"What's your relationship?"

"Are the two of you dating?"

Carter stepped up to the podium and covered Eliza's hand with his. "I think we've answered your questions."

"The public wants to know if they're voting on a party boy with a bank account and friends in high places or a serious candidate, Mr. Billings."

Carter's jaw tightened.

"Carter and I have known each for a couple of years," Eliza spoke for him. "Outside of a beer while watching a football game, I've never seen him overdrink. I dare anyone here to prove me wrong."

"You sound defensive, Miss Havens."

"I'm offended. He might not call plays well from the sofa, but Carter Billings is an honest man."

The rapid-fire questions and Eliza's revealing answers stunned Carter silent.

"You're a football fan, Miss Havens?"

"Isn't everybody?"

Carter, along with half the crowd of reporters, laughed. He stepped forward and slid his hand over hers. She flinched, but didn't pull away. "Thank you all for coming today."

"Mr. Billings?"

"Miss Havens?"

Reporters pushed forward, cell phone and small recording devices in hand, each of them begging for one more answer to one more question.

Carter slid a hand to the small of Eliza's back and guided her off the platform. Only when they were back in his room did he stop touching her.

Jay clapped a hand on Carter's back once the door closed behind them. "Well done."

Eliza released a sigh and turned toward them. "What now?" she asked.

"We watch how they spin it," Jay explained as he switched on the TV.

"How they spin it?"

Carter indicated a chair for her to sit. She sat close to the edge, as if ready to leave.

"The media has a way of taking what you say, splicing it with what you didn't say, and making a completely new story."

"I'm not sure how they could possibly do so with what we said."

"You'd be surprised," Jay said, removing his jacket and tossing it on the back of the sofa.

"How long will this take?"

Jay glanced at his watch. "We have twenty minutes before the afternoon news runs."

"Have you had lunch?" Carter asked. The way she twisted her hands together in her lap gave evidence of her nerves.

"I don't think I could eat."

"Which means you haven't eaten."

Eliza shook her head.

"How about something light? We'll have them bring it here." He lifted the phone and didn't wait for her to agree. The concierge put him through to room service. After ordering the soup of the day and a pot of coffee, two more of his staff members walked into the room. After a short debate, Carter ordered a few sandwiches to feed everyone in the room.

"I saw Bradley from Channel Four doing a wrap-up outside the lobby," Justin, one of the staffers, told them.

"And?"

"Hard to say." Justin's eyes shifted to Eliza. He smiled and shrugged.

Another staffer arrived, tossed his jacket aside. "Well?"

"Nothing yet."

Eliza glanced from each man in the room to another. Her skin grew pale.

The men spoke to each other, each speculating what the media would say. Carter sat on the arm of the chair Eliza sat in, and leaned forward. "Are you OK?"

"Fine."

Yeah, right!

"We can watch in the other room."

She glanced at the bedroom door and shook her head. "I'm fine here."

Yeah, right!

Twenty minutes felt like an hour. As the opening credits for the news rolled over the television screen, room service arrived. Jay rushed the hotel staff in and out. Nobody bothered with the food.

"Shh!"

Carter's first glimpse of Eliza on-screen filled him with a strange sense of pride. It was unfounded, he knew, but watching her walking beside him on film felt right somehow.

"After last week's blunder, gubernatorial candidate Carter Billings is on cleanup. He certainly enlisted a mysterious and charismatic partner to help him. It's hard to determine if Mr. Billings was fighting off an unwanted suitor to his current girlfriend or if his explanation holds merit. You be the judge." As the press ran a clip of Carter's press statement, Carter noticed what little color Eliza had on her face disappear. Her index finger slipped between her lips, her eyes fixed to the screen.

You sound defensive, Miss Havens.

I'm offended.

"Even with Miss Havens's obvious edge, she humored the reporters with her crack about Mr. Billings not being able to determine a ref's call during a football game. Still, this reporter isn't convinced Mr. Billings will be able to escape the now notorious YouTube video."

Jay switched to another channel. This one more sympathetic than the last, but still not what Carter had been hoping for.

Without a word, Eliza stood and walked past the crowded room and into the bedroom.

Chapter Six

Her stomach churned, and she didn't even bother to keep from biting her nails.

Eliza glanced down at her expensive dress before removing the hat from her head and throwing it on the dresser. "What a waste."

She collapsed onto the bed and grabbed her purse. She removed her wallet and found a well-worn picture. On the yellowed paper was a once happy family: her mother, whom Eliza resembled so closely they could have passed as sisters; her father, an honest, loving man; and her as a child of only nine.

The picture had been taken six months prior to their deaths. Prior to their murders.

Those memories were buried so deep, at times, Eliza would forget. After seeing her picture on every news channel, she realized how much she and her mother looked alike.

And that could be a problem.

A knock at the door had her scrambling to put the picture away and to close her purse.

"Eliza?" It was Carter.

"Come in."

Closing the door behind him, he said, "You OK?"

"I'm fine. It's you they're smearing all over town. I can't believe how much they've twisted everything."

He leaned a hip against the dresser and tucked his hands into his pants pockets. Even with all the stress, he was sexy as hell. "We didn't think one press conference would fix everything."

"I hope you won't need me. My wardrobe budget is tapped for the year." She released a nervous laugh.

"I can reimburse you."

Her jaw tightened. "Please. That's not what I'm suggesting." Besides, she couldn't remember the last time someone had paid for her clothes—well, outside of a stupid yellow bridesmaid dress. "So what's next? More press conferences?" She needed to know so she could make a graceful exit from this part of Carter's plan.

"I'm sure those will happen."

He moved over to the bed and sat beside her. She placed her purse to her side.

"You have a different plan, don't you?"

He nodded, suddenly nervous in a way she hadn't seen him before. "We've run studies and researched past candidates in similar situations. Outside of waiting four more years, I need to do something drastic to get the media's focus on the race."

"How are you going to do that?"

"It's simple. They want a family man in office."

Eliza shifted on the bed. "You're going to pull a family out of your butt?"

He laughed, and his blue eyes fixed to hers. "No. I'm going to get married."

Her smile fell. *Kathleen? Isn't he done with her?*

"That's extreme, isn't it?"

"I don't think so. Getting married fixes the image of a fight-starting party boy in a bar. It adds stability to an office that historically has been run by married men. It's the answer to my problems."

Maybe it was, but her stomach didn't like it. She swallowed hard. "I suppose."

"You agree?"

"You're the politician, Carter. You have a finger on the pulse of the voting public more than I do. I guess as long as Kathleen agrees—"

"Kathleen?" His confused stare bordered on comical.

"Who else?" He probably had a small lineup of willing women to be Mrs. Billings.

"You!"

Eliza jumped to her feet; her purse fell to the floor. "Me? Are you crazy?"

"Before you say no—"

"No!"

"Hear me out."

"No!" She needed to get out of the room. Needed to get out of the hotel. Eliza grabbed her hat and shoved it on her head.

Carter stood and stopped her from reaching for her purse. He placed a hand on her arm, and she pulled back as if stung. "Listen, Eliza, you're half the reason I'm in this mess."

"Hey," she said, poking him in the chest with a cracked nail. "I didn't invite you to that bar, and I certainly didn't suggest you get into a fight. So don't blame me for this."

"What was all that about me being an honorable man?"

"The truth of that will change the minute you try and blackmail me into marriage."

"Who said anything about blackmail? I was proposing—"

She tried to step around him, only to be blocked again. "Yeah. Well, don't. I'm the wrong woman for you for more reasons than you could possibly know. Now give me my damn purse so I can leave. I do have a life to live."

"This discussion isn't over," he said.

"You'll be talking to yourself, because I'm done."

Carter clamped his jaw shut and stared.

She folded her arms over her chest and stared back.

He cracked first, stepped back, and reached for her purse.

Remembering the gun, she moved to intercept him. "I'll get it…"

Carter reached it first. The purse wasn't big, and the moment Carter's hand touched it, his face turned to stone.

She grabbed for the bag as he lifted it out of her reach.

He undid the clasp.

"Stop."

And dumped the contents on the bed.

Eliza froze, staring at the weapon she'd carried with her all her adult life. Not even Samantha knew about it. And no one knew why.

"You want to tell me what *this* is all about?"

Her chest heaved with every rapid breath she took. "You want to know what *this* is all about? I'll tell you what it's all about. None of your damn business, that's what it's all about." As quickly as she could, she shoved the contents into the bag, the gun last, making sure the safety wasn't tripped, and then stormed out of the room.

She made it as far as the door.

She opened it and found herself faced with two suit-wearing men holding badges.

"Miss Havens?"

"Son of a bitch!"

The detectives glanced at each other and put their badges away. "We need to speak with you"—they glanced around at the audience of Carter and all his men—"in private."

Not too often in Carter's life—at least since the age of eighteen—did he ever feel off axis. Apparently, all that was changing today.

His bodyguard stood beside the detectives, and his staffers had turned down the television set and were tuned in like an uplink to the Net.

Carter took a chance and placed a hand on Eliza's shoulder. She didn't flinch.

Worse, she trembled.

"What can we do for you, detectives?"

"It's Billings, right?"

"That's right."

"We need to speak to Miss Havens—alone."

"Eliza?" As if saying her name had snapped her out of a daze, she shook off his hand and glared at him over her shoulder.

"I have this," she told him.

"If you'd come with us, we can—"

"Hold up." Carter stepped in front of her, stopping them from leading Eliza away. He might not know what she was hiding, but he wasn't about to let her leave the hotel in custody without some explanation. "I am a lawyer and was a judge before seeking office. If you have a reason to take Miss Havens—"

"I'm sure you're a brilliant attorney, Mr. Billings, but even you understand that some things shouldn't be discussed in the hallway of a very public hotel with an entourage of people at your back."

Taking the clue, Jay said, "That's our cue, gentlemen. Time to give everyone some space."

"No"—Eliza grasped Carter's arm and tugged him back—"I'll go."

"The hell you will."

"Listen, Hollywood, I get that you feel the need to protect and serve here, but you don't get it. I'll just go. Everything is fine."

"If you're in trouble—"

"I'm not."

"She's not."

Both Eliza and the detectives spoke at the same time.

"I'll call you later," she promised and then stepped away from Carter's protection and walked alongside the detectives down the hall.

What the hell is going on?

Carter met the eyes of his bodyguard, Joe, and nodded toward the retreating figures. Taking the hint, Joe followed them.

Unable to pursue without drawing attention to them, Carter watched until Eliza turned the corner and disappeared.

The woman he'd just asked to marry him was being escorted away by bona fide detectives and hadn't been surprised in the least. Expected it, even.

The gun didn't faze her.

She didn't explain it.

Twisting on his heel, almost colliding with Jay, Carter returned to his hotel room and swung his cell phone to his ear. "Go," he told his staffers. "And I shouldn't have to tell you to keep your mouths shut about what just happened."

"We're on your team," Jay reminded him.

Carter's jaw hurt with the amount of pressure his back teeth were taking. "I know. Just...Just keep the others silent."

Jay nodded to those leaving the room. "I'll spin it, don't worry. It's what you hired me for."

Rubbing a frustrated hand over his face, Carter managed a half smile while the cell phone in his hand rang. *Answer the fucking phone, Blake.*

Answer the fucking phone.

At least the detectives waited until they hit the car before starting in. "What about 'low profile' did you not understand, Eliza?"

"I'm not in the mood for a lecture," she told them. She'd had a right-shit day, starting with a press conference she really didn't want anything to do with. Moving on to the twisted media, which couldn't recognize a red light at an intersection if it were flashing in its face. Then on to a proposal from a gorgeous, successful man who, if she were being honest with herself, she had the ultimate hots for, but to whom she'd promptly said no. And ending with, but not limited to, being driven to destinations unknown by two of LA's finest!

Yeah! She'd had a shitty-ass day!

"Standing in front of every media station in the greater Los Angeles area, and at least two national channels, isn't exactly *low profile.*"

Dean, the overweight detective in the passenger seat, glared at her. The last time she'd seen him, he was chewing nicotine gum like it was crack. From the slightly yellow teeth peeking through his lips, Eliza guessed the cigarettes had won.

James, his skinny partner, drove while keeping a keen eye on his rearview mirror.

Yeah, Jim was short for James…And the fact that putting their names together spelled out James Dean wasn't lost on her.

"I'm not eight," she told them.

"But you look exactly like *her.*"

Her. Damn it, her mother had a name. Not that she'd remind them.

"*She* is dead. Has been for a long time." No one knew that more than Eliza.

Dean twisted in his seat and poked a yellowed finger in her direction. "She gave everything to protect you. The least you could do is stay hidden so she can rest knowing you're safe."

"Hide, you mean?"

"Hide, live life out of the spotlight, however you want to put it. Shouldn't be hard. Zillions of people aren't splattered all over the damn TV."

"Yeah well...Life happens." Life with a duchess as your best friend and an influential politician suggesting marriage.

Nibbling on her fingernails, Eliza took two seconds to wish things in her life were different. Wouldn't it be nice to be able to live a normal life with a sexy man like Carter protecting her?

Wasn't gonna happen.

She glanced at James, who had stayed painfully silent during their drive. "You don't have anything to add?" she asked.

"We're being followed."

Unable to stop her natural instinct, Eliza shifted in her seat and noticed Carter's bodyguard in the dark sedan following them. "It's OK. He's harmless."

"Your boyfriend's?" Dean asked.

"Carter isn't my boyfriend."

"Looked like it to me and half of America. Even those in prison with privileges."

Taking a deep breath and blowing it out through clenched lips, she sputtered, "You're reaching, Dean."

"I'm not, and you know it. You're biting your nails. You know this shit stinks."

Asshole.

"How are the cigarettes? Still smokin'?" It was mean, but he wasn't playing fair and Eliza didn't care. "I've lived my life like a good little Witness Protection Program girl. I'm done. You got that? Done!"

"I don't think you have a clue who you're dealing with if you think you're done. This isn't a joke, Lisa—"

"It's Eliza. I haven't been Lisa since I was nine." Just one of the many changes she'd had to make in her life. "Take me home."

"That isn't wise," James finally said.

"Take me home."

Jim met Dean's eyes. She couldn't help but wonder if they'd take her into custody for her own protection.

Jim took a sudden turn back toward the freeway. Toward her home in Tarzana.

She sat back in her seat, with her purse in her lap.

"I hope you know how to use that gun," Dean said.

How did he know? Of course he knew. Jim and Dean seemed to know everything about her life.

"Anytime you want to have a shoot-off, or whatever you call it, you let me know."

"I might just do that," Dean said.

Jim laughed. "You'd lose," he told his partner.

She let a half smile meet her lips.

"So. Was this a scare tactic, or do you two know something?"

Dean looked at Jim and then the rearview mirror.

Neither of them said anything.

Scare tactic. Which had worked when she was a kid trying out for the cheerleading team. Not so much now.

They turned off the freeway and down her street.

"Get back to the studio, Eliza. Brush up on your tae kwon do. Stay alert," Dean told her as he turned into her driveway. "And for the sake of God, call us if you find the butter in the wrong place in the fridge. Got that?"

Yeah, she got it.

Through their rough exterior, James and Dean were good guys. They had no idea what her life was really like, but they meant well.

"Got it."

Chapter Seven

Her phone was ringing when she walked into the house. Caller ID told her it was a private number, but Eliza knew without a doubt it would be Samantha. Blake and Carter were close. He'd probably hit speed dial the minute she disappeared down the hall.

To avoid a face-to-face with her friend, Eliza picked up the phone. "Hey."

"What the hell, Eliza? Are you OK?" Under the tone of *What the hell is going on?* was, *I'm scared for you.*

"I'm fine." She pulled back the curtains and checked the street. As expected, Joe was parked across from her house, and it looked like Jim had circled the block and was now a few houses back.

"Carter just got off the phone with Blake."

"Yeah…" Looked like Jim was staring at the license plate of Joe's car. Eliza hoped Joe didn't have a background he wanted buried.

"Yeah? Eliza? Talk to me. What's going on?"

She let the drapes fall back into place and stepped away from the window. Let the cops and bodyguards work it out among themselves. "I'm fine, Sam. Really. I'm sure Carter painted an ugly picture, but I'm good."

"The police don't escort you away for a private chat if everything is good. Carter is freaked out, and he and Blake are on overdrive trying to figure out what's happening. You can save us all the trouble by talking."

Eliza leaned against the wall in the hallway and toed off her heels. How was she going to avoid this? She'd managed to keep her past buried for years. Maybe she could buy some time and figure out a plan. "Some things shouldn't be talked about on the phone. I'm sure you understand that."

Samantha hadn't always lived the perfect life. And when she and Blake were dating, his crazy ex had bugged the very phone Eliza spoke on to gain information about their relationship.

"I understand. Do you want to meet for coffee? Come over to the house?"

As much as Eliza would have liked to ignore Jim and Dean's warnings, she couldn't. How much could she tell Samantha? And how wise was it to have Gwen stay with her?

And how soon would Carter be pounding on her door for answers?

"I need a day or two. And before you say it, I know I can trust you. I just need a little time."

Samantha blew out a sigh over the phone. "OK. Promise me you'll call or come here if you need *anything*."

"You know I will."

After hanging up, Eliza ran upstairs and changed into two outfits, one hidden under another, and then quickly locked up her house before getting in her car.

Two cars followed her. Joe stayed close, not caring that she saw him, but Jim followed a few cars back.

Within ten minutes, she was in a packed mall parking lot and out of her car.

The crowded mall would have made ditching one person following her easy. Three would take some effort.

Dean weaved in and out of people, easily seen because of the size of his waist. Joe was talking into a cell phone, probably to Carter.

Keeping her sunglasses on, Eliza found the movie theater inside the mall and noted the movie times. The latest young adult vampire movie was about to let out. "Perfect," she whispered to herself.

At the ticket booth, she smiled at the twentysomething attendant and bought a seat for the latest chick flick. "One for *Ten Million Dollar Bride*, please."

Ten bucks later, Eliza was slipping into the crowd. She diverted to the ladies' room, but not before noting Joe buying a ticket.

Inside a stall, she shimmied out of her loose-knit pants and black shirt and tucked them into her oversize purse. Her barely there shorts fit the teenage style, and the shoestring top should have been illegal to wear. She pulled her hair through a trendy black hat with a sparkly cross embellished over the brim. As she was applying gloss to her lips, a slew of giggling teenage girls crowded into the bathroom.

"Oh my God, that was the best one yet," one of the girls squealed as the others oohed and aahed over the latest teen heartthrob.

One of the girls noticed Eliza standing there and let a toothy grin brighten her face. After a few seconds of chatty teenage noise, Eliza glanced at the obvious popular girl of the group and said, "Love that shirt. Where did you get it?"

The tiny blonde lifted her chin and smiled. "Forever Teen," she said. "Cute hat."

Using the desire to impress an older hip girl to her advantage, Eliza complimented the girl's taste and, in a weird way, managed to gain her trust. The girls moved like a small mob from the bathroom, while others shoved in. Eliza slid her glasses on and melted into their group, chatting as she went about a movie she hadn't seen. Thank God the trailers of the film had dominated the movie ads for weeks.

In the small gaggle of teens, Eliza snuck out of the movie theater, right past a clueless Joe. Dean stood outside the door of the theater but didn't see her slip by.

"Do you go to Valley High?" one of the girls asked her.

Do I look that young?

"UCLA, actually," Eliza lied.

"Cool."

A city bus was pulling up to the curb, and Eliza made her break. "Nice talking to ya," she said, waving at the girls.

Eliza overpaid the bus fare and found a seat by the back door. Acting the part of clueless kid, she tucked earbuds in her ears and pretended to listen to music. A couple of rough twenty-year-old kids watched her from across the aisle, trying to get her attention with a smile.

Five stops from the movie theater, Eliza stepped off the bus just as the door was closing. After two blocks on foot, she found a bathroom at a fast-food restaurant and changed back into age-appropriate clothes. One taxi ride later and she was sipping a cocktail at an outside lounge in Santa Monica.

No Joe.

No Dean.

No Jim.

After the third time her cell phone rang, she finally turned it off.

A smile crept onto her lips. *You still have it, Lisa.* She'd managed to escape those following her and fade into the world undetected.

She'd managed to hide.

Again.

Carter debated using Samantha's key and letting himself into Eliza's home to wait for her return. But then what? She'd kick his ass out, and he'd be no closer to answers than he was when she'd stormed out of his hotel room.

Blake knew nothing. And Samantha knew even less. How was it that two women as close as they were could keep deep secrets from the other for so long? Carter thought men held the award for silence.

Apparently, he needed to reevaluate his assumptions.

Blake pulled a couple of favors and discovered that before Eliza was nineteen years old, she didn't exist. There were no school records, no teenage job, and no driver's license at sixteen. Carter would have dug deeper but couldn't shake the feeling that he was violating her privacy.

After the third time he called her cell phone, he left a simple message. "Call me."

She had to know they were all worried. Detectives don't knock on your door every day and ask to talk to you without explanation.

Or did they?

Carter ran his hand through his hair in frustration.

Every time he watched the media coverage of his press conference, he was struck with how amazing Eliza appeared before the cameras. She couldn't have been more perfect, from the way she dressed to the way she teased the reporters. If he could convince her to be his wife, if only for a little while, his political future would be that much more secure. At least that's what he told himself. He knew that marrying her might give them both a reason to give into the simmering heat between them. The hammering inside his chest wasn't due to his political career.

Her flat-out refusal of his proposal shot his plans to hell. He should have expected it. Her utter revulsion to the idea rocked his world, and not in a good way. He knew now he'd blown his proposal. But that wasn't going to stop him from making Eliza his wife. He just needed to change his strategy.

His thoughts were swimming around about how to do that when his cell phone rang.

"Yeah?"

"She's home." It was Joe, who had taken watch over Eliza's house, awaiting her arrival.

"What about the two cops? They still hanging around?" According to Joe's earlier conversation, the detectives who'd escorted Eliza from the hotel were just as dumbfounded when she disappeared in a movie theater as Joe was. "She vanished like a pro, Boss," Joe had told him. "She's done it before."

"They took off as soon as she showed up."

Carter wasn't sure if that was a good thing or a bad thing.

"OK. I'm on my way. Go ahead and take off once I get there. Get some sleep. I think we're all going to need some." Carter hung up, grabbed his keys, and left his house. Even if Eliza didn't tell him what was going on, he wasn't going to leave until he knew she was safe.

Crosstown traffic was light, and he made it to her Tarzana home in less than twenty minutes. He signaled Joe, who waved back and left once Carter parked in her driveway.

A shadow behind the living room window, followed by the curtain moving, made him realize that he was stalling. Sitting in her driveway like a stalker wasn't his style.

He pushed out of the car and marched to her door.

He knocked, but she didn't answer.

"I know you're home, Eliza," he said through the door.

After knocking a second time, he said, "I'm not leaving."

He heard the click of locks disengaging before she opened the door.

Her hair had been brushed out, her makeup scrubbed clean from her face. Even still, she was beautiful. Although there was a heaviness in her gaze he hadn't seen before. Worry, maybe, or perhaps it was doubt.

She stepped away from the door in a silent invitation for him to enter.

At least she gave him that small comfort.

He closed the door and walked into the hall.

She quickly stepped behind him and slid the dead bolt in place. The move caught him as strange, but he didn't comment.

Walking past him, she said, "If I wanted to talk to you, I would have called."

Carter followed her into the kitchen.

"When would that have been? Tomorrow? The next day?"

Water boiled on her stove inside a kettle, and the steam was starting to hum. Without an invitation to sit, Carter leaned against the wall and watched her mill about the kitchen as she made herself a cup of tea.

"Maybe."

Translation: *No.* Damn, she was stubborn.

"Are you going to tell me what's going on?"

She ripped open a tea bag and placed the packet inside a cup. Each movement was slow and deliberate. "I don't know," she finally said.

From the confusion set behind her eyes, he believed she was just as torn about revealing her secrets as he was torn up for not knowing them.

"Are you going to tell me anything? Like, did you know those detectives?" He asked both questions deliberately.

Unfortunately, she didn't fall for his bait. "I'll tell you what I want, when I want. Yes-and-no questions aren't going to work to whittle away answers."

An entire line of questions, ones he'd practiced en route to her home, now needed to be rewritten in his head. "I hope you know you can trust me." Not a question. She couldn't dis him for that.

"This isn't about trust."

He should have taken some comfort in that.

She brought the tea up to her lips and blew across the hot beverage. She peeked over the brim to look at him.

"Since we're talking about trust," she started, "what the hell was all of that about marriage earlier?"

He folded his arms over his chest. "I suppose you could say I'm following Blake's lead. Marriage solves a few fundamental problems in my career path."

She stared at him full-on now, not trying to look away. "Your problems. Not mine."

"Problems you helped play a role in." He saw the spark in her eye before she managed her first syllable of defense.

She sat the tea down and placed a hand on the counter. "That's low, Carter."

"And true, or you'd be the first to tell me I'm wrong. If I had a choice, I'd be married by Monday to help dispel all the media crap created by your and Gwen's night on the Texas town. I thought I could come to you and obtain a little bit of cooperation."

"A little bit of cooperation? Marriage is a tad more than a *little bit* of anything." Her voice rose, and her knuckles started to grip the counter.

"Yet you earn your living arranging marriages or partnerships on trite reasons less important than mine." How dare she follow a moral high ground? Maybe she'd forgotten how well versed he was on her and Samantha's business.

"You forget that our clients have to approve of the relationships we arrange. They have to like the person—"

He laughed, interrupting her. "Do you really want to pretend we aren't friends to prove your point?"

Her cheeks grew rosy, which he had to admit was much better than the pasty color she'd been sporting when he walked into the house. He felt the fire burning inside her as she shot daggers with her eyes.

"You're my best friend's husband's friend. If you're looking for a wife, you might peek into your little black book, or whatever it is you use, and draw another name."

Carter let his arms drop and took two steps closer. The angrier she became, the more his blood churned. His body responded to her outrage, but not in anger. "I don't want to draw another name."

"Well, you need to. As far as I see it, you and I hardly get along. We have nothing in common and can't be in the same room for more than an hour without getting into an argument."

True. All of what she said was true.

He moved into her personal space, felt the heat of her skin, and sensed the spark of her temper. Her eyes shifted as he approached, but she didn't slide away. A stubborn woman, she simply glared, daring him to prove her wrong. Well, he intended to do just that.

"You're ignoring one thing that proves you're the perfect wife for me."

She tilted her chin in defiance. "Oh, yeah? What's that?"

"This." He swept her into his arms and captured her lips in the space of one breath. He was banking on her willful nature to accept his kiss, and she didn't disappoint. Her lips were an explosion of taste on his.

She let out a tiny whimper as her eyes fluttered closed. Molding his body to hers, he made sure she felt his growing desire. Her soft curves ignited his body and left his brain mush.

He ran his tongue over her lips and demanded acceptance. He'd waited so long to be where he was at this point, he wasn't coming up for air even if his head grew dizzy and the lights faded.

Her fingers found his arms and gripped him hard. For a brief moment, he thought she'd push him away. He should have known better. Eliza tilted her head and opened enough for him to devour her. Their tongues dueled, both fighting for control over their growing passion. Her kiss was everything he'd ever dreamed it would be. He could smell the sandalwood musk she used as perfume. Something he'd always identified as uniquely hers. No flowers or overly sweet designer perfumes would do her justice.

Carter slid a hand around her waist and nibbled on the edge of her lips.

Her hand drifted inside his suit jacket and kneaded his back before dipping lower over his ass.

Sweet Lord, he wanted her. He released her lips only to move on to her chin and neck, trailing kisses and learning the spots on her body that made her whimper.

She sighed and tilted her hips into his. She trembled and searched for more contact. Carter slid between her thighs and lifted her with ease onto the cool granite countertop.

Eliza pushed his jacket from his shoulders.

He tossed it to the side in a rush. Even with their clothes on, her body searched for his, begging to be touched, to be fulfilled.

He wanted to make love to her, needed to prove they were more than friends. A tiny voice in the back of his head warned him that she was vulnerable tonight. Spent from a taxing day filled with reporters and cops.

But as he filled his palm with her breast and her nipple tightened into a small bud of need, he knew he couldn't walk away from her now without igniting her anger. He pinched her nipple, and she let out an uncharacteristic squeak. He brought his lips back to hers and smiled under her kiss.

Eliza gripped his hips and moved against him. She should have been pushing him away, stopping this reckless act that wouldn't end well.

She couldn't. Living her life the way she had, never knowing what tomorrow would bring, made her want this more than taking her next breath. Somewhere between dodging Jim and Dean and cocktails on the beach, Eliza realized that, through all her bravado, she might just have to uproot her entire life in order to stay alive.

That meant saying good-bye to Carter. Saying good-bye to those she'd foolishly allowed into her heart.

So when Carter found the waistband of her pants and pushed his way inside, Eliza didn't stop him. Instead, she lifted away from the counter and opened her legs wider.

He sought the damp heat of her sex, and sparks danced behind her closed eyes. Eliza gasped under his kiss as his fingers discovered her tight need and began to unravel her passion. One of her legs wound around his as she struggled to breathe.

She could feel the weight of his stare as he watched her under his hooded gaze. There was no room for embarrassment here. Only the need to find the promised release.

"Yes," she whispered, moving with him. She wanted more than his fingers dancing over her sex, but she'd settle for this.

Her cries grew more frantic, and her core dampened his fingers. He moved faster and penetrated her with a skillful digit. She gripped him with every muscle of her body as he pushed her over the edge. "Oh, Carter."

He moved slowly a few times, and she trembled in an overexcited response after her orgasm. Eliza dropped her head onto his shoulder as he removed his hand and caressed her hip.

“That shouldn’t have happened,” she mumbled. He probably expected her to fight, but she was out of energy and at a loss for words.

“Shh,” he hushed her. “We’ve been sniffing around *this* for years.”

She nodded and didn’t trust herself to speak.

After a brief hug and a kiss to her forehead, he stepped back, keeping his hands on her arms.

Eliza adjusted her clothing and met his gaze. “What about you?” she asked when she caught sight of his aroused state.

“We’re good,” he assured her with a half smile.

Her eyes dipped as fatigue took over.

“I should go,” he said.

They’d pushed through enough boundaries for one night. And if he felt secure that she’d be here tomorrow, he wouldn’t feel the need to keep watch on her all night.

Chapter Eight

Sleep eluded him most of the night. Finally, at four in the morning, Carter gave up and took a tepid shower. Which beat the hell out of the freezing-cold one he'd taken the night before. He'd do it all again. One taste of Eliza was not going to be enough. He'd known it wouldn't be. Maybe that was why he hadn't given in to the urge to kiss her over the past two years. The verbal sparring was the only release of the sexual tension that had built between them.

Not anymore. During the few hours of rest he'd managed, he cleared his head of the emotions clogging his thought processes and realized what he needed to do was learn Eliza's secrets.

He shoved into a Friday-casual suit, leaving the tie and jacket off until he needed to leave his house.

The kitchen wasn't a place he spent much time, but he could manage a small breakfast. He set the coffeemaker to brew and fired up his computer.

Searching for Eliza Havens before her eighteenth birthday had already come up empty. "You didn't drop out of the sky," he said to himself. He ran a search on her last name and, surprisingly, didn't come up with much other than the media coverage from the day before and anything concerning Blake and Samantha. There were a few photos taken of different social events over the last couple of years. In each one, Eliza's face was partially hidden from view. Even one of the two of them at Blake's Texas wedding. It was almost as if Eliza knew the camera was pointed at her and she didn't want her face to be seen.

Carter poured himself a cup of black coffee and, out of habit, turned on the TV to the news. The last he'd heard, the media coverage from the day before was still painting him in a dim light. Yet, instead of doing whatever he could to gain points in the polls, he was searching the Net to uncover Eliza's past.

What did he really know about her? He removed a legal pad from his desk and wrote her name at the top of the page.

Age? He didn't know. He guessed it to be in her late twenties.

Parents? She never spoke of them. In fact, she never spoke of family at all. He placed a big question mark by the word *parents*.

Birthplace? He assumed California. She didn't talk about living anywhere else.

School? Carter ran a hand through his hair and tossed the pen on the desk.

Jesus, he knew nothing about her. How shitty was that?

After a couple sips of coffee, he turned the page of the pad over and wrote down what he did know.

Eliza Havens. He scribbled her name and circled it twice.

He'd known her for two years. She'd been Samantha's friend for several before that.

He wrote down other words that came to mind when her image flashed in his brain: *Smart. Resourceful. Goal-oriented. Beautiful. Witty. Secretive. Carries a gun.* He circled these last words twice.

Why would someone carry a gun? Law enforcement or federal officer, but that didn't make sense. Up until yesterday, he hadn't seen her around any official of any kind. Then those two detectives had knocked on the door.

Carter dropped his hand on his desk. "Of course." He wasn't looking in the right place for answers.

It was just after five in the morning. Too early to call in favors.

He warmed up his coffee and started a search in the LAPD profile to see if he could recognize the faces of the men who'd shown up at his door.

An hour later, he had two names. Dean Brown and James Fletcher. Longtime detectives in good standing with the department. They were under the heading of Special Operations. How generic could it get?

He picked up the phone and dialed a contact in New York.

"Yeah?"

"Hey, Roger. It's Carter."

Carter had known Roger even longer than he'd known Blake. The two of them operated in different worlds now, but at one time, they'd been close. "Well, hello, Governor. How the hell are you?"

"I'm not the governor yet."

"Give it time, give it time." His friend chuckled. "What has you calling me?"

"Can't a guy call a friend?"

"Ha! You're too busy for friends. Especially those of us who never left New York."

Carter could hear the busy station in the background of the call, phones ringing and someone swearing up a blue streak. Criminal or cop, it was hard to tell. Sadly, Roger spoke the truth. There were very few people Carter kept up with unless they involved climbing to the next tier of his career.

"How's Beverly?"

"Good. Ready to pop any day."

Carter cradled his head in his free hand. He'd forgotten all about her pregnancy. "Everything's good, though? The baby and mom are doing fine?"

"She's great. Roger Junior should be here by the end of the month."

"Do you know if it's a boy?"

Roger huffed. "Doctor said the cord was in the way of a good view, but I'd like to think that cord was just my boy taking after his old man. Besides, having a girl scares the crap out of me."

Carter envisioned Roger and his two hundred-plus pounds holding a six-pound infant. What a sight. "You're going to be a great dad."

There was a pause on the line. "So, why are you really calling? Need a little help, Counselor?"

Carter took his pen and flipped the pages of his desk calendar and scribbled Roger's name on a random date a couple weeks away. He really did need to check on his friend and his expectant wife just to see how they were. "I do have a couple questions you might be able to help me with."

Roger didn't seem pissed that he was right about the reason for the call. "Shoot."

"I ran into a couple of LAPD detectives who work under the title of Special Operations. Any idea what that could be?"

"Could be anything from homicide to making sure someone like you is protected against a viable threat. Where did you meet these two?"

"They wanted to talk to my…to a friend of mine. She didn't seem surprised to see them."

"A friend, huh?"

"A special friend," Carter said.

"What else can you tell me?"

Carter debated his options. He gave Roger a small profile of Eliza. Told him she was an engaging, intelligent woman whose private life was her own. He ended his description by telling Roger that she carried a handgun.

"What's she afraid of?" Roger asked him.

"I don't know. She's not a needy woman. In fact, she managed to lose my bodyguard and the two detectives in broad daylight."

"You sure she's not a cop?"

"Positive."

"You gonna give me her name, or are you gonna make me guess?"

With all the media painting Eliza as his girlfriend, Carter knew Roger would figure it out sooner rather than later. "Eliza Havens. You know I need this kept quiet."

"Well, I guess I should stop updating my Facebook page, then," Roger teased. "I got your back. Let me do a little digging. If she is carrying legally, there will be a traceable record as to her reason why. Getting a conceal-and-carry for a civilian is damn near impossible in California. Here too," he added. "Makes me glad I'm a cop."

"Thanks, Roger."

"Oh, do you have a name on the detectives?"

Carter gave him the names, and they said their good-byes.

Eliza lifted the wig from the bottom of her closet and cringed. She'd forced herself out of bed early, fully intending to pack a bag and move on.

Now she sat cross-legged in front of her half-filled suitcase with doubts.

She and Samantha had built an amazing friendship. Little Eddie was like a nephew to Eliza, and she couldn't imagine not seeing his chubby little face grow up. Even Gwen and all her pent-up haughty ways had grown on her.

Then there was Alliance. The business Samantha had started and they now ran together. Eliza envisioned some of the women she'd grown to know through Alliance. Some of them came from ugly families who'd used their children like pawns on a chessboard to get what they'd wanted. These women searching out husbands to keep them financially stable did so to get what they wanted and to tick off their families. Each story was unique. Each one believable.

When she thought about it, Eliza's story wasn't as sad as some. At least her parents had loved her before their deaths.

She remembered their voices at times in the night when everything was still and quiet. The soft way her mother would speak to her and tell her a bedtime story. Her father always called her "pumpkin" in his deep, booming voice.

Her parents had this crazy love that wrapped around her and kept her safe.

And in one night, all of that shattered into a zillion pieces.

Eliza swiped a tear from her face and forced the painful memories aside. She missed having a family to call her own and had found some of that love with her friends.

She shoved away from the suitcase and jumped to her feet. After a fast rummage through her drawers, she found the outfit she was looking for and put it on.

She wouldn't run. Not yet. She'd take Jim's advice and duck out of the public eye. Brush up on a few moves that kept her confident, if not safe.

And she'd watch.

She'd listen.

And run like hell if her past wanted to catch up with her and threaten those she'd grown to love.

Dean sucked in a full lung of nicotine and let it stream out between pursed lips. He'd tried kicking the habit over the years and finally gave in to the fact that he was a smoker. Wasn't going to change no matter how much gum he chewed or how many bogus psychological bullshit tapes he listened to.

He'd been a cop since his early twenties, had said "I do" twice, and then had given up half his shit twice again to say, "I sure as hell don't."

There were very few constants in his life. Jim was the closest thing to a brother he'd ever had, and even his own daughter didn't go out of her way to call, even on Father's Day.

He tapped the end of his cigarette against the ashtray and turned up the volume of the news.

Eliza's image flashed on the screen, and he upped the volume even more.

She'd grown into a beautiful woman. Seeing her on TV made him a little sick. It had been a few days since he'd seen Eliza, and the news had backed off. Until today.

"Gubernatorial candidate Carter Billings has taken a slight dip in the preliminary polls after the Texas brawl recorded last week. Even with the eyewitness account of Eliza Havens, the people aren't ready to vote on such a young and unattached candidate. Billings's rival in the polls, Darnell Arnold, wasted little time learning more about Miss Havens and holding a press conference of his own."

Dean left the cigarette in the tray and leaned forward in his seat. His fist clutched the remote, and his eyes narrowed.

"Seems Mr. Billings has been known to spend quite a bit of time with Eliza Havens. Some even say, if Billings wins the election, there may be a rare wedding of the newly elected governor while he's in office. This assumption was vocalized in Mr. Arnold's interviews." The reporter cut out of the scene, and Arnold stood in front of several reporters. As usual, the politician didn't talk politics, he talked crap, and the people listened. Dean had been around enough years to identify bullshit when he heard it. It helped that he knew Eliza Havens better than anyone could.

"What do we really know about Miss Havens?" Arnold asked. "She might have several influential friends—foreign friends, I might add—but it seems this woman appeared out of nowhere. There are no school records, no birth records. I've heard of politicians unknowingly hiring an illegal alien, but to elect a governor who might place an illegal as the first lady of our state should be avoided."

"Son of a bitch!" Dean yelled at the set. "She's legal, you ass-wipe."

The news ran footage of Eliza's press conference as well as a few shots of her at various functions. Many of which she stood by Billings's side. Most of the shots hid some of her face, but not all.

One in particular reminded Dean of her mother. And if *he* noticed the similarities, so would others.

The broadcast switched to another story, and Dean forced himself from his favorite chair before grabbing the phone. He hoped to hell Eliza wasn't serious about this guy. He and Jim needed to convince her to disappear, and he knew from experience that getting the cooperation from women in love was like stopping a cockroach from snacking on a forgotten doughnut.

Chapter Nine

After a grueling workout full of kicks and punches Eliza had forgotten she knew how to throw, she managed to clear her mind enough to concentrate on only the objective facts of her life.

Her mother and father had died nearly twenty years ago. Although she did resemble her mom in many ways, the chances of anyone finding out her true identity tilted the scale from slim to none. Yet Jim and Dean seemed more worried than they had reason to be. That begged more investigation.

Eliza had been told to never whisper an ounce of truth about her life, or she stood the risk of putting others in danger. She was certain the cops meant the average Joe with minimal resources for security.

Lucky for her, her Christmas card list was packed full of wealthy, influential individuals who had security details at their disposal. Much better than any state-paid employee carrying a badge had available to his or her family. Lord knew that cops often put their own families at risk when they busted big names in crime. That didn't stop them from doing their jobs, and she sure as heck wasn't going to walk away from the life she'd built for herself.

Then there was Carter. Her stomach pitched thinking of his touch. He took his time and seduced her fully. Looking back, she wasn't sure why she'd let him. She'd been vulnerable, not in a normal state of mind. She supposed he'd known that on some level and hadn't pushed her for more.

She wouldn't forget his mind-blowing kisses and her explosive response to him any time soon.

The last thing he needed was a temporary girlfriend to tarnish his reputation while running for office. Their short trip on lovers' lane would have to be a stand-alone affair.

Too bad. She wouldn't mind exploring his other obvious bedroom talents. Maybe in five years, after the election and his term in office. That was, of course, if he didn't pursue a wife during that time. Eliza wasn't about to be the "other woman."

Eliza pulled down the busy two-lane road en route to Samantha and Blake's home in Malibu. No one appeared to be following her, and the road in front was congested with summer traffic.

Telling Gwen about the risk of moving in with her was a must. Chances were the British-born lady wouldn't risk the move no matter how much she craved adventure. Although, in a weird way, Eliza would enjoy the other woman's company. Running interference if Carter knocked on the door wouldn't suck, either.

He'd left a short message on her cell phone telling her that he was thinking about her. Then he went on to say he needed to fly to DC for a couple of days. She didn't want to be disappointed, but she was. One minute, she wanted to see him; the next, she didn't. Dating in high school wasn't this confusing.

Eliza pulled up to the Harrison estate and buzzed the gate, all the while smiling at the camera pointed at her car. The slow hum of the motor opened the long levers and pulled the massive steel open wide enough for her car to pass. Once the gates closed, she continued up the drive.

Mary, Samantha and Blake's cook, met her at the door. "Samantha is putting Eddie down; she'll be with you in a minute," the older woman said.

Eliza stepped into the grand foyer and set her purse and keys on a table. “Thanks, Mary.”

“Do you want to wait in the kitchen or the den?”

Usually, Eliza would have joined Mary in the kitchen, but considering the sensitive nature of the pending conversation with Samantha, she thought it best to hide. “The den, if you don’t mind.”

A wave of uncertainty crossed Mary’s features, but she didn’t say a thing. “Of course. I’ll bring coffee.”

“That would be great.”

They both walked down the hall, but Eliza veered off to the main gathering room in the house. They had a formal living room, but like most homes in America, it was only used during the holidays and special occasions. The Harrison home should have felt cold and uninviting because of its sheer size. It wasn’t.

In the corner of the den was a big plastic chest filled with Eddie’s toys. Several board books with tiny teeth marks covered the coffee table, and at least one unidentified stain was smack-dab in the middle of the sofa.

Yep, even with all the money in the world, a two-year-old ruled the house.

Eliza sat on the couch and leaned back. Instantly, a squeak sounded from behind her. She reached around and found a plush toy with an internal noisemaker.

She laughed. Lord, these things must drive the adults crazy after a day. Samantha had told her more than once to avoid noisy toys as gifts.

Eliza stuck to the rules her best friend had laid out, and Carter would always bring the biggest and noisiest toy. That past Christmas, Eddie responded to Carter’s gift with glee. Even with a short attention span, the little guy played with the One Man Band playground for nearly an hour. It still took up a coveted spot in the child’s room.

Eliza made a mental note to find an interactive noisemaker for the next holiday.

She picked up a Dr. Seuss classic and thumbed through the pages.

Footsteps sounded in the hall before Samantha strolled into the room. "I thought he'd never go down."

Eliza tossed the child's book aside and smiled at her friend. "Naps are so boring," she teased.

"I don't know about that. I'd love a nap." Sam picked up a few scattered toys and tossed them into the toy box.

"You don't have to clean up for me."

"I'm cleaning up for me," Sam said. "There's an amazing home under all of this, and the only time I see it is when he's sleeping."

Eliza gazed around the room. The house was brilliant, with bright primary colors scattered about. Some of the breakables had been relocated to the top shelves or removed from the room altogether, but the Malibu mansion was fit for a duke, duchess, and a toddling little earl.

Samantha fussed with the room's mess for a minute or two before Mary returned with coffee and homemade cookies. Once Mary left, they talked about chocolate chip cookies, two-year-olds, and how far the kids could make the mess spread before Sam finally sat down. "So"—Sam leaned forward, took a deep breath—"you're not here to talk about cookies."

Eliza sat the coffee down. Her palms felt damp. "No. My plan was to come here and say good-bye."

"What?" Sam shouted.

"Was—as in, I'm *not* leaving."

Sam placed a hand over her chest and sat back. "Don't do that."

"Sorry. I'm…This is hard. You keep some secrets so long that saying them out loud breathes new life into old haunts."

Sam reached over and placed a hand on Eliza's knee. "You don't have to tell me if it hurts too much. But I hope you know by now that any secret you want me to keep, I will."

"I know. What I can tell you has to be in confidence. I don't expect you to keep it from Blake or Gwen." *Or even Carter, for that matter.* But she left that unsaid. "It wouldn't be fair for me to ask you to keep this from them. They need to know that being around me might be a risk."

Confusion spread over Samantha's face, but she didn't say anything. She relaxed and waited for Eliza to continue.

"I was in the Witness Protection Program…Well, I still am, technically. Though I've blown that with my appearance beside Carter a few days ago."

Sam opened her mouth and then closed it.

"My father witnessed…" How much should she reveal? Enough to let Sam understand the risk of continuing her friendship. "A murder. A couple murders." More like a massacre. Dead was dead, however, and adding layers to that carnage would only bring misery. "I was nine. So what I'm telling you is what I've learned since. I didn't see anything." Which added to the frustration of living her entire life partially removed from the world.

"You've never spoken of your parents," Samantha said quietly. Patiently.

Emotion rolled over Eliza in hot waves. She was never quick to tears but they were close. So very close.

"My parents did the right thing. My father couldn't have lived with himself otherwise." She stood now and started to move. She picked up a small red plush toy that sat on a chair. "He turned state's witness. We didn't have much, so walking away from our life didn't bother them as much as it might some. I guess, in that, I was grateful. It wasn't like my grandparents lived close by. My father's dad might still be alive somewhere. I'm told my mom's parents are gone."

"Where are your parents?" Samantha asked after a long pause.

Eliza sent her a wry smile and shook her head. "We were careful. But not careful enough."

Sam pulled in a quick breath as the reality sunk in.

"I've been alone for a long time, living in one anonymous state-run dump after another. I moved often, just in case someone watched. The two cops who showed up at Carter's press conference were assigned to my case when I was sixteen. I'm not in trouble with the law. My only crime is stupidity."

Eliza pushed the hands of the toy over the eyes on the head. *See nothing. Be nothing.*

"If you knew helping Carter was a risk, why do it?"

"It was the right thing to do. I'm the one who suggested to Gwen that we go to that bar. I knew the guys flirting with us were edgy." Eliza released a long-suffering sigh and continued. "I felt responsible. I couldn't stand by and let Carter's campaign slide into the dark abyss without trying to help."

"He would have understood."

"Maybe. It doesn't matter. Seems the media has pegged me for an illegal at this point. I may have decreased his chances of getting into office instead of helping." All the risk had been for nothing.

There was a moment of silence.

"Why did you want to run again?"

Eliza sat the stuffed animal on the bookshelf before turning to her friend. "Dean and Jim, the detectives, made certain I remembered why I was in hiding. The man who murdered my parents is still alive, Sam. In jail, but not unconnected. He has an extended family who would love revenge."

"Revenge on a child who had nothing to do with his incarceration?"

"Dillinger and Capone might strike a pose for a good Hollywood movie, but they were animals who didn't leave families unharmed. Their threat is what scared people into keeping their lips shut. There are many Capones out there. They come in all nationalities. All ages. The guy gunning for me made it clear that he'd find me. That it was his mission in life to eliminate my father's seed from this earth. There's no reason to think he's found God and has changed his mind."

"How old were you when your parents died?"

"Nine."

Unlike Eliza, Sam was known to shed tears. They now welled behind her eyes. "Oh, Eliza. I'm sorry. What kind of friend am I that I never knew any of this?"

Eliza smiled and tried to joke. "Carter might look like he belongs in Hollywood, but I'm the better actor."

Sam blinked back tears and forced a smile. She stood and walked over to Eliza. "I don't know if I should be mad that you didn't tell me this earlier or honored that you trust me enough now."

"It's a burden, Sam. Knowing me can be dangerous."

"You don't know that for sure, or you would have run."

Eliza nodded. *Maybe.* "I might still. But at least you'll know why. I'd hate it if you disappeared and I never knew why."

"Don't say that. You're not going anywhere."

"I don't want to."

Sam frowned. "You're not. You have friends who are capable of protecting themselves and you."

Eliza leveled her gaze at Sam and sighed. "I'm counting on that. If you didn't have means, I wouldn't have come here today." She wanted safety for Sam and her family more than for herself. At least that was what Eliza wanted to believe.

"Harry?" The guard called his name from a few feet away. In his hands was a newspaper rolled into a tube and secured with a rubber band. "I have more wallpaper for you."

Harry smiled as Devin approached, wondering what news the paper would bring now. Each and every day in prison morphed into the next with nothing to look forward to. Word from the outside was the only sunshine available.

Many of the criminals he'd been incarcerated with had a family member or two who would visit on occasion. Not Harry. He'd destroyed his family and any hope of seeing the remaining members ever again with his greed and selfishness. If and when he made parole, he didn't have the right to search out his daughters.

Harry stood and extended his hand for the paper. "Thanks," he offered the guard.

Devin shrugged and walked away.

A low hum of anticipation brought a spark of warmth deep inside. Instead of opening the paper on the closest table, Harry opted for a little solitude and walked up the flight of stairs to his cell. There was still thirty minutes before the inmates were forced to their overcrowded bunks and barred rooms. But Harry would gladly give up that little bit of freedom for a glimpse of his grandson.

His two other cellmates weren't occupying their small space when Harry sat on his bunk and opened the paper. He skipped the front page and the financials and went straight to the entertainment section. He blew out a sigh when he saw them. A wedding party with bride, groom, and a handful of attendants. In the groom's arms was a toddler, smiling for the camera. Harry's gaze landed on a young woman in a wheelchair as his thumb stroked the picture. If only he could make her whole.

Regret clogged his throat.

A buzzer sounded in the building, signaling the end of their free time. Less than a minute later, Lester and Ricardo returned to the cell.

Lester had bunked with Harry for a couple of years. He was quiet most of the time, except when he stopped taking his meds and ran on the manic side of his personality. Like Harry, Lester was doing time for fraud. He'd been caught stealing the identity of unsuspecting small-business owners and cleaning out their accounts. He wasn't violent, which worked well with Harry.

Ricardo had joined their room only a few months earlier. He was built like a linebacker, so Harry kept his distance. The man said very little unless it was with his fist. Harry didn't trust him and could only guess what he was in for. In the early days of Harry's imprisonment, the violent felons weren't kept in the same cell blocks with those like him. Budget cuts and a lack of state funding for the prison system had forced all offenders in with each other.

Harry was no slouch. He stood at over six feet tall and never missed a meal. He wasn't a fool, however, and never thought for a minute he'd stand a chance in a fistfight with Ricardo.

"Whatcha got, Harry?" Lester asked as he squeezed in the tiny space between the bunks. "Oh, are those your girls?" Lester had seen other pictures and knew some of Harry's story.

"Yeah."

"The baby is getting big."

Ricardo slid a glance over his shoulder and took in the page. "I thought your daughter was already married."

"She is."

On the top of the page, the article said the couple was renewing their wedding vows. Harry pointed to the title and let the reporter's words do the job of explaining what the picture depicted.

Ricardo started to turn away and then stopped himself to take a closer look.

Harry felt the need to pull the paper aside but refrained himself.

"Friends of the bride?" Ricardo asked, pointing to the others in the picture.

"I guess," Harry said, not knowing any of the people in the pictures personally. He recognized the names, but not the faces.

When Ricardo turned away, Harry carefully folded the paper and placed it in his stash with the others.

Chapter Ten

Carter was running on five hours' sleep in the past three days. What he truly needed was a big bed and six hours of silence so his body could feel normal again.

That was asking too much.

He had two messages on his personal cell phone. One from Roger in New York telling him to call him back when he could manage a secure line and the other from Detective Dean asking for a few minutes of Carter's time.

After a few frustrating attempts of connecting with his buddy on the East Coast, Carter gave up and drove himself to the police station where Dean and his partner, James, worked.

Although Carter had attempted to avoid an audience by driving himself, several sets of eyes shifted his way as he walked into the police station.

Carter glanced over the heads in the room, searching for one of the two cops he'd seen escort Eliza from the hotel a few short days ago.

"Looking for someone in particular, Counselor?"

Used to the title, Carter answered quickly. "Dean Brown?"

"Down that hall. First door on the right."

Carter nodded his thanks and walked past a few sets of eyes. Before he rounded the corner, his cell phone buzzed in his pocket.

Impulse had him opening his messages. Blake's name popped up on the screen with a short note: *We need to talk. Drinks tonight?*

Carter sent a quick yes and a promise to call, then slipped the phone back into his suit pocket.

The smaller office housed six desks and a handful of detectives. Dean and James were sitting across from each other at the far end of the room. Both of their heads snapped up when one of the other detectives greeted him. "I didn't know we were on the campaign trail," came one snarky comment, followed by a laugh.

"I'm here to see—"

"Billings," Dean interrupted, "nice of you to come."

The other detectives stood aside as Dean and his partner walked to Carter's side. They shook hands with cordial smiles. "We haven't formally met. This is my partner, James Fletcher, and I'm Dean—"

"Brown. I know."

Dean's eyes narrowed.

"You wanted to see me."

James shifted onto the balls of his feet and nodded toward the hall.

"How about a cup of coffee?" Dean offered. "Guaranteed to rot your gut and keep you awake for the next twelve hours."

"Sounds good." Carter followed them out of the busy office and down another hall. They stopped at a coffeepot that looked as if it were last cleaned sometime back when Prince was singing about 1999. They filled a couple of Styrofoam cups. From there, they found a secluded room Carter recognized as one where interrogations took place. He couldn't help but wonder if he was there for some sort of official questioning. Though he knew he'd done nothing wrong, these two did remove Eliza from his side a short time ago. He couldn't be too careful.

The door behind them shut, and Carter wasted little time. "Do I need a lawyer?"

Dean glanced at James, and James at Dean. "No," James said as he pulled out a chair and offered it to him.

After sitting, Carter attempted the coffee. The bitter taste slid down his throat like a slug and threatened to come back up. Not only was it bad, it was cold.

"You're not here—not officially, anyway." Dean sat on the edge of the table and crossed his arms over his chest.

"There are a dozen cops in the other room who saw me walk in. If this was supposed to be in private, you should have informed me."

"Not private, just not official. If we met outside of the station and someone saw us, it would broach more speculation. My guess is the media loves to follow you around town with cameras shoved in your face."

Carter couldn't argue with that. "So why *am* I here?"

"What is the nature of your relationship with Eliza Havens?"

He was surprised by the question and wasn't about to answer it. "Why do you want to know?"

"She's important to us."

"Important how?" Did these cops forget they were talking to a lawyer? If there was anyone well practiced in the art of obtaining facts, it was he. Not to mention his ability to elude questions like the politician he was.

"Are you dating her?" James asked from the other side of the table.

"Are you an uncle…a cousin?" Carter asked.

"You're not going to answer our questions, are you?"

"Give me the reason behind this meeting, and I'll consider your questions." He wouldn't answer them, but he'd consider them.

"Eliza is a stubborn woman."

Carter chuckled. *Understatement of the year.* "And?"

"We have reason to believe that she could be in danger. If we knew the nature of your attachment to her, we might be better equipped to help keep her safe."

The smile attempting to break because of the "stubborn" comment disappeared when the word *danger* was uttered. "What kind of danger?"

Dean exchanged a look with James, but neither of them elaborated. From the firm set of Dean's jaw, they weren't going to, either. "Someone needs to start trusting someone here. You guys called me, remember?"

James pushed away from the table. "It would be best for Eliza to disappear for a while."

"Disappear?" Carter didn't like the sound of that.

"Yeah. Only, she isn't seeing the wisdom of our years. If you're close to her, maybe you can convince her."

Disappear? Danger? Carter was starting to find the clear dots on the page. The lines between said dots were muddy, with more questions than answers. He needed more answers. The best way for him to secure those answers was to bluff and let these men think he knew more than he did. "You said yourself Eliza is a stubborn lady. You guys have obviously known her for a while."

"Longer than anyone," Dean said behind his coffee cup.

James cleared his throat, obviously attempting to shut up Dean. "Our only goal is keeping her safe. You've spent enough years with your head in the business of law, Mr. Billings. You know how budget cuts keep our hands tied. Eliza needs protection, and we can't always be there to render it."

"Protection from whom?" As the words left his lips, he knew he'd given away the fact that he knew little.

"Telling you that isn't possible. We brought you here in hope of getting Eliza to listen to reason. She understands the risks. She knows she should leave."

Carter thought of the recent wedding, of Eliza's friendship with Samantha, and her love for Eddie. "Not gonna happen."

"Meaning you won't help us?"

"Meaning you had it right the first time. Eliza isn't prone to doing something because she has to. She does only what she wants." He thought briefly of the god-awful yellow bridesmaid dress and her unease when speaking with the media. OK, maybe she did do things she didn't enjoy, but she did them for someone else.

"We thought you might say as much," Dean said before pushing away from the table and poking his head out the door. "Keller?" he yelled.

Footfalls sounded beyond where Carter could see, combined with a tapping of nails.

Dean's gaze slid low as another cop entered the room with a four-legged friend at his side.

The German shepherd waggled his dark eyes from one man to the other. His tongue lapped to one side of his mouth as he panted.

"This is Zod. A newly retired member of our force."

"Why is he here?"

"You're going to give him to our mutual friend."

Carter's brow shot up. "I am?"

"You are." Dean thanked Keller, and the other man left the room. "Zod is fluent in German commands. Ones I'm sure Li—Eliza remembers. If we gave her the dog, she'd probably laugh in our faces. Maybe, from you, she'll keep him."

Like anyone who watched the evening news, Carter knew the damage a police dog could do. What worried him wasn't that Eliza could stay safe with one at her side, but why she needed him.

"You really think this is necessary?"

"It's an added layer of security we can slip Eliza without too much of a fight. Making her move in with a friend—or a boyfriend—to help keep her protected isn't something she'd agree to easily," James said.

Dean huffed out an exacerbated breath. "She's more stubborn than my ex-wife."

"Which one?" James asked, laughing.

"Both."

"She's really in that much danger?"

Dean nodded.

"And you're not going to tell me why or who might be after her?"

"We're telling you to give her the dog and watch her back. If anything looks suspicious, we need to know." Dean removed a card from his wallet and handed it over. "If you weren't running for office, I'd suggest you stick to her like a shadow until we know she's safe. Your high-profile life is what started this mess, and the last thing Eliza needs is more media exposure."

The sick feeling deep in Carter's stomach started to spread. He needed answers.

He needed them yesterday.

Carter stood and both men followed. James secured a leash on Zod and offered the other end to Carter.

"Zod? That's really his name?" Sounded like a sci-fi god.

Zod responded to his name with a bark.

"He eats special food. One of the deputies will bring a case of it out to your car."

A stat call to Roger was in order. Eliza couldn't be the only one able to call off the dog.

"Witness Protection Program." Roger's words resonated through Carter's hands-free connection in his car.

"I should have guessed that earlier," Carter informed his friend.

"Digging information up is like peeling layers of duct tape away from each other. You'd be better off going to the source to find answers."

Carter glanced over to Zod, who pressed his nose to the crack in the window for a sniff. He'd tried Eliza's home, but she wasn't there. And she wasn't returning his calls. A message from Blake revealed that Eliza was having lunch with Samantha in Malibu.

"I don't know if she'll talk."

"Most don't. But then, most avoid the spotlight and split once their identity is revealed."

She hadn't run. Yet Carter knew she wanted to. He wasn't positive why she stayed, but he would do his best to keep her rooted in her new life.

Zod grew bored with the world outside the car window and settled into the passenger seat of Carter's car. The K-9 rested his head on the armrest between them, and his cold, wet nose brushed against Carter's dress shirt. "What do you know about police dogs?"

"As much as the next cop who doesn't work with them, why?"

A car behind him honked when he didn't notice the light at the intersection had turned green. Zod's eyebrows pitched, but the animal didn't lift his head.

"I have one staring at me right now. A present from Eliza's friends at the station."

Roger blew out a long-winded whistle. "No shit?"

"No shit!"

"That's huge, Carter. You need to be careful."

It wasn't himself he was worried about. "The dog isn't for me."

"I gathered that. If the cops want one of their own with your girlfriend, they believe there is a viable threat. Criminals don't care who's caught in the cross fire."

Carter turned off the overcrowded Pacific Coast Highway en route to his best friend's estate. "I know the score, Roger. What I don't know is how to speak German to a dog. I need some direction here."

"You're in the car, right?"

"Yeah."

"Then I'll have to call you back. Wouldn't want Fido to misfire." Roger laughed over the line.

"His name is Zod."

Roger laughed harder. "Who says cops don't have a sense of humor?"

Carter rolled up to the gate and used the remote access he had to the estate. He waved at the cameras as the gate slowly opened to let him pass.

"Gotta go," Carter told his friend. "I'll call you later."

"Be careful, Governor."

As Carter clicked off the call, he remembered his campaign and realized how quickly he'd forgotten about it during his concern for Eliza. His gaze shifted to his beautiful distraction's car parked in the driveway. He smiled at the thought of seeing her again and felt his gut warm. He missed her.

The question was, did she miss him?

Zod strolled along beside Carter as he walked up the steps to the house, and sat when they reached the door. One of the housekeepers let him in and only gave the dog a passing glance.

Carter considered leaving Zod outside but decided against it when he saw a gardener walk around the house. Even though he used the leash, Zod stuck to Carter's side and moved when he did. *Smart.*

The housekeeper directed Carter toward the family room. Already, he could hear Eliza's voice mixed with Gwen's and Samantha's. The women were laughing. Something Carter had forgotten about doing for the past few weeks.

Gravity shifted, and suddenly he felt very tired. He rubbed a hand over his face before he faced the women.

"Mrs. Harrison?" the maid called into the room. "Mr. Billings is here."

Samantha darted her gaze to the door, which Carter caught; then his eyes found Eliza and stayed there. Their eyes locked. She appeared drawn, exhausted.

He knew the feeling. "Hey," he managed before Gwen shoved out of the chair and walked toward him.

"Carter?" She wrapped her arms around him and kissed both his cheeks before dropping to her knee to address the dog.

A play of emotions crossed Eliza's face. He supposed his own face mimicked hers. Part hesitation, part excitement. The last time they'd seen each other, he'd all but molested her. OK, he had—not that she'd minded. Still, it met with the question of how he should act now. Carter guessed it would be best to follow the woman's lead with a room full of spectators.

"Who's this?" Gwen asked, oblivious to the emotions rolling inside Carter.

"A gift," Carter managed, his eyes never leaving Eliza's dark, questioning gaze.

"A gift?"

Eliza blinked a couple of times and dipped her focus to Zod. She sucked in a deep breath, and the smile she'd worn as he'd stepped into the room faded.

"For Eliza."

Eliza shook her head and pivoted on her heel.

Samantha joined Gwen and let Zod sniff her hand. "So you know," Sam said.

Eliza glanced over her shoulder…and waited.

"I know what?" Carter asked.

Sam glanced up from her crouched position next to the animal and stared at Carter. A brief look to her best friend, and Samantha asked, "What's his name?"

"Zod."

Gwen started to laugh, and Eliza shook her head, all the while her back turned away from the room.

"Zod?"

The dog barked a few times at the sound of his name. "Don't look at me," Carter said. "I didn't name him."

"If you didn't, then who did?" Gwen asked.

Samantha twisted toward Eliza, who refused to look at them. Then Carter glanced at Gwen's confused expression.

"Sam," he started, "would you…Could you and Gwen take Zod so I can talk with Eliza alone for a minute? He could use some water…or something."

Sam took the hint and reached for the leash. "Sure. C'mon, Gwen."

Thankfully, Gwen and Sam left the room without question, both chatting as they walked away. Once they were gone, he waited for some outward sign that Eliza knew he was standing there waiting for her to do something…anything.

"I don't want him," she finally spoke.

Not *I'm not taking him*. Not *I want you to take him back*.

"Apparently, you need him."

She blew out a quick breath. "Don't try and pretend you don't know why."

She still wasn't looking at him. Her back was so stiff it must have hurt. She appeared ready to run. Bolt out of the room at the first sign of trouble.

"I know two things," Carter started. "A couple of your friends I met the other day asked me to give you the dog."

She kept shaking her head. "And the second thing?"

"That the police are trying to protect you." He left out that he had discovered she was probably part of the Witness Protection Program, hoping she would volunteer that information. "I'm not sure why, Eliza."

Carter took a chance and walked closer. When he was a foot away, he lowered his voice. "What's going on?" he nearly whispered in her ear.

"It's complicated."

"I'm a good listener."

"They shouldn't have come to you. I don't need a guard dog."

"Dean said you'd refuse him if he and his partner had given one to you."

"Dean would be right." Eliza finally turned toward him. Her eyes pierced his. "I still don't want him."

"But you'll keep him…right?"

Her jaw tightened; her eyes darted toward the door the animal had walked through. "I don't know."

Carter placed a hand on her shoulder, and when she didn't shrug him off, his insides doubled in. Somewhere in the back of her eyes, he noticed fright. It only lasted a minute before it was gone. "For a little while. Please. I can't be with you all the time."

"I didn't ask—"

"And you live alone. Tarzana isn't the safest city in the valley."

"It's not the worst, either," she defended.

"Are you going to tell me why—why Dean and James asked me to give you this dog, why they know you to begin with?"

Eliza swallowed a couple of times, obviously struggling with her words. "They're being paranoid. Overprotective cops who think everyone is the enemy. They're cautious is all."

"You carry a gun in your purse, Eliza. That's more than caution."

She shrugged away from him and moved to the window to stare outside. After a few minutes of silence, she told him what he'd already been told. "I'm part of the Witness Protection Program. Dean and Jim were assigned to my case when I was a kid. The guy they're worried about is serving a life sentence, so there really isn't anything to get worked up about. Zod is overkill. I'm not in any real danger, or they'd have moved me on by now. They're just paranoid. Have been since the press conference."

Carter felt strain in his arms and realized his fists were clenched. Hearing confirmation of his earlier concerns angered him. "Who? Who are they protecting you from?"

"It isn't important."

"Bullshit."

She swiveled on him, her hands resting on her hips. "I've already told you why. What you'll probably hear from Blake once he and Samantha talk. I would never ask my best friend to keep this from her husband, and I know you'll talk to him. But no more, Carter. I see no need to place you or Sam and her family in any more danger."

"I can take care of myself."

"Maybe you can. But what about Sam? What about Eddie? The Witness Protection Program isn't set up for petty theft."

"I know that."

"Then you know I can't reveal any more than I have. Against my better judgment, I'm standing here and not running off like a scared rabbit. That doesn't mean I won't if there is any real sign that someone is after me."

"Dean is giving you a police dog. They're worried."

"Paranoid. Not worried."

"What's the difference?"

"Because they gave me a dog and not a human escort, that's why. I know what I'm talking about, Carter. I've lived with this my whole life. If there were any real threat, they would ambush me and make sure I had twenty-four-hour protection until I could disappear or be as protected as the president of the United States."

Carter wasn't sure if he should be relieved or upset.

He was uneasy, regardless of her explanation. "You'll keep the dog?"

"Will it end this conversation?"

For now. "Yes."

"Fine. I'll keep the dog."

Carter accepted it as a small victory. She'd told him some of the truth, and he'd accomplished the goal of maneuvering a guard dog into her home.

What Eliza didn't know was that he planned on being beside the dog every moment he wasn't working. And if he couldn't be there, then he'd find a way to have others by her side.

Chapter Eleven

An impromptu dinner party began once Blake returned home. In truth, Eliza was comfortable with the distraction. Zod sat on the floor between her and Carter and eyed the people at the table. Police dogs like the massive shepherd were trained to ignore offerings of food from strangers, but that didn't stop *some* people from trying to feed them.

"I'm surprised you managed to get away this long, Carter." Sam was pushing food around her plate, obviously not interested in eating. "I don't think we've spent over an hour in your presence since the campaign began."

Carter's gaze drifted briefly to Eliza, then quickly to the dog.

"I could use a few days off."

Gwen placed her hands in her lap. "Do governors take holidays?"

"I'm not the governor yet." Carter smiled at Gwen and started to slip another piece of his dinner under the table to Zod. Zod glanced at the food, ignored it, and rested his head in his paws.

Eliza caught Carter's hand and placed it firmly on top of the table. He lifted one side of his mouth in a sly smile.

"But when you are, will you have time for yourself?"

"I'm sure I'll figure it out," Carter said. He gave up on feeding the dog and left the morsel meant for Zod on his napkin before reaching for his drink.

"Even our government officials take vacations," Eliza explained to Gwen. "Speaking of vacations, where's Neil?" Eliza directed her question to Blake.

"He's driving Jordan and her nurse back from summer camp."

Eliza shook her head. She'd forgotten all about Jordan's week-long outing. Samantha's sister had the mind of a child and didn't trust many people. As Sam and Blake's bodyguard, Neil had taken on the role of Jordan's protector too. The whole idea of a bodyguard had bothered her when Samantha and Blake first got married, but now Eliza viewed Neil as one of the family. Although the man didn't say very much, his size and deathly stare would scare any would-be assailant away.

"How did it go this year?"

Samantha smiled. "Well, I think. She's adjusting to changes much easier in this last year. I think Eddie stimulates her."

"Eddie stimulates everyone—at three in the morning," Blake said, laughing.

"It's not that bad." Sam swatted his arm.

"So Neil will be home tomorrow, then?" Gwen asked.

Eliza noted the lift in Gwen's chin as she directed the conversation back to Neil.

"Before noon."

"Maybe he can help me move then."

"Move?" Sam questioned.

"In with Eliza. You haven't forgotten, have you?" Gwen's gaze shifted around the table.

"Oh, Gwen...I don't know. Things are kinda crazy right now." Eliza had revealed enough about her past and the current concerns for her safety to Gwen earlier. Surprise and pity were the woman's first reaction, but she obviously wasn't worried about her own security enough to shy away.

Gwen waved her hand in the air. "Oh, posh. I'm not frightened of anyone following you from your past. Besides, having more people around you and not less would be in order."

Movement at Eliza's feet caught her attention as Zod sat up, licking his jowls. A quick glance to Carter's guilty face confirmed her suspicion that he was still attempting to feed the dog at the table.

"I don't have security like Blake and Sam do, Gwen. It's not as safe."

"But it's safe enough for you? If you don't want me there, please say—"

"I didn't say that," Eliza interrupted.

"Then it's settled. Neil can help me move my things in tomorrow. If there are safety measures to be taken, I'm confident Neil can help. Don't you agree, Blake?"

Blake's eyes traveled around the table before he spoke.

"In light of the circumstances, and with your approval, Eliza, I'd like to have the Tarzana house wired with safety measures and monitoring."

She started to argue, but Gwen cut her off.

"Brilliant idea."

"That sounds expensive," Eliza finally said.

"But necessary." Carter folded his arms over his chest.

"I don't know if I want my privacy invaded with cameras."

"Small price to pay for protection."

Eliza nodded toward the dog that was sitting up and staring at Carter. "That's what he's for."

"What about when the two of you aren't home? Wouldn't you like to know if you had any visitors around while you were gone?"

Carter had her there.

"I can't afford it."

At least two people huffed at the table. Just because all of Eliza's friends were loaded didn't mean she was. Sure, Alliance had managed to put money in her pocket and some in her savings, but dripping in cash, she wasn't.

"Technically," Sam started, "the Tarzana home is mine, so I wouldn't expect you to pay to have a monitoring system installed."

Eliza passed a glare to her friend.

"I love you, Eliza. I don't want anything to happen to you."

Some of the building resentment faded with Sam's words. "You're not playing fair."

Sam winked at her husband. "I'm playing to win."

"Brat."

"Glad we have that out of the way." Carter pushed away from the table and glanced down at the pile of forgotten scraps sitting inches from Zod's nose. "What is wrong with this dog?"

Eliza giggled.

"Seriously. What dog lets perfectly good food lie by its nose without taking a nibble?"

"Police dogs only eat special food from one source. If they were tempted by steak, then the bad guys would learn to keep a T-bone with them whenever they committed a crime." Eliza scooped up the food and placed it on her plate. She patted Zod on the head and praised him.

"You're kidding."

"Nope."

Carter scratched his sandy-blond hair and wrinkled his brow. "I couldn't get my dog to chase a ball growing up."

"I doubt Zod knows how to play ball." In fact, if she remembered right, police dogs didn't even play with other animals. Which was kind of sad when she thought about it. This dog was a working machine.

She hoped she wouldn't need him for long.

Eliza watched Carter check his text messages, his e-mail alerts, and his voice mail. As each hour passed, his eyes languished between hardly open to forcibly awake. If he had a passing thought about their intimate moments, he didn't let on. Sure, Eliza could read the concern in his words, his tone, but he didn't say anything that wouldn't be considered polite.

While visiting in Sam and Blake's family room after dinner, Carter's eyes gave up the battle of staying open, and his chin dipped onto his chest. Zod sat at his feet with his nose tucked into his paws.

"Poor thing," Gwen whispered, nodding toward where Carter slept.

Carter's chest rose and fell in slow degrees. Eliza felt a warm pull inside her heart. "He's running too much."

Sam patted Blake's knee as she stood. "I'll have a room readied for him to stay over."

Blake shook his head and glanced Eliza's way. "I don't think he'll stay."

"Why ever not?"

"He told me he's going to follow Eliza home."

Sam sat back down. "That's a good idea."

"I can make it home on my own."

"That's not the point. He's worried. We all are."

Eliza had started to argue when Carter's hand slid from the back of the couch and to his lap, waking him. He blinked a few times and noticed everyone watching him. "I fell asleep, didn't I?" Embarrassment colored his cheeks.

"We were about to place bets on when you'd start to drool," Blake teased.

Carter ran a hand through his hair, giving it the perfect amount of messy. Eliza easily pictured him as a child with drowsy eyes and thick pajamas. She was certain he was just as irresistible then as he was now.

"You should spend the night here," Eliza suggested.

"You both should," Samantha said.

"Thanks for the offer, but I have that meeting with Mr. Sedgwick early tomorrow."

"The retired real estate broker?"

"Yeah. He's been threatening his children and grandchildren that he is going to leave all his property to his next girlfriend if they don't start getting along." When Eliza first started working alongside Samantha, she'd thought that arranging temporary relationships would be among the young or middle-aged. But then there was Sedgwick, who'd reached his seventy-sixth birthday in the winter and vowed to be married by spring. His spoiled, deadbeat children squabbled about everything, and Sedgwick was in need of a strong woman to knock some sense into his kids' heads.

"If we do find him a companion and something happens to him, those kids are going to scream and tie us up in litigation for years."

"That's what I think too," Eliza told Samantha. "I need to find a bingo parlor filled with large German widows close to his age."

"But he wants a young wife."

"He wants a companion," Eliza insisted. "Someone to share his time with. His children don't spare him any of their precious time unless he's shelling out money. It's sad."

Eliza stood and the others in the room followed.

"You'll call me tomorrow?" Sam asked.

"Keeping tabs on me?"

"Damn right."

Eliza would do the same if Sam were the one in her situation, so she took it as concern from a friend and not an overprotective measure.

"We'll work scheduling the security system in tomorrow morning. Do you plan on taking Zod with you when you're out?" When the dog heard his name, he stood and wagged his tail.

"Restaurants don't allow animals."

Carter mumbled something under his breath, but Eliza ignored him. "I should be back before noon."

"Perfect," Gwen said. "That will give me time to gather my things." Gwen leaned in for a hug.

Eliza thanked Sam for dinner while Carter and Blake headed for the door.

Once their good-byes were said, Carter stood outside with Eliza.

"I'm not going to be able to talk you out of following me home, am I?"

Carter shook his head and sent her a cocky, tired smile.

"Fine." He couldn't keep up the pace of politician running for office and personal bodyguard for long. She turned toward her car, Zod at her side.

"What, no argument?"

"I'm too tired to argue," she said over her shoulder.

Carter chuckled and proceeded to follow her home.

Lunch with Sedgwick proved to be the highlight of Eliza's day. Even with the older man's constant chatting about the world going to hell and how the youth today didn't know how good they had it, his noise didn't compare to the noise of Eliza's home.

Zod greeted her at the door with a need to go outside. Before the dog was finished, her phone rang. With the phone to her ear and the back door to the house open so the dog could get back in, Eliza listened to Neil detail the long list of servicemen who would descend upon her in less than an hour.

"Parkview Securities is sending four electricians within the hour." Neil's tone was short and to the point. "They have gray uniforms with black lettering for their logo and names."

Eliza giggled. "This is important why?"

"Knowing who is walking through your door *should* be a priority. I would think you'd understand that."

The smile drifted from Eliza's face. Neil didn't sound very happy with her or the situation.

"OK, Boss, what else?"

Zod finished outside and walked back in the house. Eliza shut the door and continued to listen to Neil's monotone voice.

"Two of the electricians will work inside the house, two outside. They will wire all the doors and windows and place cameras in common rooms and hallways."

"I don't want my bedroom monitored."

"Bedrooms and bathrooms are excluded."

There was some comfort in that, she supposed.

"A fifth man will arrive a couple hours after the others to set up the monitoring system. His name is Kenny Sands. He's the owner of Parkview. He's five-ten, about a hundred-eighty pounds. He will need to show you and Gwen how to work the system and explain how to access your system when you're away from home."

"Is Gwen on her way?" Eliza glanced at her watch. It was just past noon.

He hesitated. "We will be there by two."

"So who is going to watch these cameras, Neil?"

"You'll have twenty-four-hour surveillance from the same eyes watching Samantha and Blake."

In other words, handpicked virtual bodyguards who worked with Neil.

"Any questions?"

"Just one."

Neil was silent on the line.

"How come Samantha didn't call me with these details?" A phone call from Neil was out of character.

"I told her I would take care of it."

"She's afraid I would talk her out of it?"

"Something like that."

"And there's no arguing with you."

"Few have even tried."

Eliza laughed. "I'll bet."

Chapter Twelve

Carter's phone buzzed in his pocket. He glanced at the text message from Neil that read only one word.

Done!

Although the information Jay was telling him about the latest polls was important, the room around him faded as Carter's thoughts turned to Eliza. Her house was secure, and she wasn't alone. Not that Gwen would offer much in the way of protection. At least Eliza had company when he couldn't be there.

The night before, when he'd dropped her off, he didn't want to leave. He had walked around her home, making sure there wasn't anyone lurking in the shadows, and hadn't said a thing. Her arms had been crossed over her chest in an obvious sign of *Leave me alone*. Carter took the hint and moved along.

"Did you hear me?" Jay asked.

Carter shook his head. "I'm sorry. I'm distracted."

"That's obvious." Jay scowled and tossed his pad and paper aside. "What the hell is up with you lately?"

Carter rolled his head from one side of his neck to the other, all the while searching for the answer Jay wanted. "I have a lot on my mind."

"Which is obvious to me and the voting public. Care to share so I can fix your problems and we can move on?"

"You can't fix my problems, Jay."

"The hell I can't. That's what you hired me for. I find your problems before they submerge from the depths of the Atlantic. So what is it? Family? A woman? What?"

Jay was the best. He'd been in Carter's employ for a few years. Started out as an assistant and worked his way to campaign manager. Jay had earned Carter's trust when, two years ago, Carter's uncle, Senator Maxwell Hammond, decided to pay an unexpected visit to Carter's office unannounced.

Jay recognized the senator on sight, but when the man announced he was Carter's uncle, Jay thanked him for the introduction and then asked if he had an appointment.

Carter wished he'd seen the old man's face when Jay slighted him with the question. Maxwell should have been a five-star general in a former life. He commanded attention when he walked in a room and seldom did anyone question his authority.

Jay questioned.

As Jay had assumed, the unexpected and unwanted visit from his uncle took a minute for Carter to absorb. Carter considered himself adaptable, but Uncle Max was the self-ordained patriarch of Carter's family and a first-class son of a bitch if there ever was one.

Jay had managed to divert Max until Carter could figure out why Max had sought him out.

Carter and Jay worked frantically, searching Carter's cases involving Max's colleagues and friends. Sure enough, a son of a diplomat was due to appear in Carter's court within the week. Prepared for the *suggestion* from his uncle, Carter met him for drinks that night at the hotel where his uncle was staying. There was small talk, a few "How is the family doing?" questions, and then Max proceeded to try to bend Carter's decision to Max's will. Max smoothed the collar of his perfectly tailored suit jacket along his chest. The man was fit, barely carrying an extra pound around his belly, but the years in office were catching up with him. Streaks of gray peppered his brown hair. He was blessed with good looks and charisma, the two things money couldn't buy in politics.

"I understand one of the Prescott boys is going to be in your court next week. Some kind of domestic issue."

"Is that so?" Carter lifted his drink to his lips, completely prepared for what was coming next.

"Kids make mistakes."

Not this one. Joe Prescott II was one spoiled bastard who had managed to escape justice for every misdeed he'd been guilty of since his teens. At twenty-three, the rape and physical evidence the prosecution had on Joe's crimes would wipe the perpetual smirk off the kid's face for a long time. Although Carter had yet to hear the case, the eyewitness testimony and physical evidence were ironclad, apparently.

The evidence was what every cop wanted and what every lawyer loved. As a judge, it made his job easy.

Joe had waived a jury trial in hopes of bribing the judge.

Carter hoped the police didn't screw something up and testimony or evidence wouldn't have to be thrown out. Shitheads like Joe and his political friends needed to understand that some judges didn't sell out. No matter who asked.

"Baseballs breaking windows are accidents. Tying defenseless women up and assaulting them…not so much."

Max took a swig of his drink. "The girl is unreliable. From a bad family."

"That makes it OK?"

"Don't be stupid. Prescott is a good kid. He's changed."

Carter sat back in his chair and watched the unease from his uncle. He couldn't help but smile and enjoy his moment of uncertainty.

"Prescott gives everyone with a Y chromosome a bad name."

Max's glass hit the counter with a thud. "The case needs to go away."

"To protect your political dollars?"

"Make it happen."

The last thing Carter wanted was more politicians like his uncle running the country. Knowing his uncle Max like he did, Carter said little more about the case and was determined to do all he could to send Joe to jail.

Less than a week later, Joe Prescott II was found guilty beyond reasonable doubt and had his own escort to the state penitentiary, where he should have had plenty of time to contemplate his misguided life.

Should have.

Max never spoke of the trial, never spoke of the case. However, after only fifteen months in prison, an executive pardon exempted everything Joe Prescott did and set him free.

Carter was livid. He knew what had happened. He knew the ties Uncle Max had pulled to set the kid free.

"Well? Is it Eliza?"

Jay's question snapped Carter out of his past memories and back to the present.

"Why would you ask that?"

"She's beautiful. An easy distraction."

That she was. Even though Carter trusted Jay, he wouldn't reveal any of his true concerns when it came to Eliza. "I had a life before I decided to run for governor."

Jay tossed his head back and laughed. "No, you didn't. I was there, remember?"

"Just because it wasn't displayed for your eyes doesn't mean it wasn't there."

"Don't give me that crap. Dating and an occasional toss don't constitute a love life. And outside of your job, you don't do squat.

You've made this job a cakewalk up until that stunt in the cowboy parking lot."

The cowboy parking lot had mucked up his momentum and helped his rivals take the lead. If only Eliza would agree to marry him. Then he could keep an eye on her and make the good citizens of California see that he was the right person for the job.

"Is this distraction of yours going to keep you from the luncheon in Chicago tomorrow?"

"No." Lunch in Chicago to raise funds tomorrow, San Francisco the next night. How in the world was he supposed to snag a wife—no, make that snag Eliza—when he was jet-setting all over the country?

And what if someone was watching her?

What if the dirtbag responsible for her parents' deaths wanted to speed up Eliza's date with death? A familiar burn in his stomach started to warm his insides. "Remind me again…Who are Montgomery's supporters?"

While Jay rattled off the governor of Illinois's allies in Congress, Carter did his best to not think of Eliza and the four-legged furry friend protecting her when Carter couldn't be by her side.

"For a police dog"—Eliza waved a three-inch-high heel at Zod while she yelled—"you sure have a thing or two to learn about manners!"

Zod tilted his head to the side and continued to pant. Not an ounce of guilt marred the dog's expression.

Eliza eyed the puncture marks in the heel and felt her blood pressure soar all over again. She had half a mind to send Jim and Dean a bill.

The front door to her home opened, and a calm female voice announced the breach into the interior of the home as if it were a flight arriving on time at O'Hare. *Front door!* Equally annoying was the back sliding door opening, or a window. Only when the system was armed would an actual alarm blaze a siren that would wake the neighborhood.

It was overkill. All of it. "Bad dog," Eliza scolded one last time before dumping the shoe on the counter.

Gwen sailed into the kitchen with a garment bag in her arms. "I thought I heard you in here." Gwen wore the perfect smile, under the perfect nose, without one hair out of place. Eliza was sure that the girls Gwen had gone to school with probably hated her for her perfection.

"I'm telling Cujo here to lay off the shoes."

Gwen set her bag down and wagged a finger in Zod's direction. "Are you misbehaving?"

Zod's tongue rolled out of his mouth as his big brown eyes glanced between the two of them.

"I'll give the dog points for taste. He only eats expensive. My guess is his original owner was a man."

"Why do you say that?"

"He hasn't touched my running shoes."

"Perhaps he needs more exercise," Gwen said. "Our dogs back home run the grounds of Albany and seldom sit inside."

Albany was Gwen's family estate. Eliza had been there on occasion to celebrate with Blake and Samantha. Gwen's idea of a yard was hundreds of acres of land. Eliza's postage-stamp backyard didn't compare.

"I'm still not sure why you'd want to live here and not the virtual palace you grew up in." Eliza picked up the ruined shoe and plunked it in the trash.

Zod stared. It was as if the dog knew he could take you out and didn't give a rat's rear end that he messed with your stuff.

"There is more to life than a big home."

"Big homes don't suck." Eliza loved Samantha's Malibu estate. The views, the pool. The kitchen was even tempting, although Eliza's idea of cooking consisted of a microwave and a toaster oven. She always said that if she had a cook's kitchen, she'd learn how to bake a pie.

"I've had luxuries my entire life, and though I appreciated them, I know I took them for granted. For once, I'd like to earn my own way."

Eliza laughed. "You haven't lived until you've eaten dehydrated noodle soup for lunch and dinner."

A look of horror passed over Gwen's face. "That sounds ghastly."

"Be careful what you wish for, Gwen. I've had next to nothing, and it's less than fun. I can see how earning your own way might sound enlightening to you. For the rest of us, it's old-fashioned hard work."

"I'm not afraid of hard work," Gwen defended herself.

"I'm happy to hear that. We have a mixer we're attending tonight. Fancy ordeal at the Royal Suites in Beverly Hills. Very upscale. The kind of thing you should fit in quite well with."

Gwen flashed a smile and lifted her chin. "I'll be eager to learn what you and Samantha do."

Eliza heard a muffled sound behind her and noticed Zod inching toward the back door and another pair of forgotten heels.

She yelled in German at the dog to stop and then picked up her shoes.

"I find it hard to believe that Zod will ignore beef but eat shoes."

"We might not want to tell anyone his weakness, or we might find a shoe salesman ransacking the house."

Chapter Thirteen

The mixer was black-tie and formal gowns, the kind of affair Eliza endured but didn't love.

The fake smiles and meaningless endearments rolled off the tongues of the attendees like cheap lines at a beer bar. "Nice to see you again…Don't you look lovely…What a smashing gown…"

Who in the real world used a word like *smashing*?

Uptight, rich yuppies who managed to invest their trust funds and make money, that's who.

The first time Samantha brought Eliza to one of these functions to work the room, prospecting for clients and the women willing to marry them, Eliza had nearly tripped on her formal gown. Back then, she couldn't talk current affairs of the rich and connected. Gwen, however, was a natural. A daughter of a duke who understood the rich better than Eliza ever would, Gwen veered away from Eliza as soon as they left their coats with the doorman.

Eliza didn't drink at these functions, but always kept a glass of wine in her hand—managing maybe one sip. A salesman might try to work the room as an outsider, but she didn't play that way. She tried obtaining the trust of her clients by acting as one of them.

Thus far, her strategy had worked.

No one guessed she had a compact 9mm strapped to her thigh. At affairs like this one, a purse would be cumbersome, and leaving a firearm unattended was never smart. There were many events in the past year where she'd left her gun at home. Thanks to Dean and Jim, she didn't feel as if she could do that anymore.

Even now, she felt the heavy weight of someone's stare and turned around to see if anyone was watching her.

She was about to give up on her search when her gaze landed on the broad shoulders of a familiar frame.

Over the rim of his glass, Carter caught her gaze and sent her a wink.

What is he doing here?

Warmth spread in her stomach and traveled south. His dominating presence and charismatic smile snagged more than one attractive woman's attention as she walked by. The suit had a tailored fit that made department store suits appear rumpled and old.

Though most of the men wore bow ties, Carter kept it simple with a navy blue tie in place of a bow tie. Very patriotic.

Carter went back to talking with the group he was standing with before he shook one man's hand and started walking toward her.

Several eyes followed him as he made his way to her side.

Once there, he leaned down and kissed her cheek as if it were a normal greeting for them both. "Sorry I'm late," he said a little louder than Eliza had expected.

"Late?" she whispered. "I didn't know you were coming."

"Really?" He removed a glass of wine from a passing waiter's tray as he spoke. "I'm sure I mentioned it last night."

"I'm sure you didn't."

"Must have slipped my mind."

Sure it did. Eliza sipped her wine, not meaning to, and watched Carter wave to a guest across the room. *What was he up to?*

"Aren't you flying out of town tomorrow?"

"First thing in the morning."

"How many hours sleep did you manage last night?" He appeared more rested than the previous night, but not by much.

"A few."

"A few? You're going to get sick if you keep this up."

Carter lifted his eyebrows and flashed his Hollywood smile. "Is that concern in your voice?"

Was it?

"No…yes."

Amusement passed his lips.

"Oh, stop. Of course I'm concerned. Illness spreads, and we do run in the same circles." Her excuse was lame, but it would have to do. Instead of waiting for Carter to laugh in her face, she attempted to turn away.

He managed to capture her around the waist and slid his hand to the small of her back. "C'mon, I have some people I want you to meet."

"I'm here for work," she said as he directed her across the room.

"So am I."

Walking away would have made a scene, so Eliza kept to his side and ignored the comfortable position of Carter's fingers pressing against the small of her back. When they arrived at a gathering of men drinking and laughing, Carter's hand didn't move. In fact, he moved even farther into Eliza's personal space.

"Gentlemen," Carter interrupted the conversation, "I'd like you to meet a friend of mine. Eliza Havens, this is…" Carter rolled off several names, all of which she should have remembered but promptly forgot.

Carter proudly stated that Eliza was part of a firm titled under acquisitions and mergers. He didn't elaborate on any details and derailed any personal questions about the two of them. The men were polite and appeared enamored by anything Carter had to say. Very little politics was discussed, and most of it only scratched the surface of the current events plaguing the state. Carter told the others that they were attempting to enjoy a night off without deep debate. Of course, if the men wanted to join him at a campaign function, there was one planned at the end of the month to help raise funds. He'd talk politics in depth at that time.

As the conversation dried up, Carter moved Eliza to another set of people and repeated his introductions.

Within a half hour, her drink was gone and she had another one in hand.

Carter's palm sat firmly on her back, with his fingers often squeezing her side when one of the men in the group let his eyes linger on her cleavage for more than a second.

Out of the corner of her eye, she noticed Gwen working the room. Something she really should have been doing.

Instead of letting Carter's nearness distract her, Eliza attempted to remember the names and marital status of the people Carter was introducing to her.

Stenberg, a lawyer, probably in his sixties. He lifted his drink to his lips, and Eliza saw the gold band.

Next.

McKinney, an investor of some sort. No ring. Had to be in his seventies. "Mr. McKinney, was it?"

"That's right." He had a slight Irish lilt to his voice.

"Is your wife here, or does she stay away from these affairs?"

Carter nudged her side, and she nudged him back.

"No wife, I'm afraid."

Carter kept the conversation light. "McKinney and I are the bachelors on the block."

Stenberg sighed. "McKinney might not have a stunning woman on his arm like you, Billings, but that doesn't make him a bachelor."

McKinney tossed his head back and laughed. "My last divorce wasn't my doing, no matter how the media painted it."

"The media does have a way of mucking things up, don't they?" Eliza asked while making a mental note to keep McKinney on her Alliance radar.

From that encounter on, Carter attempted to stop Eliza from probing the personal life of the guests by asking about a man's wife or a woman's husband. The ones where he didn't mention a significant other gave Eliza the information she needed.

Eliza placed her empty glass on a tray and shook her head.

Carter excused them and led her toward a lighted doorway to the outside patio.

"Where are we going?"

"You look like you need some air."

She did. The fact that he'd noticed made her heart skip an extra beat.

The air outside was still warm, with a slight breeze coming in from the east. "Feels like a Santa Ana setting in."

"As long as it doesn't produce any fires."

Summer, wind, and fires were a constant in Southern California. More than earthquakes.

"I think we'll be OK."

Carter stopped by the edge of a pole and reluctantly let his arm drop to his side. "You're a natural in there. Do you and Samantha come to these things a lot?"

"Samantha used to do this all the time. Before Blake. I've been solo for most of the last two years. With Gwen coming on, it should ease up the number of these that I'll have to attend."

"Does it work? I mean, do you just ask if the men are single and ask if they're interested in a dating service?"

"I'm much more subtle. Most of our clients are referrals. But it doesn't hurt to mingle and find new ones."

"I guess it's not very different from getting set up in college."

"Only, our clients all have something to offer and something to gain."

Carter thought about how Samantha and Blake's marriage had started out as an arrangement and ended up with a happily ever after.

He glanced and caught Eliza watching him.

"What?"

"Why are you really here, Carter? And don't tell me it's to work. You haven't talked politics all evening."

He stepped away from the pillar he was leaning against and took a step closer to her. "You're right. I'm not here for my quest for office."

Instinct told her to move back, but she kept her feet planted in place.

"Why, then?"

"For you. I knew if I'd asked to join you tonight, you probably would have said no."

"I don't need a bodyguard."

"See? I knew you'd say that. I didn't want to come as a bodyguard. I wanted to come as your date."

Her mouth dried up, and her jaw slacked like a guppy out of water.

"My date?"

"Right."

"Why?"

Carter wove one of his hands around her waist and moved closer. "I think about you all the time. Have for a while."

"Really?" All of her one-word answers were starting to annoy even her.

Carter just smiled and moved in with calculated ease.

"Really. So what do you say, Eliza? Can I ask you out on a date? Dinner? Maybe a movie?"

Dinner and a movie? Oh man, when was the last time she'd done that?

But this was Carter standing way inside her personal space, heating her body with his.

"Do you have time for dinner and a movie?"

"I'll make time if you say yes."

Eliza forced her eyes away from his, but they rested on his chest. His very big, very firm, very yummy chest. "I don't know, Carter. We don't have a long history of getting along."

"We seem to be doing OK tonight."

"We're in a crowded room."

"Restaurants are crowded—movie theaters too."

She laughed. "I don't know."

Carter lifted her chin and stared into her eyes. His fingers trailed along her jaw with one simple stroke that fired all of her senses and surged energy down her spine.

"It's dinner. We both eat. And I could use a real night off."

Eliza fixated on his lips and felt the tip of her tongue sneak out of her mouth to moisten hers.

Carter sucked in a quick breath.

He was dangerously close. Close enough for her to absorb the masculine scent of his cologne, the very fragrance that lingered on her skin after their one brief intimate moment.

"Have dinner with me, Eliza." The deep tenor of his voice rumbled in his chest.

"Dinner? I can do dinner."

A sly smile lifted his lips, and he moved even closer. His kiss hovered close, and she moved closer.

"I want to kiss you," he said, stroking her chin with one hand and keeping her tucked into his side with the other.

Eliza gave a tiny nod and waited for him to make good on his remark.

"But I think I'll wait." His words registered even though he didn't move away.

"Wait?"

"I rushed you the last time. I don't want to repeat the same mistake twice."

Eliza tore her eyes from his lips and caught the mischief dancing behind his eyes. "Kissing me was a mistake?"

"Kissing you was a taste of heaven. Rushing you into that kiss, that was a mistake. I won't rush you again."

What if she wanted to be rushed? Talking about kissing and the act of kissing were very different monsters. Right now, she was hungry for a taste of his lips. Before she could take action, Carter pulled away.

"I'll pick you up tomorrow night, six o'clock."

"How should I dress?"

"Casual."

She could do that. What she didn't think she could do was rest until he delivered his promised kiss.

Chapter Fourteen

Dean ripped open a plain envelope with his name scribbled on the front that sat on his desk.

A note was stapled to a receipt from a department store. *Your shoe-eating dog loves the taste of leather. What did you do, give him a cowhide to gnaw on?*

It was signed simply *E*.

Dean scraped his jaw with his palm and covered a laugh. Sure enough, Eliza had sent him a bill for two pairs of shoes. Looking at the price, he knew Eliza had gone ahead and bought a more expensive pair than she usually wore.

He tossed the note on his desk and logged in to his computer. With Eliza on his mind, he typed in the name of the felon responsible for Zod's presence in her life and waited for the man's current location to pop up.

The prison records stated that he had been moved within the jail he'd been housed in for over a year. Dean wrote down the cell number, determined to find out who bunked with the scumbag.

He typed up a quick e-mail to the warden asking for details and sent it off.

Dean already knew the man in jail had "good behavior" privileges. Newspapers and the television would be accessible.

It would be a lot easier if the man assaulted someone on the inside. Then his chances of seeing Eliza on the news or in the papers would be more difficult.

Dean wasn't that lucky.

At least Eliza was sailing under the radar and had managed to keep her face out of the news for the past week.

Dean patted his jacket pocket by habit, searching for his pack of cigarettes. He bit his lower lip in an effort to squelch the need for nicotine. Eliza's comment when she'd seen him hummed in his brain. He wanted to quit and had purposely left the pack at home. He hadn't smoked for thirteen hours, and already, his nerves were fried.

He sucked down his cold coffee in an effort to replace one chemical with another.

Damn warden is taking his time getting back to me.

Dean glanced at the time he'd sent the e-mail. It had only been twenty minutes.

He'd picked a hell of a time to quit smoking—again.

They skipped the movie and played miniature golf. Carter knew if he sat down in a dark theater, he'd fall asleep within minutes. That wouldn't bode well for his being voted "date of the year."

What he wasn't expecting was his date to be Little Miss Hole-in-One.

For the most part, they went unnoticed on the small golf course. Filled with families and teens, the patrons were too engrossed with one another to identify him as the potential next governor of the state. For once, he was happy to be invisible.

Carter leaned on his putter as Eliza lined up her ball.

"There's no way you'll make that with one swing."

"Is that a challenge, Hollywood?"

"Even the sign says par is three."

"Par schmar. It's all in the angles, just like bowling and pool."

Carter narrowed his eyes and waited while Eliza tapped the ball up an embankment and through a narrow hole, coming within two inches of the hole before stopping.

"Told you."

One tiny tap and the ball went in. "That's still one under par. You'd have to make this—and the next three—in one shot just to catch up."

Carter dropped his ball and attempted to see the angles Eliza had referred to. "I didn't know you were so competitive." He tapped the ball, watching it roll up and then right back down before it landed within a foot of where he'd started.

Eliza laughed. "Why do things halfway? Do it right, or don't do it at all."

He hit the ball again and made it through the hole. "Who taught you that?"

"My dad, actually. He was an optimist who believed anything was achievable with hard work and determination." Her voice softened, and Carter glanced up from the ball to see her gazing into the sky. He'd never heard her talk about her parents. Considering the events in her life, she probably never did.

"Was he a hard worker?"

Eliza sighed. "Eighteen-hour days. He held a nine-to-five and then picked up extra work after hours. He believed in mothers staying home to raise their children."

Carter tapped the ball, overshot his mark.

Eliza kept talking. "My mom took care of the house, cooked—she baked bread. I remember our whole house smelling like yeast and dough. Some kids wanted their moms to bake cookies. I used to live for a thick pad of real butter smothered over oven-hot freshly baked bread."

Carter couldn't relate; his own mother wouldn't know the right side of a spatula.

"We always ate dinner as a family. My dad would come home between jobs, shower, and sit down to three courses before moving on to his next job. He never complained. When I would moan about him not being around, he'd remind me how lucky we were to have so much. Most of my friends at school were latchkey kids who didn't see either of their parents."

"I wish I could have met them," Carter said in a low voice.

Eliza shook her head and smiled. "They would've liked you. And forgiven the fact that you're a Republican."

"Ahh"—he laughed—"Democrats."

"Optimistic. For all the good it did us."

"They raised a smart girl."

She pointed her putter toward the forgotten ball. "You can distract me with compliments, but I know you're one over par already."

Carter hit the ball again, missed, and endured Eliza's laughter. "You really suck at this."

"Do you always gloat when you win?" He was smiling along with her and knew her competitive nature wasn't mean-spirited.

"Yep."

Carter moaned.

Later they found a casual restaurant with an outside patio overlooking the ocean. "I hope this is OK."

Eliza lifted her hands in the air. "It's a crab shack. What's not to love?"

The noise from the restaurant drifted outside. There was a playoff game playing inside, with plenty of people watching in the bar. "I needed a break from fine dining."

"I'll bet." She picked up a menu and peered at him over it. "You do know that women are told never to pick crab to eat on a date, right?"

"They are?"

"It's messy and usually expensive. Nothing says class like eating with your fingers."

Carter found himself worrying if he'd picked the wrong restaurant. He'd enjoyed playing golf and listening to Eliza talk about her parents, and he hoped to keep the night moving in the same easygoing direction.

"So what are you going to order?"

"King crab legs with extra butter." Her answer was quick.

He tossed his head back and laughed. "What about first-date impressions? Aren't you worried about setting your gender back a notch or two?"

She placed her menu back on the table. "I like crab."

"Even if it's messy?"

Eliza nodded over to a couple at another table. "I'll wear a bib."

He folded his hands and leaned forward. The confidence and ease she had in her own skin excited him. She'd tucked her rich dark hair into a small clip, but a strand had fallen loose. He brushed it behind her ear and let his finger linger on her skin. He could get used to touching her. There wasn't a time in recent memory where they'd managed to get alone for as many hours as they had on this date.

He liked it.

They talked about the first time she'd eaten crab and discussed the uselessness of the tiny fork provided by the restaurant. When dinner arrived and hot butter escaped the crab and dribbled down Eliza's chin, Carter leaned over and wiped her face clean.

Her eyes caught his, and for a minute, the conversation stopped. All he could do was stare.

She was beautiful. If she were sitting a little closer, he would have taken advantage of the pause in conversation to kiss her. As it was, he sat across the table. He had to settle for capturing her hand and stroking the inside of her wrist.

"Eating crab is a two-handed game, Hollywood."

He glanced down at her small hand in his. She wasn't pulling away, and that left him hopeful. He lifted it to his lips, watching her observe his movements as he kissed the back of it. Her smile fell, and desire sparked in the back of her eyes. He probably looked like a sap kissing the back of her hand, but he couldn't bring himself to care.

On a sigh, he reluctantly released her hand and continued with dinner.

Later, as he drove up the narrow street on the way to her home, they were both laughing about the latest YouTube video in which the princess of Denmark caught some old guy staring at her cleavage.

"I wonder how he explained that to his wife," Eliza said, giggling.

"I'm sure he lied and said he was checking out her jeweled necklace."

"You have to love social media. There's more to watch online than there is on TV."

Carter pulled into her driveway and moved quickly to help her out of the car. Instead of walking her up to the door, he took her hand in his and kept her next to the car. "I had fun," he told her. Politics had escaped his mind all night, and he'd nearly forgotten that he'd turned off his phone before picking her up. God only knew what awaited him when he turned the damn thing back on.

"Not a bad first date."

"So, did I pass for a second date?"

"Maybe."

Oh, he passed, but she wanted to see him squirm.

The curtains moved beyond the front window of the house. Not only did Eliza have a police dog waiting for her, but Gwen was probably still awake as well.

"What if I bribe you with lobster and Dom Pérignon?"

"Maybe I don't like champagne."

Carter inched closer until her body was edged between his and the car. "I've been in two weddings with you. Not only do you like champagne, you love the good stuff."

Her eyes fixated on his lips. "I could eat lobster," she uttered.

He bent down and captured her lips. Like heated butter, she melted in his arms and moaned into his kiss. Her soft lips opened, and he explored her offering. The length of her body met his as he eased his weight closer and pinned her to the car. The last time he'd kissed a woman thoroughly outside a door, or over a car, had to have been in high school. Their kiss would be only that, passionate and steamy, but it would begin and end with a kiss. For some odd reason, knowing they wouldn't go further excited him even more.

His arousal pressed against her stomach. Eliza had to know the effect she had on him. It was more than a physical attraction. All night they'd talked, laughed, and were enamored with each other's company. When Eliza snarled at something he'd said, he delivered a like response. Instead of their banter escalating into something ugly, they laughed off their differences in a playful manner.

As he kissed her now and felt her pulling him close, it wasn't a question of if he would make love to her, but a matter of when. The thought thrilled him as much as the anticipation might kill him.

He ended the kiss with a soft whimper. "I should walk you to the door before Gwen releases the dog."

Eliza leaned her forehead against his chest. "If you told me a month ago that I would have a roommate and a dog, I'd have laughed you out of town."

"You have both."

"I do. And you should get home to rest anyway. Don't you have to fly out tomorrow?"

Yes, he did.

He kissed her again briefly and then walked her to the door.

Zod barked at their approach, and Carter heard Gwen call the animal back.

"I'll call you in the morning."

"You don't have to do that, Carter."

"It's not about *have* to."

She smiled, obviously pleased. Just like kissing her hand, the little things he did brought the biggest smiles to her lips.

He'd have to remember that.

"We have a problem." Dean tossed an old newspaper on Jim's desk and waited for Jim to pick it up.

"What am I looking at?"

"The entertainment and celebrity section of the *Hollywood Tribune*. Check out page five."

The Harrison wedding party snagged the center portion of the page, with Eliza standing beside the bride.

"OK…so? We saw this a few weeks ago. This paper is old. Why is it a problem now?"

Dean leaned against the desk and crossed his arms over his chest. "I took the liberty of checking on little Ricky. As you know, they moved him to San Quentin last year." Neither of them had been happy to find Ricardo back in California.

"Old news."

"Guess who his bunk mate is."

Jim tapped his fingers against the newspaper and attempted to think up an answer to Dean's riddle. "No clue."

"Does the name Harris Elliot mean anything to you?"

For a split second, Jim's confusion filled his face. Then his jaw dropped.

His eyes pitched back to the photograph.

"Samantha Elliot Harrison's father."

"Bingo."

"Christ."

"According to the guards on the block, Harry offers stock tips to the cops who bring him pictures or newspaper clippings about his daughters. How much you wanna bet there's a picture like this one somewhere in Harry's cell?"

"Fuck."

Chapter Fifteen

Eliza sat across from Karen's desk and regarded the blonde bombshell with hope. Karen ran Moonlight Villas, an assisted-living facility, and happened to be one of Alliance's clients—well, hopeful clients.

"So what's this meeting about? Did you find a husband for me?" Karen was stunning, intelligent, and completely capable of finding a rich man on her own, but she'd chosen Alliance to search out a rich husband so she could spend time making a difference in other people's lives.

Unfortunately, Karen's beauty intimidated several eligible men. "The only one I have right now who meets your cash requirements is a very mature man who simply wants to spite his children."

Karen narrowed her ice-blue eyes. "How mature?"

"Seventy-six."

"Ouch."

Eliza shrugged. "I know. He's a very nice guy. I think he wants to scare his children into submission. What he really needs is a plump, old Italian woman to mother him and hit the kids with her wooden spatula."

Karen tossed back her head and laughed. "Sounds like my aunt Edie."

"She's Italian?"

"Kinda. My late uncle Joe was full-blood Italian, so you might say she had regular injections of Italian. She talks with an accent and everything. They lived in New York for years before they found out Joe had emphysema. Then they moved here for the nice weather. Aunt Edie has been a widow for ten years now."

Eliza found herself tapping her foot. "Any chance Edie would like to be set up on a blind date?"

"With your rich guy?"

"Why not?"

"I don't know," Karen said. "She's happy with her bingo on Wednesdays and Bunco on Fridays."

Eliza leaned forward. "How about this? I set you up to meet Stanly, and you can talk to him. If you don't agree that he needs the firm hand of an older woman, then I'll continue to find him a young one such as yourself."

"I hate to sound greedy, but what's in it for me?"

"If your aunt Edie and Stanly Sedgwick hook up, I'll ask Sedgwick to donate funds to the Boys and Girls Club. You volunteer there, right?"

Eliza could see Karen contemplating her options. Although Karen might seem shallow for wanting to snag a rich man for his money, deep inside she wanted to help many of the broken systems set up for the youth of the country.

"Would you set this guy up with your aunt?"

"I don't have an aunt, but I would if I did."

"OK…I'll meet him."

For the first time, Eliza felt the part of Cupid. She liked the thought of finding Stanly the right wife and not a stand-in young one he could flaunt around his kids and grandkids.

Eliza handed Gwen a set of earmuffs to mute out the sound of gunfire.

"Is this truly necessary?" Gwen asked as she gingerly placed the ear protection over her perfectly coiffed hair.

"I have guns, Gwen. They're more dangerous to you if you don't know how to use them."

"That's absurd. If I don't handle them, how can they harm me?" Gwen glanced at the two handguns Eliza owned sitting on the bench and scowled.

"Outside of someone pointing them at you and squeezing the trigger, I guess they can't. However, you're the one who insisted on moving in." Eliza lowered her voice and glanced around to see if anyone had entered the indoor shooting range behind them. They were early and had the place to themselves. "So you're going to have to have a couple of lessons on firearm safety."

Gwen looked like she was about to argue, so Eliza fired her final manipulating blow. "I'd be devastated if something happened to you because of my past. The least I can do is show you how to defend yourself with a gun."

Gwen tilted her head to the side. "I insisted on moving in." Her voice was too loud due to the earmuffs.

"And I insist on this."

"Oh, all right." She twisted toward the counter and placed one small hand on the larger .357 revolver.

Eliza moved beside her and began her lesson. "My guns are always loaded. You should assume any gun you pick up is."

Gwen pulled her hand back as if burned.

"It won't jump out and bite." Eliza picked up the weapon and opened the chamber. After a brief explanation of how to check to see if the gun was loaded and how to hold it, she fired off a couple of rounds. Even with the ear protection, the sound vibrated through her skull. The paper target hung less than ten yards away, and Eliza's aim was spot-on. As it should have been—she'd been shooting since she was ten.

When it came time for Gwen to try, Eliza stood behind her. "Brace yourself with one foot behind the other. The force of the bullet leaving the chamber will feel like someone is pushing you back. Don't let go."

Gwen nodded and followed Eliza's example of aiming at her target. As she concentrated, the tip of her tongue snuck out between her lips much like a child. A brief perplexed expression passed over Gwen's eyes before she squeezed the trigger and the bullet flew. She didn't drop the gun, thank God, but her arms did fly up. Eliza gazed down the room, but didn't see a hole in the target. When she looked over to her friend, Gwen was smiling from ear to ear.

"That wasn't bad at all," Eliza said.

"I didn't hit the target."

Eliza pushed a button and summoned the target to move closer. "Try again."

Gwen did, this time blasting a hole through the paper, but not the outline of the person on it. Still, she was thrilled. All apprehension and nerves dissipated. After a case of forty rounds, they moved on to the smaller weapon.

Gwen was a natural. By the time they left the range, she was talking about when they could return.

"Many men would argue with me, but I believe women have better aim than men."

They were driving home and stopped at a light. Eliza scanned the cars behind them and waited for her turn through the intersection.

"Have you always owned a gun?"

"Yes."

Gwen settled into her seat. "Our security has guns at home, but we've never been allowed to touch them. I suppose if I had insisted, someone might have shown me, but I never saw a need."

"And probably never will."

"It's quite empowering to hold something so dangerous," Gwen said with a lift in her voice.

Traffic started moving as they talked. Eliza scanned the cars behind her.

"Always remember that when you shoot, you shoot to kill." Eliza had shown Gwen every tip Dean and Jim had given her.

"I don't think I could hurt anyone."

"You could if they were bent on harming you."

"I don't know."

A car swerved out of the turn lane and tucked behind them as they drove. All the talk about guns and protection was making her paranoid. The newer-model Mercedes was popular in LA and probably not the same one she'd seen outside the range when they left.

"I'm sure if faced with death, we can do all kinds of things."

Gwen waved a hand in the air. "It won't come to that."

"Let's hope not."

Gwen made a noise before changing the subject. "When will you see Carter again?"

Hearing his name brought a smile to her lips. "He's in Sacramento until tomorrow."

"The flowers he sent were lovely."

They were. Instead of falling back on a dozen roses, Carter decided on orchids and white lilies. As much as Eliza hated being so damn girly about his attention, she couldn't help but sigh every time she walked into the living room and saw them. There was nothing casual about her feelings. Carter had effectively wriggled his way into her thoughts a dozen times a day. She didn't even want to consider her inappropriate thoughts at night.

Eliza caught Gwen staring at her from the corner of her eye. "What?"

"Nothing."

Yeah, right. The word *nothing* from a woman always meant *something.*

She turned off the busy street and checked her mirror for the Mercedes. Sure enough, it turned down a different street and didn't follow them home.

Paranoid.

Zod barked from behind the door and darted out as they walked in. Eliza watched him sniff around the yard before relieving himself. She slipped out of her shoes at the door, but instead of tucking them off to the side, she tucked them inside the coat closet. There was no use tempting the dog into misbehaving.

Gwen played the messages while Eliza set the guns on the kitchen counter to clean them.

There was one hang-up, a message from Sam inviting them for lunch on Saturday, and a message from Karen asking for a callback.

Gwen decided to shower and remove the gunpowder from her skin, and Eliza called Karen back.

"Stanly was more nervous than a teenage boy on his first date."

"He's sweet."

"I understand why you'd want him to find the right woman and not the woman for now."

"So you agree he needs to have a real wife and not a temporary one?"

"I do. If he were twenty years younger, I'd take him for me," Karen said.

"Twenty?"

"OK, thirty. Aunt Edie might be too much for him, but it's worth a shot."

Eliza couldn't have been happier. "Did you meet the kids?"

"No. We met at a coffee shop. I think his driver was on the phone with someone while he waited, so my guess is the kids know he met with a younger woman."

She hoped Stanly's kids were sweating. "Should I ask Stanly if he wants to meet your aunt, or are you going to do that?"

"I asked if he would have dinner with Aunt Edie and I on Thursday."

"Does he know it's a setup?"

"I don't think so. But I noticed the relief in his eyes when I told him I couldn't see him romantically and suggested we have a nice dinner with my aunt."

"Which is for the best. His Viagra prescription is probably expired."

"Ewehh," Karen said, laughing. "He's so focused on teaching his kids a lesson that we agreed to get together Thursday to keep them guessing. When I told him about Aunt Edie's risotto, he couldn't resist."

"What will you tell your aunt?"

"Only that I'm bringing a friend for dinner. She's used to that."

"I want a report first thing Friday morning."

"Sure thing."

Chapter Sixteen

"This is becoming a habit, detectives." Carter leaned against the door frame of Dean and Jim's office and crossed his arms over his chest. "And I'm not taking another shoe-chewing dog home to Eliza."

Jim stood and thrust out a hand for Carter to shake. Dean followed.

"Thank you for coming."

Like before, they ducked into a conference room for privacy.

"How's Zod working out?"

"Other than the shoe thing, he's fine. Eliza won't make him go places with her, but he is at the house."

Dean and Jim exchanged a look.

"What is it?"

"We assume Eliza told you why she needs the dog."

"She told me."

"Did she tell her friend, Mrs. Harrison?"

"Samantha is Eliza's best friend. What do you think?"

Again, the two cops looked at each other.

"Do you know if Mrs. Harrison has any connection to her father?" Jim asked.

"The one in prison?" Carter hadn't seen that question coming.

"Yes."

"They've been estranged since his conviction, according to Blake. Why?"

When Jim glanced over to his partner again, Carter waved a hand between the two of them. "Why?" he demanded.

"Mrs. Harrison's father is jailed in the same place as the man responsible for Eliza's parents' death."

"Sam has nothing to do with her dad. I don't see how this is a problem."

"Just because Samantha doesn't want anything to do with her father doesn't mean her father isn't interested in what is happening with his daughter. We know for a fact that wedding photos have made their way into Mr. Elliot's cell. Can you see where this is going, Counselor?"

Carter's pulse leapt, and he felt an uncharacteristic urge to scratch his palms. "Eliza was a child when her parents were murdered." Even as Carter voiced the words, he knew these men would shatter any hope he had of their fears being for nothing.

Dean opened a folder he'd brought into the room and handed Carter a photograph. In it was a woman who looked exactly like Eliza snuggled next to a robust man in his forties. Beside them was a young girl with her dark hair in a ponytail and a missing tooth within her silly smile.

"Not only does Eliza look like her late mother, she sounds like her too."

Carter ran his finger over the photograph. Eliza was a beautiful girl, even then.

"If Eliza insists on staying in her current life, she has to be better protected."

Carter's mind was twirling. He hardly registered the noise beyond the door of their conference room until it opened and a familiar furry face walked in.

"This had better be good." Eliza walked beside Zod and stopped talking when she noticed Carter sitting in the room. "What are you doing here?"

"We asked him to come," Dean said, closing the door behind her. He gave the dog a pet and pulled out a chair.

Carter stood and gravitated closer to Eliza. Her dark hair slid over one shoulder and looked like silk. He reached for her hand and linked his fingers with hers. The itchy palms faded with her touch.

"What's going on?" Eliza's cocky smile faded as she looked at the expressions in the room. "What happened?"

"Nothing—not yet," Jim said.

Dean tucked his hands in his pockets. "You need tighter security."

"Why? Cujo here is doing a great job."

"Only if he's with you. I'm told you leave home without him."

Eliza glared at Carter, and he knew what a snitch felt like after getting caught by his friends.

"Big scary dogs with huge teeth and biting tendencies aren't welcome in many places."

"Which is why you need a bodyguard."

"I have a killer security system and a roommate with good aim. I think I'm good." In all her tough talk, Carter felt her damp palm squeeze his.

"It's not enough."

Eliza was shaking her head, and Carter felt her denial before she could say the words. "I'm not going to have someone tagging around behind me, Dean."

"What about me?" Carter asked.

"Don't you have an office to get into? You can't be my personal bodyguard."

The hell I can't.

"It's a bodyguard, or you have to disappear." Dean's tone shifted from informative to direct. "This isn't a joke."

Eliza shook her head.

"Dammit, Eliza!" Dean yelled.

Everyone jumped, even the dog.

Carter let her hand go and stood in front of the other two men. "I need a minute alone with her."

Jim stood and made to exit the room.

Dean glared. "Fine, but think about this before you say no again." He pointed a finger at her. "Your picture was found in Ricardo's cell."

Dean slammed out of the room, with Jim in tow.

When Carter turned around, Eliza's face had grown white. Her eyes glossed over, and she didn't look at him when he knelt beside her. He grasped both her hands in his and held tight.

"Is he lying?" she asked.

Carter couldn't be sure, but Dean's words were floating around in her head and making her think. "Why would he?"

"To get his way."

"Dean seems to care about what happens to you. I don't think he'd lie to make you bend to his will."

She blew out a long-suffering sigh and squeezed her eyes shut. "Damn," she whispered under her breath.

To Carter, the key to fixing the problem was simple. All he had to do was convince Eliza.

"I have the perfect solution."

"An underground bunker in New Mexico?"

He was already on his knee, so he took a chance. "Marry me."

Her eyes sprung open. "Haven't we been over this before?"

It wasn't a no.

"Sure, but that was to help me get into office. Now it's to protect you from a crazy man who is responsible for your parents' deaths. We can take care of both our problems with one signature."

Eliza's eyes took on a softer edge. "Getting married will screw up your love life with other women."

She still hadn't said no. Carter's palms went damp.

"The lady I'm currently dating won't think I'm cheating on her."

Eliza gave a painful smile. "You're out of town all the time. How can you be my bodyguard?"

"As my wife, I can arrange security fit for the president."

"I don't know..."

"Is it me? I thought we were doing rather well. Didn't you like the flowers?"

"I loved the flowers."

"My skills with the crab fork turned you off?"

She was laughing now—and not saying no. "We're talking marriage."

"Your best friend and mine married for more trite reasons, and it turned out OK. I don't want to have you disappear in that New Mexico bunker. I'm still owed the lobster dinner, remember?"

She was considering his offer and not saying no.

"If the threat disappears, we can both back out," she said.

His heart squeezed in his chest. He wasn't sure if the squeeze was pain at the thought of her leaving or joy in the fact she was considering his offer.

"This is America."

Slowly, she started to nod. "There should be a wedding. Nothing too big, but something to convince the press we're not getting married for your campaign."

"We can't delay. The sooner you're my wife, the better." His heart skipped in his chest.

"Gwen and I are experts at planning weddings. We can be married by Monday." Eliza was looking at his chest as she spoke.

Carter placed a finger under her chin and gazed into her eyes. "Is that a yes?"

"I think...Yeah, that's a yes."

Something inside of him bloomed. Eliza was going to be Mrs. Carter Billings. Instead of worrying about what could go wrong, he only saw bright lights and happy endings.

She returned his smile, and he leaned forward to seal their deal with a kiss.

Nothing could have prepared Eliza for the next week of her life. Nearly as soon as she'd said yes to Carter's proposal, there were around-the-clock guards on her like glue. They approached her when they changed shift so she knew who they were on sight, but kept out of her way the rest of the time. They were like ghosts in suits. Well, some of them wore plainclothes and didn't look like bodyguards at all, but Eliza knew they all carried guns and could kick some serious ass if needed. Joe, who had worked as a personal bodyguard at times for Carter, worked closely with Neil to manage the new detail of surveillance.

Samantha and Gwen didn't seem surprised at all with the announcement that she and Carter were getting married. In fact, they congratulated her as if they'd both expected it. Sam's explanation for her reaction was simple. *You're a logical woman, and Carter is a logical choice.* Part of Eliza wondered what had happened to love before a woman walked down the aisle. Whom was she kidding? Marriage to Carter was a logical decision, and emotion wasn't involved enough to carry any weight in her decision to say yes.

Even when he'd leaned down on one knee to propose, which she thought was sweet, he hadn't professed love. No, he'd offered a solution to their problems.

Logical.

Even when the man asking to be her husband was as captivating as any rock star and as intelligent as any supreme court judge, he hadn't said he was the perfect man for her. No, he'd spoken of bodyguards and safety.

Logical.

Even when the thought of being Mrs. Carter Billings had left her breathless…

Not logical. Sexual, maybe.

"Earth to Eliza…Come in, Eliza." Sam waved her hands in front of Eliza's face to capture her attention.

"Sorry."

"It's OK. I know you're under a lot of stress. So, what do you think?"

Eliza glanced down at the flowers and pointed to the first bouquet that appealed to her. Orchids and lilies. Just like the ones Carter had sent her a little over a week ago.

"Perfect…And the cake?"

Eliza pointed to a simple and elegant design. "I'm not sure of the flavors. I don't know what Carter likes."

Gwen sat to the right of Eliza and scoffed. "He doesn't prefer chocolate. I found that strange when so many men gravitate toward the flavor. Perhaps you should pick vanilla or some such combination."

It was upsetting that Gwen knew Carter's tastes better than Eliza did. Then again, Blake and Carter had been best friends for years, and Eliza had only known him for a few. It could be worse, she realized. Samantha and Blake had been married within a week of their introduction.

Eliza checked off a couple of vanilla combinations—one with strawberry filling, another with cream.

Done!

"What's next?"

They had talked with a caterer the day before and also picked out classic evening gowns for both Samantha and Gwen.

Because of the last-minute celebration, the wedding would take place on Samantha and Blake's property, which wasn't a hardship with the Pacific Ocean in the background and majestic views on every corner of their home.

"I spoke with the photographer we used in Texas, and they're making arrangements to come here. Apparently, it's even hotter in Texas now than it was two months ago, and the photographer is free."

"I would think he'd be booked." Eliza knew Sam must have offered a huge bonus and maybe a private jet to manage a photographer on such short notice. Calling Sam on it would only bring an argument. Besides, Eliza had endured the color yellow for Sam's last wedding, for God's sake.

"I guess not," Gwen added with a coy smile.

Yeah, someone got a kickback.

Samantha picked up her notebook and checked off tasks. "We only have a few days, and a wedding dress might be difficult to find. I say we get started on that this afternoon."

"I want simple." Eliza had never been the kind of girl to fantasize about her wedding. Maybe that came with not having parents or family in her life. She always assumed she'd be married by a justice of the peace or some cheesy Elvis impersonator in Vegas.

She was surprised by her own suggestion that she and Carter have a ceremony. Maybe standing beside Samantha at all her weddings was wearing off on Eliza.

A half hour later, the three of them were on their way to a boutique in search of the perfect last-minute wedding dress.

Carter scrolled through his smartphone in search of wedding rings while Jay ran down a list of tasks and meetings scheduled for the coming week.

"Governor Montgomery has invited you to a state dinner in two weeks. It will take some rearranging, but it would probably be best for you to attend. His endorsement will put votes in your pocket."

Solitaire or a rock set with other stones? "When is this dinner?" Carter asked.

"Two weeks from this Friday."

A week after the wedding. A perfect time to show off his bride. "I'll need two invitations."

"Oh?"

Solitaire was Carter's first choice, but Eliza liked more bling than she let on. Underneath all her rough exterior, she had the heart of a girly girl.

"Yeah. And I need to clear my schedule from Saturday through Wednesday of this week."

Remembering Eliza in the awful yellow dress at Samantha and Blake's last ceremony, Carter clicked over to a rare yellow diamond collection on the site. He expected to see something ugly, but what he found was anything but.

In fact, it was perfect.

Carter saved the picture to his phone and checked his watch. He would have to call the store manager to open up after hours, but that shouldn't be a problem.

Jay cleared his throat.

"Sorry." Carter tucked his phone inside his jacket. "You can clear my schedule, right?"

The scowl on Jay's face expressed his irritation. "Of course," he said through pursed lips. "Can I give an excuse?"

Carter stood and shoved his hands in his pockets. "Eliza and I are getting married this Saturday at the Harrison estate. I have you down for a plus one. We plan on taking a few days for a honeymoon, and then we're back on track."

Jay's jaw dropped.

"While we're gone, I need you to touch base with those two detectives you met last month who intercepted Eliza after the press conference, and then you'll need to work on a security detail for her and our home."

Jay closed his mouth and threw his hands up in the air. "Hold on. You're getting married?"

"Saturday."

Jay extended his hand. "Congratulations. Smart move. This is going to go a long way to fix last month's fuckup."

Carter didn't deny or confirm his reason for marriage. "Try and give an excuse about a private affair that I'm attending. I'll have you release an announcement after Saturday. I'd like to avoid a circus."

"Sure. No problem. Now, what about the cops?"

Carter shook his head. "It's complicated. They'll give you what you need to present to the FBI to obtain the necessary security."

"The Feds?"

Carter patted Jay's shoulder. "It's complicated." He gave Jay Dean's card. "You'll see these guys again at the wedding." Carter checked his watch again. "I've gotta go."

I have a wedding ring to buy.

Chapter Seventeen

The wedding was in three days, and Carter hadn't had a moment alone with his fiancée since she'd said yes.

"I thought you said we were going out to dinner." Eliza peered through the windshield of the car with a frown.

"We are." Carter pulled up to the valet and unfolded from the car. He offered Eliza a hand and told the driver that they would be back by midnight.

Blake's pilot met them by the stairs of the private jet and welcomed them aboard.

Carter knew Eliza had flown on the plane for several occasions over the past couple of years, but the light in her eyes didn't fade when it came to the luxury.

"Are you going to tell me where we're going?" Eliza asked as she fastened her seat belt.

His hands grew moist. "As soon as we're airborne."

"Afraid I'll bolt?"

He laughed. "Maybe." *Exactly.*

The pilot taxied the plane onto the runway and announced their departure.

The cabin pressurized, and the engines effortlessly pulled them in the sky. Once the plane leveled off, Eliza said, "You might have guessed, but surprises and I don't get along. I don't mind a big bow on a present, but—"

"I'm taking you to Tucson. To meet my parents."

"Oh." Her jaw went slack.

"I told them I was bringing you to dinner."

"Do they know we're getting married?"

"Yes."

Eliza started to nibble on the end of one fingernail, and he found it cute. "Your dad is a retired police officer, right?"

"New York PD for thirty years."

"Is he the reason you became a lawyer?"

Eliza must have realized that she was chewing on her nails and quickly removed her hand from her mouth.

"In a way. I noticed how hard my father worked growing up and how much he would yell at the TV whenever he saw his work dissolve because a lawyer screwed up. My friends and I used to play detectives and lawyers."

Eliza chuckled.

"I'd stage a crime scene, and my friend Roger would collect the evidence."

"Sounds like a nerd version of cops and robbers."

"It was. My father worked his entire life for a system that's broken in many ways. I always wanted to be someone who helped fix the system for men like my dad."

She shifted in the large leather chair and kicked off her heels. "I've always wondered how you can afford to run for office. Seems most men like you come from family money. I can't imagine your dad becoming rich on a cop's salary."

"No. I had my eye on law school, but I knew the cost would prohibit my efforts. I was searching for an investment with a quick return when I met Blake. He was starting up a shipping company and wanted investors. I took half a year off school and gave Blake my tuition money."

"That had to be hard."

"It was. But Blake was…Blake. He didn't try to sell me on the idea, just said that he would triple my money. He was determined to screw his father by being successful, and I believed he could do it."

They both knew how that had turned out. Blake's shipping business had bloomed and turned into millions.

"So, are you partners with Blake?"

"Silent. I took what I needed to finish college and gave him full run of the rest of my investment."

"Wow. I had no idea. I thought you guys were only friends."

"Friends first, business associates second. I've never questioned what he does with the money, how he invests it, or anything."

"Makes me wish I had money to invest."

Carter shook his head. "His company isn't public, but I'm sure Sam will put a good word in for you."

"What about my fiancé? Shouldn't the wife of a silent partner count for something?" she teased.

He liked the sound of that. *His wife.* "I might be able to arrange something."

They laughed, and when the pilot said they could walk about the cabin, Carter stepped over to the minibar and opened a bottle of wine.

"What about your mother? What's she like?"

"My mom's great. Funny. Doesn't take herself too seriously. She gave up a lot to marry my dad but has never looked back."

"Gave up a lot? What do you mean?"

Carter handed her a glass of pinot grigio and sat back down.

For anyone who bothered to look, Carter's family was public record. However, he didn't go out of his way to announce what he told Eliza next.

"My mother is a Hammond. As in Senator Hammond."

A brief blank expression on Eliza's face faded as she realized whom Carter meant.

"Maxwell Hammond?"

"Right."

Eliza blew a whistle through her lips. "That's some big money and influence."

Carter took a drink of the wine and let the crisp flavor float over his tongue. "They used all of it to try and break up my mom and dad. It didn't work."

"That's sweet. I mean, it sucks that your extended family would go through those efforts, but cool that it didn't work."

"It was ugly, from what I'm told. She never really mended her relationship with her brother, and he's been anything but loving every time I've ever seen him. Outside of big family functions, weddings, funerals, we don't see him or my mom's side of the family." In a way, Carter running for office was exactly what his mother's family would have wanted. But he wasn't doing it for them. He was doing it for his father. The joke was on the Hammonds.

Eliza asked a few things about his family and his years in New York.

He told her about Roger and Beverly. He suggested they visit them and the baby girl who'd been born the week prior, once things settled.

"Mr. Billings, Miss Havens, we are on approach. Please fasten your seat belts."

Carter moved to the seat beside Eliza and belted in. She glanced out the window and started to bite her nails. He grasped her hand and held it between them. "They're going to love you."

"I'm not nervous," she said defensively.

Yeah, right.

Eliza wasn't sure what she'd expected, but the people responsible for Carter's existence weren't it.

Abigail Billings was a young sixty, with only minimal lines on her face to give away her age. Her strawberry blonde hair looked as if she spent time every month in a stylist's chair.

Carter's father went by the name of Cash, and Eliza could see the humor behind the man's gaze when he sized her up at the door.

"So you're the woman tying my son down," he said with a cocky grin after their brief introduction.

Abigail swatted her husband in a playful manner, and Eliza took the opportunity to see just how much like Carter his parents were. "I think we should wait until after we're married before I break out the restraints."

Cash burst out in laughter, and Carter's face grew red.

"Oh, I like her, Carter," Cash said as he placed a hand behind Eliza's back and led her into their modest living room. Their Arizona home sat beside one of the many golf courses peppering the landscape. It wasn't a mansion, but it wasn't typical suburbia, either.

"We've been so excited to meet you, Eliza. We didn't know Carter was seeing anyone seriously." Abigail offered refreshments, and Carter sat beside Eliza on the sofa.

"Eliza and I have known each other for years."

"So you said on the phone," Cash said.

"It's only recently that we started dating." Eliza could see that Carter's parents were going to drive this question, so she did her best to keep things as honest as possible. Although their faces were filled with excitement, there was a small measure of apprehension there too. Carter was their only child. Eliza didn't think it would be normal for any parents not to question a child's swiftness to the altar.

"Eliza is a close friend of Samantha," Carter explained. "I think we both avoided dating because of our mutual friends."

She caught Carter smiling her way and grinned back. What he said was certainly true for her. Of course, he left out the part where they argued most of the time when they were in the same room.

"It appears you overcame those concerns."

Carter lifted his chin. "You can see why," he told his father.

Eliza felt her cheeks grow warm with Carter's praise. He sounded convincing, even to her ears.

"So why the rush wedding?"

The need to nibble on her nails grew strong, but Eliza squelched it and tried to relax and let Carter answer his father's direct question.

"A couple of reasons, really. First is because I want to claim Eliza as my wife to the world."

"How very caveman of you," Eliza teased. Claiming her meant protecting her. She did her best not to read any deeper meaning into his words.

Carter grasped her hand and held it.

"And the second reason?" Abigail asked.

Carter's face softened as his eyes searched Eliza's. "I would think that is obvious."

Wow. Eliza's heart flipped in her chest. Carter really had missed his call to Hollywood. If she weren't aware of his real reasons for marrying her, she'd have believed he was a man desperately in love.

Abigail released a long sigh.

Cash stood and moved to his son's side.

Carter pulled Eliza to her feet before accepting his father's handshake and bear hug. "Congratulations, son."

Eliza felt a small pang of guilt when Cash hugged her and welcomed her to their family.

They ate dinner in comfortable conversation. Abigail asked about Eliza's family, and she told her they'd died when she was young. There was only a moment of sadness that passed over the other woman's face, but then Carter turned the conversation to other things.

Eliza couldn't help thinking about her parents while seated alongside Carter's. They would have loved Carter and applauded his desire to protect her. Then again, if it weren't for their deaths, Eliza wouldn't have been marrying the man at her side.

Abigail addressed Eliza and pulled her out of her thoughts. "Has Carter warned you about my brother?"

"He's said a few things."

"He's a typical politician. Believe none of what he says."

"Hey!" Carter scolded his father.

"Present company excluded."

"He's right, Eliza. Max believes he is the authority on everything and everyone. If you show him a weakness, he'll exploit it." Abigail was serving coffee in the living room while she delivered her warning about her brother. "He's managed to overshadow my father after years of trying."

"Is he really that bad?"

"Worse. The only thing I can praise him for is my sister-in-law, Sally. Truth be told, I don't know why she stays with the man. She's undeniably sweet and an utter pushover. Perfect for Max."

"That's sad." Eliza couldn't imagine not having a backbone and allowing a man to rule over her.

"If given the opportunity, you'd get along fine with her. Chances are Max won't allow a friendship to develop, so please don't think it's you."

"Are they all coming to the wedding?" Cash asked.

Eliza knew that Carter had invited his grandparents and Max and Sally. After learning more about his uncle, she couldn't help but hope the last-minute invitation wouldn't be accepted.

"Max and Sally are coming. I haven't heard from John and Carol." John and Carol were Carter's grandparents. She found it odd that he addressed them by their first names.

"I'll pin my mother down for an answer tomorrow and phone you with the information."

By the end of the evening, Eliza felt as if she'd known Carter's parents for a long time. She looked forward to seeing them at the wedding and knew they would be the anchor of sanity while navigating Carter's family.

"Your parents were surprisingly real," Eliza told Carter once they were alone in the car on the way back to the airport.

"You were expecting blow-up dolls?"

"You know what I mean."

Carter switched lanes and navigated onto the freeway.

"Everyone says the same thing. My dad was a cop for years. It's hard to not be *real* after that. People anticipate a Kennedy when they consider my mother's upbringing."

Eliza could see how that would be expected. Abigail might be polished, but she wasn't pretentious at all. "You're lucky to have them."

Carter glanced her way, and his expression shifted into sorrow. He grasped her hand and gave a gentle squeeze. "I'm sorry."

"Don't be."

"I am. I should have realized that meeting my parents would remind you of yours."

"My parents were happy too. Spending time with your parents reminded me of the good times."

"I wish they could be here for the wedding," Carter told her.

"If they were alive, we wouldn't be getting married." Her attempt to correct Carter resulted in his frown.

"I guess," he mumbled.

What does that mean?

Their flight home was uneventful and quiet. Eliza wasn't sure what she'd said to upset him, but she could feel his mood shift. Between the silence, the wine, and the late hour, Eliza found herself nodding off on the plane.

Security followed them from the airport to her house, where Carter dropped her off without even a hug.

Sleeping was impossible. Memories of the good times with her parents morphed into the time following their deaths. The empty shell of her life twisted into bitter feelings and a hard shell around her heart. For years, she didn't let anyone in.

That had changed somehow. Her deep friendship with Samantha and the affection for the people in her life, for Carter, made her vulnerable.

She once again questioned if she was doing the right thing. Curled up in a ball on the side of the bed was Zod. Outside of guard dogs, Eliza had never owned a pet. Pets equaled roots, and she knew better than to plant those.

Yet here she was, forty-eight hours from her wedding, with thick wooded roots growing everywhere.

What happens when it falls apart? She held no illusion that it wouldn't at some point. Happiness didn't last forever.

Stop thinking, Lisa! She twisted her pillow so the cool side hit her face, and curled into a fetal position. *Stop thinking!*

Chapter Eighteen

"You've got to be kidding me." Eliza stared down Gwen, Sam, and Karen and backed away from the silk scarf they held up for her to put on.

"C'mon, Eliza. You're getting married tomorrow, and if there is one thing I missed out on with my marriage to Blake, it was a bachelorette party."

Bachelorette party? Is she kidding me? "You get married every friggin' year."

"But it isn't the same!" Samantha and Karen shoved their way into the house and waved at the cute security guard sitting in the car at the end of the drive.

Zod started to bark at the sudden appearance at the door. Eliza told him to stand back in a language he could understand.

"Are you surprised?" Gwen asked as she placed a fake tiara on her head.

Surprised? She was settling into a long episode of *Home and Boring Television* to lull her to sleep. After only a text from Carter since their trip to his parents, Eliza was a mite apprehensive about her decision to marry the man.

"I'm stunned," Eliza told her temporary roommate.

"Since you invited Karen to bring Sedgwick to the wedding, I thought it was OK to ask her to come," Samantha pointed out as they walked into the kitchen with bottles of expensive wine in their hands.

Eliza smiled at Karen, knowing she could trust her. "Of course it's OK."

"We wanted to take you to Hollywood. There's this great place on Sunset that was perfect. But your security detail nixed our plans."

Deep inside, Eliza was charmed by the ladies' effort. From nowhere, Gwen produced a small cake in the shape of a tied knot with Eliza's and Carter's names on it.

Samantha uncorked a bottle and poured everyone a glass. "You know, I miss this place sometimes."

"Mrs. Sweeny still cooks fish every Friday night and stinks up the neighborhood," Eliza reminded her friend.

Samantha wrinkled her nose. "Really?"

"And the yippy dog across the street barks all day," Gwen added.

Sam shook her head. "I still miss it. In a weird way."

"Psychotic way."

Gwen shook her head. "I disagree." The hoity British accent added to Gwen's claim. "It might be quaint, but it's liberating."

"This coming from a woman who has lived a life of privilege."

"Privilege and restraint. That security detail that is keeping us from scantily clad men shaking their bottoms for our eyes followed me around London most of my life. I know better than anyone here does how straining that can be after a while. Living here without those bonds has been relaxing beyond words."

Eliza tipped back the wine and enjoyed. "I hear ya." She could only hope the security guards were temporary.

"Is someone going to explain why they're here?" Karen asked.

Samantha didn't miss a beat in her cover-up. "Tomorrow Eliza is marrying the man who may be the next governor of California. They insisted on security."

Karen released a simple "oh" and didn't say anything else.

With their wineglasses filled, they returned to the living room and turned on the stereo.

Eliza's thoughts wandered to what Carter might be doing…

"You're getting married tomorrow." Blake pointed at Carter while holding his shot glass. "This calls for a celebration."

"Like you celebrated the night before your marriage?"

"No. I screwed that up. But I've made up for it every year since."

Carter glanced over to Neil, who tipped his shot glass back and downed his third shot within the hour.

"So that's why you want a wedding every year." Carter enjoyed the slow burn of the twenty-year-old whiskey and listened to his best friend boast.

"I get married every year because I made Sam marry me in Vegas. She deserved better. But you…You're doing it right the first time."

Am I? Blake knew that Carter was marrying Eliza for her safety. The fact that it wouldn't hurt his campaign couldn't be ignored, either.

"If you say so."

"It doesn't matter why you're getting married," Neil said, reading Carter's mind. "What matters is that tonight is your last night as a single man. Any self-respecting bachelor is entitled to inebriate his brain before he gets married."

Carter turned to Blake. "You didn't get wasted."

"I was too busy writing up a contract with my lawyer. You're not."

Damn. Carter hadn't even thought of that. Not that he worried that Eliza would attempt to marry him for what she could gain out of the deal. But considering her cold demeanor the other night, maybe…He shook the thought from his mind.

"C'mon, Carter. Your drink is dry, and we have a full night ahead."

The noise from the radio droned out his groan.

The sound of a "full night" held very little appeal.

Eliza held a silver-wrapped box next to one in scarlet red.

"We didn't have time for a bridal shower and a bachelorette party, so we're combining both." Karen's eyes were glazed over, and Gwen was tipsy and giggling with every word.

The first gift was a skimpy white silk teddy with a belted robe that would barely cover her bottom.

"It's beautiful, Karen."

"Open the other one," she insisted.

The red box was smaller and rattled when Eliza shook it. "Should I be afraid?"

"It won't jump out at you, if that's what you mean." Karen's sly grin made her nervous.

Sure enough, the second box was scandalous. "Handcuffs…really?"

Gwen's giggling spread among them. It felt good to laugh. With her life on edge, Eliza hadn't laughed enough lately.

"Mine next," Gwen said as she thrust gifts into her hands. "I'm a bit more practical, I'm afraid. I wouldn't even know where to buy a sex toy."

Samantha and Karen both said "Melrose," at the same time. Another fit of laughter ensued.

"The first gift is something new."

Inside the elegantly wrapped box was a pair of drop pearl earrings with tiny diamonds dangling on a gold chain. "They're gorgeous. You shouldn't have."

"Don't be silly. They suit your dress and will frame your face beautifully."

"They're too much, Gwen." They had to have cost a small fortune.

"Rubbish. Now open the next gift. Something borrowed."

The long box was light and adorned with a gold bow. Inside was a tiara with a veil fastened to the back.

"I had a coming-out party when I was sixteen, and my father gave me the tiara. I hope you'll wear it."

"Are these real?" Eliza picked up the crown and ran her fingers along the stones.

"Of course."

"I don't think I've seen that many diamonds in one setting in my entire life," Karen said.

"Me either." Eliza started to shake her head. "This has to be worth a small fortune."

"Probably. Image was everything to my father." There was longing in Gwen's voice.

"I'm honored."

Gwen leaned forward and kissed Eliza's cheeks.

"Oh, and here." Gwen took a small envelope from the box and removed a coin from inside. "A sixpence for your shoe."

"A what?"

"You know, something old, something new, something borrowed, something blue, and a sixpence for your shoe."

Eliza palmed the coin before returning it to the box.

Inside the next box, Samantha gifted her with something blue. A garter and a baby-blue corset with matching panties.

"Carter is going to love that," Gwen announced.

Eliza's first thought was how right she was. Then it dawned on her that she and Carter hadn't been intimate. OK, if she counted their brief moment of insanity in the kitchen, then maybe they had been. But not really.

And who said they would be on their wedding night? Theirs was a marriage of convenience. The expectations weren't the same, were they?

"Eliza?"

The thought of Carter removing her wedding dress and discovering the soft-blue lingerie brought warmth to her thoughts.

"Eliza?"

Would he like it? Did he enjoy that kind of thing? What man wouldn't love that kind of thing?

"Helloooo?"

"What?" Eliza snapped.

Karen tossed her hand up in the air, and Zod shot to his feet and ran to the window.

"We lost you," Karen said.

Zod barked and Gwen told him to quiet.

"I'm sorry. I was…thinking about Carter."

"I'll bet you were."

Zod kept barking, and Eliza felt a chill dart down her spine. "*Was ist es?*" she asked the dog.

The women in the room stopped talking and making fun of Eliza's lack of conversation.

Eliza turned off the lights, stood to the side of the curtains, and pulled them back.

"It's probably a cat," Karen said.

The K-9 shot to the back of the house.

Eliza shuddered. A dark memory tugged at the back of her mind. She followed Zod to the back door and grasped her purse as she passed it.

He scraped at the door, and Eliza didn't hesitate opening it.

"What's happening?" someone behind her asked.

She found her handgun and released the safety. The door opened, and Eliza stood there poised.

"*Holt*," she instructed the dog.

Zod stood on four legs and barked into the darkness.

"Who's there?"

Samantha rushed to her side. "What is it?"

"I don't know. Stand back." She flipped on the outside light and saw nothing.

"I'm sending my dog," Eliza shouted in the dark corners where the light didn't reach.

No one outside said a thing, but Zod kept barking.

Eliza waited two seconds and sent him in. "*Suche!*"

Zod took his command and bolted into the backyard. He ran to the back fence and jumped up half its length. He doubled back and sniffed the side yard.

A noise from the opposite side fence sounded, and Zod rushed to the other side.

"Miss Havens?" a man's voice called from beyond the fence.

"Don't move," she yelled to the voice.

"Oh shit." The man yelling sounded like the guard Carter had stationed on her once he'd asked her to marry him.

"Don't move!" Eliza rushed to the side yard. "*Stehen Sie hinunter!*" She instructed Zod to hold his attack. But God help the guard if he moved. Zod was instructed to attack anything that moved.

By the time Eliza made it to the side yard, Russell, the guard, was pinned to the side fence and frozen in place by a vicious dog growling and barking at his prize.

Eliza grasped Zod's collar and shoved her gun into her pocket. "Did you see anyone?" she asked the guard.

Russell hadn't moved from the fence, and his eyes never left Zod. "Only the dog."

Eliza swiveled back to the yard and searched the dark corners.

Who was there? Who had been there?

—

"We're fine," Eliza explained to Carter over the phone thirty minutes later. "It was probably a cat." Though she knew that Zod wouldn't react to an animal the way he had.

"I don't like it."

"I'm sure I overreacted. We've been drinking a little. I'm fine, really."

"I still don't like it. You should stay with me tonight."

"The night before our wedding?"

"Of course. Why not?"

"It's unlucky." Lord, even she knew seeing the groom the morning of the wedding was bad luck.

"That's ludicrous."

"Yeah well, that's how my mind works sometimes. I'm fine. If there was anyone in the backyard, Zod scared them off. I'm sure they won't be back tonight. Russell didn't see anyone, either," she added as extra ammunition for her argument.

"Still..."

"I'm fine, Carter. I promise."

"If something happened to you—"

"It won't. But it's sweet that you care."

"We're getting married tomorrow. Of course I care."

Did he? Did he really? "I'm nervous," she admitted.

"About tomorrow?"

"Yeah."

"I am too, a little."

How nervous? "Are you still in? 'Cuz if you want to back out—"

"No! I'm excited, nervous, and everything a groom is supposed to be before the day of his wedding. I'm not having second thoughts."

Eliza smiled into the phone and cradled it closer to her ear. "Me too," she sighed.

"So we're in?"

She nodded. "Yeah. We're golden."

"Good," he said. "Now let me come over there and get you."

"Not happening, Carter. Gwen and I are fine. My guess is Neil will have two more guards on duty before midnight."

"Three."

Eliza laughed. "See? We're fine."

"Ahh."

"Enjoy your last night as a single man."

"I'd rather fast-forward to tomorrow."

"If you can do that, California is guaranteed to elect you."

Carter chuckled.

"I'll see you tomorrow, then," Carter said.

"I'll be the one in the white dress."

"I'm looking forward to it."

Eliza held on to the phone for a long time after he'd hung up.

Chapter Nineteen

How in the world did Samantha do this every freaking year? Eliza sat ramrod straight in a chair while Gwen fussed with her hair and Tracy, the makeup artist, carefully applied mascara to Eliza's lashes.

"You have the most expressive eyes," Tracy told her.

"Really? What are they expressing?"

"Nerves, oodles of nerves."

Eliza couldn't argue that. If it weren't for the fresh coat of polish on her nails, she'd be nibbling up a storm.

Samantha stepped into the room wearing the striking three-quarter-length gown that rose high on her waist. The gown was perfect for an outdoor wedding. Ever practical, Eliza insisted that the gowns be something the women could use again. The color was a cross between wine and burgundy, and it screamed of understated elegance. Gwen and Sam decided on swept-up hair and simple diamond pendants for their necklaces. The two of them were stunning. Eliza couldn't help but smile.

"You'll be happy to know that Carter is here and already working the room downstairs."

"Is he as nervous as our bride?" Gwen asked.

Eliza met Samantha's gaze in the mirror while Tracy applied another layer of shadow on her eyes.

"He looked good. He asked about Eliza."

"Making sure I'm here."

"I don't think he doubted that."

There was a knock on the door right as Tracy backed away. "Done."

Samantha opened the door and let Carter's mother enter.

"I hope it's OK," she said as they shut the door behind her.

"Don't be silly." Eliza wanted to stand up to greet her, but Gwen was attaching the tiara and fixing the veil down the back.

"I thought I'd assure you that everything is ready. Even my stuffy brother managed to make it on time."

"And your parents?"

"They're here as well. Please don't worry about them. The last thing they enjoy is a scene. I know weddings can perpetuate family drama, but mine would be horrified to find themselves in the paper for ill behavior in public. Now, in private, that might not be the case."

"I understand the sentiment, Mrs. Billings. My father hated the media and avoided scandal at all costs," Gwen said. "There." The last pin attached the diamond tiara to Eliza's head, and Gwen stood back. "Lovely."

Eliza stared at her reflection in the mirror. The gown crossed in the front, dipping enough to show off some cleavage. The style was similar to Gwen's and Samantha's. Only, hers was floor length, with a slight train. Her bare arms kissed by the summer sun had a healthy glow, contrasting the white silk beautifully. Her mother would have loved it. Her father would have cried. Just thinking of them, remembering them, brought a well of tears behind her eyes.

"Oh, don't you dare!" Tracy scolded. "You can cry after the pictures."

Gwen laughed and Samantha moved to Eliza's side. "You're going to take his breath away."

"My son is a lucky man."

Eliza hid behind her smile. Abigail didn't need to know their marriage was somewhat forced under a bizarre set of circumstances. "Thank you."

"I have something for you." Abigail reached into her purse and removed a small box. "It falls into the old and blue category. Samantha told me you were covered with borrowed and new."

Inside the box lay a tennis bracelet with ice-blue aquamarine and diamond stones layered on top of platinum.

"It's gorgeous."

"When Cash and I married, we managed to anger nearly everyone in my family, except my nana. She gave me this to wear on my wedding day and asked that I hand it down to my daughter or daughter-in-law on her wedding day." Abigail removed the bracelet from the box and attached it to Eliza's wrist.

Again, guilt about the circumstances of the wedding plagued her, but she accepted the jewelry and hugged Carter's mother. "Thank you."

There was another knock on the door. "Ladies? Are you ready?" Blake asked.

Sam opened the door a small crack. "We're coming."

Abigail turned for the door. "I'll see you after the ceremony."

Gwen fussed behind Eliza, making the dress drape perfectly, and Samantha handed her the floral bouquet.

This is it.

"Ready?" Samantha asked.

"I'd better be."

They opened the door to find Dean standing in the hall. His mouth fell open when his eyes met hers. It had seemed only fitting to ask him to walk her down the aisle. Eliza always felt closer to the man than any assigned to her case, and he couldn't exactly say no. Besides, she'd told him at the time, if pictures of the two of them managed to make it to her enemy, he'd see that she was surrounded by protection. From the man walking her to the altar to the man accepting her as his bride.

"Wow," he managed.

"You clean up well yourself." Eliza attempted to lighten the growing knot of excited nerves. But there was still a hint of water behind Dean's eyes.

Downstairs, the music started to play, and Gwen shuffled in front of them to take her place.

Dean offered his arm and leaned in to whisper, "I feel I need to offer you some kind of advice."

"You don't have to."

"Good. I managed to get married, but I suck at *staying* married."

Eliza chuckled and turned to look at Dean. He was completely serious and somewhat offended that she was laughing. She leaned up and kissed his cheek. "Thank you."

"For what?"

"For caring."

He winked. "C'mon. It's about time I hand you off to someone else for a while."

Eliza continued to laugh as she walked down the stairs.

All eyes were on his bride, which suited Carter perfectly. When she stepped out into the sun and glanced up the grassy path to his side, her eyes met his, and his nerves flew away with the breeze. He knew how sappy it would sound if he told anyone his thoughts, but it didn't matter.

Eliza was the picture of perfection. Every man's dream. And she was about to become his.

She was smiling at something Dean had said, and the laughter behind her eyes made her glow even more.

Dean handed her over and waited until Carter looked his way.

"Take care of her," he said.

"I will."

Carter took Eliza's hand, squeezed it, and turned toward the minister.

The minster spoke of tomorrow, of now…of love. He encouraged both of them to consider each other every day of their lives. He addressed the audience and asked if there was anyone who thought the two of them shouldn't marry.

For a moment, Carter held his breath. God help anyone who said a peep now.

They didn't.

He glanced down at his bride, noticed the slight smile on her lips, and knew she was thinking the same thoughts.

When the minister addressed him and asked if he would hold, cherish, and always keep sacred his union with Eliza, he said he would and felt the commitment to his very core.

Maybe it was the expression on his face, but when it was Eliza's turn to devote herself to him for always, Carter believed her.

The minister asked for the rings, and Carter turned to Blake. His best friend produced the ring he'd picked out for Eliza to wear. It was the first time she would see it.

When he turned to her, her gaze drifted from his face to his hand. Her face washed of color, and he thought for a moment that he might have to hold her up. Her jaw dropped, and she quickly swiveled her eyes toward him. They glossed over, and a brilliant smile manifested behind her mask of nerves. "With this ring, I thee wed."

Carter accepted her ring, a simple gold band with a beveled edge and brush finish, and then finally the minister pronounced them husband and wife.

Both of them released a collective sigh, which brought a slight chuckle from the audience.

For a brief moment, it was only the two of them. The minister wasn't there, the audience…the sea. No one. Carter stepped into her space, wrapped his hand around her waist, and lowered his lips to hers.

He didn't care that flashbulbs recorded the moment, didn't care that his loving parents stood by and watched. This was for them. It was in that moment he knew that marrying Eliza meant more than protecting her from her past.

This was deeper.

This was lasting.

He ended their kiss and held on to her so she wouldn't fall.

He paused for the camera when the minister pronounced them Mr. and Mrs. Billings.

She squeezed his hand, and he shuffled them down the aisle.

According to his tip, recreation time tonight would confirm or deny what he'd been told. It was impossible to deny the future governor a few moments of airtime on the local channels. Especially when that man was getting married.

The media ate that shit up.

He glanced around the roomful of blue-uniformed inmates and knew that many of them would hold out hope that the next governor would grant them a pardon.

He didn't hold out that hope.

And if his tip was correct, there would be no question left in his mind what he needed to do.

The only way he could resolve what his meager existence had become.

Even then, it wouldn't leave him whole.

But it was something.

It was something.

"Senator Hammond. The pleasure is mine." Eliza prayed to God that Carter was nearby, but he was across the room talking with Blake and one of his influential friends.

Eliza extended her hand, and Carter's uncle leaned down, pretending to kiss her cheek. "Congratulations."

"Thank you." What else could she say? Eliza glanced over in Carter's direction, hoping that he would feel the weight of her stare and come to her rescue.

"I certainly hope you're prepared to be a political wife, Eliza. The strain is taxing, I'm told."

Where are my supernatural powers when I need them? C'mon, Carter. Look over here. "I'm sure it's not that bad."

Hammond laughed, although his smile appeared forced, tight. "How is it I've heard nothing of you until last month with that unfortunate incident in the Texas bar?"

Carter!

"Discretion is key, isn't it?"

Hammond hesitated. "I suppose."

His words hung on the air like a thick cloud of smoke.

"Max, it's wonderful of you to have come on such short notice."

Eliza had never felt like kissing another woman before as she did at that moment. Abigail stepped into the conversation and dominated it in seconds.

"It seems your son has followed in your footsteps, Abby. Instant marriage with someone the family barely knows," he whispered so no one close by could hear.

"The best matches, I'd say. Speaking of, where's Sally?"

Maxwell glared at his sister, his hatred thinly veiled.

Lord, how could Abigail stand it?

"She's helping Mother. Perhaps you can lend a hand."

Abigail smiled and clasped Eliza's arm. "Perfect idea. Come, Eliza, let me introduce you to the matriarch of our clan."

They left Max standing alone, clutching his drink.

"Holy cow!" Eliza exclaimed when they escaped his presence. "Is he always so intense?"

"Yes. Sadly. He didn't say anything truly nasty, did he?"

"No. But I don't think he likes me."

Abigail dropped an arm around her shoulders. "That's a very good thing. I'd have worried if he had."

"Are you going to tell me why all the badges are here?"

Carter glanced over at his father and considered lying. Instead, he stalled. "What do you mean?"

"So that's how you want to play it. OK…" He turned toward the guests and nodded in Dean's direction. "Dean is a cop, but not Eliza's family. My guess is the man he's talking to is his partner. They've talked to four other people here other than the wedding party. Of course, there is Neil, but we know he's a retired marine. He still works for Blake, right?"

Carter swallowed his drink. "Yeah, technically."

"There's a rookie, a police dog with the valet, and those are only the ones I see. So I'll ask again. Why all the badges?"

Carter hesitated. "It's complicated, Dad. This isn't the time or place."

Cash lowered his voice. "Are you in…Has there been a threat?"

Across the room, Eliza laughed alongside one of their guests. "I'm fine."

Cash followed his gaze. "You know I'm here to help."

For the first time in a while, Carter remembered how effective his father was as a cop. Maybe it was time to do some investigating on his own. As much as Dean and Jim were there to help, they weren't free with the details that had landed Eliza in her current position.

Carter waved Neil over and asked the man if he had a pen. He scribbled Ricardo Sanchez's name on a napkin and handed it to his father. "He's in San Quentin," he whispered in his father's ear. "Look back ten years."

Cash shook his son's hand. "Have I told you how proud I am of you lately?"

Carter patted him on the back. "It's been at least an hour."

A photographer snapped pictures throughout the day. During Blake's long-winded toast, Carter stood beside Eliza with a possessive hand around her waist.

When they cut the cake, Carter dribbled only a speck of icing on her nose. He avoided a messy chin by capturing her hand and licking off her fingers. For a moment, he caught her eyes and saw a spark of desire flood in them.

They hadn't spoken of their wedding night, of what the other expected. In Carter's mind, he figured he'd let her set the course. With the slightest hint of passion, he would consummate their union and give into the sizzling chemistry that had been brewing for years. The thought of removing her wedding dress to see what she wore underneath brought heat to his cheeks and desire to his blood.

He finished chewing the cake while she watched, and because he knew she wouldn't pull away, he dipped his head to hers and kissed her. She was sweeter than the cake and breathless when he moved away.

They had another hour, tops, at the reception before he could remove her from the crowd and gauge her desires. He could hardly wait.

Chapter Twenty

Plucking tiny grains of rice from her hair in the back of the limousine en route to the airport, Eliza took a full, deep breath for what seemed like the first time that day. "Wow, that was crazy."

Carter leaned forward and helped her disengage the small grains. "Crazy good?"

Her cheeks actually hurt from all the smiling. "Yeah, crazy good."

He nodded and tossed the rice to the floor. "Have I told you how gorgeous you are?"

"Yeah, you did."

"Well you are." He laughed.

The car moved into traffic, leaving the guests behind to continue the party.

Eliza brushed rice off his shoulder. "You missed your Hollywood calling, Carter. I'll bet you didn't even rent this tux."

"Is that a compliment?"

"Yeah, it is." She left her hand on his shoulder and slid it to his neck.

"Are you going to say 'yeah' all night?" He placed a hand on her thigh and lifted an expectant brow.

"Maybe," she said to be trite.

His eyes narrowed with laughter. "Now she says maybe."

Even if their marriage was one of convenience, there was no reason not to enjoy it. If there was a lesson learned from Samantha and Blake's union, it was that denying a physical attraction proved fruitless when the man you desired happened to be your husband.

She pressed her lips to his and tasted his surprise. He pulled her into his arms and deepened their kiss. His hand stroked her bare arm as he moved his lips to her ear. "Are you sure?" he asked.

Eliza glanced at the glass separating them and the driver. "We're adults, we kinda like each other, and the bonus is we're married."

Carter sat back and held her face in his hands. "I never assumed…"

"I know. Which makes it even better."

He kissed her again, this time with more fervor, more desire. Heat swelled in the pit of her stomach and traveled south. Her hand slid inside his jacket and met with the hard ripple of muscle under his shirt.

Carter moved away again. "We need to start talking, or I'm going to embarrass us both," he said.

She wiped some of the moisture off her lips and put a bit of distance between them. Carter glanced out the back window to the car that followed.

"How long of a flight do we have?"

"Too long."

The bodyguards would be on the plane with them, which meant they wouldn't be alone until they reached the hotel in Kauai.

The driver maneuvered them through the airport and onto the tarmac. He stopped when they arrived at Blake and Samantha's jet. Much to Eliza's surprise, there were half a dozen paparazzi clicking pictures of them as they boarded the plane.

"Looks like news of our nuptials spread."

Russell and Joe flanked them as they climbed the steps into the plane. Eliza swiveled at the top of the steps and sent the photographers a presidential wave. Carter shook his head, and his eyes crinkled with laughter.

Once inside, she asked Carter to help her with the zipper of her dress. He groaned as he slid it down her spine. They both eyed the bed on the plane and smiled at each other. Eliza was sure where his thoughts led. "I don't think so, Hollywood. Two bodyguards, a pilot, and a copilot are too much of an audience for me."

"There's a door."

"Not a thick one. What if we hit turbulence?"

"Kauai is five hours away," he debated.

Eliza held up her dress with one arm and placed the other on his chest. "How long have you known me?"

"Over two years."

She shoved him out the door. "Five more hours won't kill you." She shut the door behind him and changed into a more practical dress.

Carter felt the ungodly urge to bang his head against the seat of the airplane. Eliza eyed the door to the bedroom more than once. The bodyguards were happily tucked into a service section of the plane and wouldn't even notice if they slipped into the room. About the time Carter opened his mouth to suggest they "rest," the captain asked them to fasten their seat belts and expect some turbulence.

That was two hours ago. Outside of a trip to the bathroom and a refill of sparkling wine, they were glued to their seats.

"I just realized something," Eliza said as she sipped her wine. "I've never been to your house. I didn't even pack my things. And what is Gwen going to do?"

"I wouldn't worry about Gwen. I think she likes her new life. And I'm sure Neil will tag a team of watchful eyes on her for safety."

Eliza hadn't thought of that. "Gwen will love his attention."

"What does that mean?"

"Just that—she'll love Neil's attention. I think she has a thing for him."

Carter swiveled in his seat. "For Neil? Are you sure?"

"She hasn't said so directly. But she does that dopey, girly look whenever she talks about him. Don't you dare tell him I said that."

He laughed. "I left high school some time ago. I admit I didn't see that coming."

"No one is coming." Eliza stopped short when she realized what she'd said. "I mean, I don't think Gwen has done anything about her attraction."

Carter winked. "Something tells me she won't. And I can't imagine Neil initiating a relationship with Blake's sister."

"Because he works for Blake?"

"It's more complicated than that. If there is an attraction, then I'm sure Neil will take extra care to ensure Gwen's safety. So don't worry about her. I can text Jay when we land and have him hire a moving company if you want. Your things can be in my home before we get back."

"I'd rather do it myself. Besides, I'll have extra hands around me for a while to help." She glanced to the front of the plane and the bodyguards that were playing cards. "How long do you think we'll have to have them around?"

"I honestly don't know."

Eliza wasn't sure, either. And when the guards could move on, would that mean her marriage to Carter could too? Damn, she wasn't married a full day, and already she wondered how long the union would last.

The aircraft dropped a couple of feet as it hit unstable air, and Eliza clutched the handrest of her seat. Carter covered her hand with his. "Smaller airplanes have a harder time hiding bumps."

"Mr. and Mrs. Billings, we will be up here a little longer. The weather in Hawaii isn't ideal for landing. We are waiting for a break to make our descent."

Eliza swallowed hard. "Did you fly a lot as a kid?" she asked to take her mind off the nasty flight.

"Holidays when my parents couldn't avoid the Hammond gathering. You?"

"Not much. I don't remember any flights with my parents. After, there were a few. But nothing like this."

"The turbulence or the private jet?"

"Either."

"If you fly as much as Blake, it makes sense to own your own ride."

They hit another air pocket, and Eliza's wineglass tipped over.

Carter pushed it away to avoid it soaking her dress.

"You fly all the time."

He nodded. "I do. Which is why I've been talking with Blake about a co-op."

The plane sunk, then leveled out.

Eliza swallowed hard. "You want to own your own plane? Isn't that expensive?"

"Not if you fly all the time."

"Please…"

"OK, yeah, they're costly. But when I travel, I have people with me. I need to go quickly, and I don't have time for domestic schedules. Besides, I've hitchhiked off Blake enough. It's time to put some of my slush fund to use."

"Slush fund?" Somehow Eliza didn't think he was talking about a simple savings account. Or a 401(k). "My slush fund is in a coffee can back home. It would take a hell of a lot of coffee cans to come up with a private jet."

They hit a couple more bumps before the jet sailed through the air.

"Life happens once. I have money. I might as well use it."

What does that mean?

Eliza glanced down at the rock he'd put on her finger. It was Kardashian huge, to the point where she wondered if it was real. After listening to Carter, she knew better than to ask. She needed to thank him for it at some point, but now didn't seem right.

The aircraft started its descent, and her ears popped with the change of pressure.

Eliza released a sigh when they made it to the ground. Not that she was overly anxious that they would crash, but the flight had rattled her nerves.

Rain pelted them as they left the plane. The airport was flooded, and the car that was supposed to be waiting for them had been delayed.

It was still light outside, which somehow made everything a little better, but still, the flight had been long, and they were now two hours behind schedule. Not that they had a schedule, but for them, it had been a long day, and a plush bed in a five-star resort sounded divine.

"Apparently, a road washed out, but the locals think it will be fixed within the hour."

"I thought Hawaii was always sunny. Like California." The humidity licked her skin, and she knew her assumption was just that.

"It rains a lot here this time of year. It doesn't last long, though."

It didn't. But the locals had a hard time getting the road passable, and it was nearly two more hours before they made it to the hotel.

With a flower lei around her neck, Eliza passed through the lobby in a daze. The wicker decor and open-air foyer would simply have to wait to be appreciated. Right now, a hot shower and a bed was all she wanted.

In their room, a fruit, cheese, and wine basket met them. It was from Carter's parents.

"I like your parents."

"They like you too. Why don't you take the first shower?" Carter suggested.

It was well after midnight on their body clocks when Eliza slid into the hot, pulsating water. *What a day.* She thought back on several moments when she'd envisioned her parents' faces, their smiles. They might not have been there in body, but she'd felt them in spirit.

Even though it was late, she dressed in the lingerie meant for this night. Hopefully, Carter would shower quickly or stand the risk of her falling asleep on him.

Eliza scrubbed her face clean but went ahead and put on a little lip gloss. She nibbled her fingernail before realizing what she was doing. "It's Carter, Lisa. Get a grip. No need for nerves," she whispered to herself. After running a final brush through her hair, she smiled at her reflection before stepping from the bathroom.

"The shower is all..." Her words died on her lips.

Carter had removed his coat, tie, and shoes and had laid on the bed to wait for her. His features softened in slumber, and the slow, steady rise and fall of his chest brought a wave of pleasure over her. He was sound asleep.

Without waking him, she took a blanket from the closet and draped it over him. She removed her silk robe and slid between the cool sheets and cooed.

He didn't so much as stir.

Eliza turned onto her side and watched him sleep.

Sunlight filtered in behind her closed eyelids and pushed the cobwebs from her brain.

Something tickled her nose, and she moved her head to scratch it. The musky scent mixed with that of soap met her nose.

Carter.

Before she opened her eyes, Eliza realized two things. First, she was intimately wrapped around her husband, who at some point in the night had managed to slip out of his clothes and into the sheets with her. The second was that her husband wasn't asleep.

The sound of his heart beating in his chest met her ear, which was cradled in the crook of his arm. One of her legs was draped over his as if it had the right to be there.

His fingers gently stroked her back and thigh.

How had she managed to get so tangled? Cuddling wasn't her thing. Normally.

With Carter, there didn't seem to be a normal.

With as little notice as she could muster, she started to move away.

Carter wouldn't have it. His hand on her thigh pressed firm and kept her in place.

Eliza opened her eyes and viewed his naked chest for the first time. Well, she'd seen him by the pool at Sam's, but this was entirely different. After taking a brief moment to admire the sculpted way his chest looked from her angle, she closed her eyes and sighed.

This was something she could get used to.

She opened her eyes again and repositioned her cheek on his chest.

"You're not going anywhere," he told her with laughter in his voice. "I worked up the nerve to touch you here"—he tightened his grip on her thigh to indicate what he meant—"about twenty minutes ago, and I've wanted to travel higher ever since. Only, I didn't want to wake you."

His words brought warmth over her skin. She envisioned his internal debate while she slept. Funny, she didn't think of him as an insecure person. But apparently, when it came to seducing her, there was a hint of doubt. "I'm not the one who fell asleep last night."

He groaned and clicked his tongue. As he spoke, he made good on his threat and inched his hand up her thigh with a slow ascent. "Guilty. I'm sorry about that."

"We were both exhausted."

She spread her palm over his chest. Her new ring sparkled off the sunlight streaming in from the window.

"I woke around three and climbed in with you. I hope you don't mind."

His fingers danced over the curve of her hip, maneuvered under the silk of her panties, and she shivered with anticipation of more. "I don't mind."

Carter shifted to his side, and Eliza gazed into his eyes. "Good morning," he whispered.

He captured her lips in the softest of kisses. A slow, gentle exploration. She could still taste the mint of his breath, which left her feeling guilty for not having the same fresh taste to offer him.

The slow pace he set with his kiss proved he didn't mind. He probed her mouth open with little nips until his tongue played with hers. Eliza didn't realize she was rigid beneath him until all her muscles relaxed. Carter pressed her into the soft cotton sheets and ran his free hand up her waist, pushing aside her nightgown.

He kissed like a man who should be paid to do so. He didn't leave anything untouched and only moved away when he needed to breathe. When he did, she ran her fingers over his chest. When did he find the time to work out? Or was the muscle definition from his gene pool? She'd thought about touching him more than she'd admit. Thinking about it and enjoying the feel of his warm skin were nowhere near the same.

He brushed his thumb beside her breast, coaxing her skin awake.

"You're really good at that," she told him as he moved to kiss the side of her neck.

"At kissing?" He playfully bit her ear.

"At making me feel like the only woman in the world."

His hand left her breast and moved to her cheek. He leaned back, and she opened her eyes to find him staring at her with his dark-blue eyes. "You are the only woman in my world, Eliza."

Who knew Carter's thoughts ran deep? The compassion she found behind his eyes made her admit something she'd never done before. "It's Lisa. My name before…It was Lisa."

His hands hesitated on their discovery trip over her body, and he lowered his voice to just above a whisper. "Have you ever told anyone else that?"

"No," she whispered. "I never wanted to until now."

The smile on his face reached his eyes, and he held her closer. "When we're here, I'll use your real name."

Tears welled in her eyes, which was silly. Her heart wasn't filled with sadness, but joy in having trust in another human being. "I'd like that."

She slid her thigh between his and moved deeper into his embrace. She sought his lips and languished in his taste. His stiff arousal pressed firmly against her stomach. *He sleeps in the nude.* She notched the information into her brain and soaked in his slow, titillating touch.

The leisurely kisses proved maddening as her skin heated and her body began to ache. Carter didn't seem to feel the same urgency to move faster, and yet he kept devouring her mouth, face, and neck.

Eliza found a sensitive spot on his hip and dug her fingernails into his dense muscles, marveling at his perfection. Everywhere she touched she liked, wanted more. Soon the friction of his leg pulsating between hers wasn't enough. She followed his hip and ran the tip of her finger over his erection.

Carter groaned and moved his lips and tongue to the flesh below her collarbone. Her breasts ached, wanting his touch. With a gentle nudge, she guided him to where she wanted him. Lord, he took his time pushing away her nightgown before swirling his tongue around one pert nipple. He licked her as if she were made of the finest cream, and he wasn't going to stop until the bowl was empty.

Suddenly, the clothing she wore felt like a noose around her neck, and the urgency to feel him skin to skin overwhelmed her. She stopped teasing his erection and tugged at the fringes of her lingerie. He took the hint and stripped it away.

High color reached his cheeks as his gaze traveled down her nearly naked body.

"I work out," she teased.

"I can tell. I always knew you'd be spectacular."

She squirmed under him, constantly aware of his heated sex and how close it was to bringing them both pleasure. "You thought about me?"

"All the time." He kissed her nipple again, and the one scrap of clothing she had left on dampened.

"Even when we argued?"

He moved lower, kissing under her breast and tasting her stomach. "Especially when we argued. You're all fire and passion. I've always wanted a sample of that." He ran a finger under her panties.

She gasped when he found her moist, aroused state.

"You're killing me," he said.

She laughed and lifted her hips to help him ease off her panties. He watched as she wiggled her hips.

"Death by sex. I don't know if that's happened in real life. Fiction, maybe."

He found her sex again, the way he had before all those weeks ago in her kitchen. "I want to taste you—all of you. But I don't think I can wait much longer," he told her.

The waiting was killing her too. "Then don't wait, Hollywood." She opened her thighs a little wider, enticing him.

Carter reached to the table on his side of the bed. There, he found a condom he must have placed there the night before.

"I'm on the pill," she told him.

He hesitated with the package. "Are you suggesting we don't use this?"

Am I? She was a twenty-first-century woman; she'd never slept with a man without one. The risks weren't worth the pleasure. "I…I don't…I've never not," she told him. "But if we wanted to…" *What am I saying?* "If we didn't use it, we'd be safe. We've never talked about these things."

He palmed the condom, leaned in, and kissed her again. "I'm clean," he whispered between kisses. The awkward moment she'd just had disappeared like pixie dust on the wind.

He stopped kissing her long enough for her to open her eyes.

"Make love to me without a barrier, Lisa."

Hearing her name from his lips for the first time made her want to cry. "I'd like that."

The grin that stretched over his lips spread for miles. He tossed the condom to the floor and moved between her legs.

He gazed into her eyes as he slowly pressed his heated flesh into hers. It had been quite a while for her, but Carter murmured for her to relax and take him in. His eyes rolled into the back of his head, and he dropped his forehead to hers. "So wonderful," he whispered.

And it was. The heat, the tenderness of his touch. The trust she felt for the man making love to her. She'd trusted men before him with her body, but never without protection and never with her given name. He was her husband, and somewhere this felt more like an act of love than just sex.

The word caught on her mind, and she swept it away. Love opened people to vulnerability, and Lisa hated feeling vulnerable.

With a tilt of her hips, Carter was seated inside her and releasing tiny gasps. His fit was perfect. She was already contracting around him, wanting more.

Eliza had never imagined Carter to be so complete in his lovemaking. She'd fantasized about him in bed more than once, but never thought he would make her want to roll him on his back and take over, yet at the same time want to wait and see what he would incite from her next.

"Carter?"

He thrust his hips to hers and pulled away slowly. "I feel like a teenager again. I want to devour you slowly one minute and work you over the next."

She wrapped her legs around his waist and grinned. "You've devoured. It's time for the work-over."

"Thank God. Hold on."

For a minute, Eliza thought he was teasing, but then he started to move. Holding on became increasingly difficult as he pressed her deeper into the bed with each pass of his sex over hers. The intensity of his pace and the speed in which he brought her desire to a peak startled her. He found the perfect stroke and friction.

She gripped his back and moaned. "Yes..." She tilted her hips, moving faster. He kept her there, hovering over her release. "More," she cried. "Please."

He gave a soft laugh and surged into her with such intensity she couldn't breathe. Her orgasm was instant and full of fireworks.

Breathing was an effort, and Carter wasn't anywhere near done. He whispered sultry things in her ear that kept her captivated.

The sheer masculine power that was consuming her made her want to weep.

"I want to make you scream," he told her. He pinched her breast with his words, and she nearly did. Her teeth found his shoulder, and she gave him a love bite that made him moan.

Perhaps their playful banter out of the bedroom would transfer into their love play. *How fun would that be?*

Carter brought her to the edge again, making her breath hitch in the back of her throat. "Yes," she gasped.

And then he emptied inside of her. The feel of his warmth filling her catapulted her into a place of rainbows. Her body couldn't get enough of him as she shuddered, milking him dry.

Carter collapsed on top of her, his heart beating wildly in his chest. Eliza—no, Lisa, he reminded himself—struggled for air, and damn, that made him feel like a god. Her body accepted every last drop of his seed. That felt damn good. He'd had sex without condoms when he was young. With Lisa, it was a gift. One he would cherish and hold dear.

"Hot damn, Hollywood."

"You like?" He hoisted his weight off hers enough to look at her satisfied face.

The inner muscles of her womb constricted around him.

He groaned.

"If I told you how amazing that was, it would feed your already overinflated ego."

He kissed her nose. "And *we* wouldn't want that."

She wiggled her hips and ran her foot down his leg. "No, *we* wouldn't."

With a swift move, he positioned himself under her but kept himself tangled intimately within her.

She sat tall and thrust out her perky breasts. He palmed them both instantly. He hadn't paid enough attention to this lovely addition to her body.

"This position does have possibilities."

"Yes. Yes, it does." Carter pulled her down for a kiss and explored those possibilities.

Chapter Twenty-One

They ate, drank, laughed, and made love like happy fools on their honeymoon. Carter wanted to play the happy fool for as long as he could. Sadly, their time on the island was drawing to a close.

They sat under the stars with tiki torches and hula dancers. A native Hawaiian band played the drums so the women wiggling their hips could do so to a beat. He and Eliza drank sissy drinks and applauded the dancers when they finished.

"I can't believe we leave tomorrow." Eliza leaned into him, comfortable in his embrace.

"I was thinking the same thing."

"Wouldn't it be wonderful if we could just stay here? No bad guys, no phones, no shoe-eating dogs?"

The last thing he wanted to think about was the man responsible for her distress at home. Reality started to crash around him. He'd married her to keep her safe, but what if he couldn't?

God, he hated that thought. His eyes traveled to the guards who kept constant watch over them.

But what if it wasn't enough?

He kissed the top of her head and stared at the fire pit in the middle of the luau. "I'll keep you safe."

She swirled her finger on his thigh, drawing invisible shapes. "I know. But if something were—"

He jolted with the words she attempted to utter. "It won't! Nothing will happen to you."

She tilted her head up and kissed him softly. When she pulled away, she placed a finger on his lips, keeping him silent. "If…I wouldn't blame you."

In an instant, he pictured her lifeless and pale. The vision left him ill. He tightened his jaw and forced the image away. "I'll never let that happen. Don't think like that. Don't talk like that." His harsh words brought a scowl to her face. "Please," he added. Telling Eliza to do anything was like daring her. "Please," he said again.

She stopped and attempted to smile. "OK."

When they made love that night, he didn't leave an inch of her untouched, unloved. As she fell asleep in his arms, he lay awake, thinking of her words, of her worry. He had to do something to remove the threat. In order to do that, he needed every scrap of information, every piece of evidence about Ricardo Sanchez. His day tomorrow would begin with a flight home, and then a conference call between his father and his best friend was in order.

"Don't you look like a contented kitten," Gwen said shortly after Eliza walked in the door of the Tarzana home.

"Hawaii was beautiful."

"It's more than that."

Zod sniffed her hand in greeting. "How are you? Eating any stilettos?"

"Stop playing with that dog and talk to me. I've not had sex in ages, so I must live vicariously through my friends. Tell me and you mustn't leave out the details." Gwen tugged on her arm until they were both seated on the couch.

The blonde bombshell was a walking contradiction. Little Miss Prim-and-Proper one minute, with every inch of etiquette followed, and then Little Miss Sin-and-Sex the next. Eliza loved that about the British-born lady.

Eliza tossed her purse on the sofa and kicked off her shoes. Before Eliza could start the lengthy session of girl talk, Zod barked.

"It's me," Samantha's low voice sounded from behind the front door.

"Come in," both Gwen and Eliza shouted at the same time.

Zod did a regulatory sniff and then circled a couple of times before sitting at Eliza's end of the couch.

"You haven't started yet, have you?"

"Started what?" Eliza asked. "And how did you know I was here?"

"Carter called Blake to tell him he was on his way over and that you were coming here to pack. I told Blake I was gonna help and… *Oh my God*, you're glowing. How was it?"

Samantha and Gwen sat forward with big eyes and anticipation. Their mouths hung open.

"I heard her excuse, Little Miss I-Haven't-Had-Sex-in-Ages, but what's your excuse?"

Samantha clapped her hands. "So you did have sex."

Eliza remembered the cameras and audio surveillance in the room. "You know others are listening, right?"

Sam waved her hands in the air. "Who cares about that? Details! I want details. Carter has had the hots for you forevah."

"No, he hasn't."

"We can debate that later. Spill." Sam shoved an unruly lock of red curly hair behind her ear and grinned like a child.

There was no walking away from what these women wanted. Eliza sucked in her bottom lip and let her body warm with the memories. "Unparalleled. He was amazing. Warm, sensual, and he took his ever-loving time. I loved that—hated it too." She sighed. "It was worth the wait."

Gwen began asking detailed questions, starting with when and where. Did they play in the plane or on the beach?

It was impossible not to get caught up in the recall. With these women, she knew nothing would go farther than these walls.

"What are you grinning about?" Carter asked Neil when he walked into the room. The larger man resembled a sixteen-year-old who'd just found his father's stash of scotch.

Neil leveled his gaze at Carter and suppressed a laugh.

"Did Sam arrive OK?"

"She did," Neil said.

Carter moved from one man to another. "Samantha is with Eliza and Gwen packing, right?"

"Right."

"So you were listening to them? Watching them?"

Neil had access to the surveillance equipment at the Tarzana house, but Carter never thought of him as a spy.

"Long enough to know that Sam arrived and they're starting to pack." The grin on Neil's face faded. "So…Where are we?"

"We're about to call Cash and see what he found out."

Carter dialed in the video call, and Blake put Cash's image on the big screen.

"Hey, Dad."

His father sat at a desk and waved at the screen. "Will you look at that? This would have made my life a hell of a lot easier when I was on the force. Is this how all of you kids talk now? No phones?"

"We text, e-mail, and talk on phones. How was your flight home?" Carter asked.

"Fine, fine. You look rested. How's Eliza?"

"She's great. Packing."

"We like her."

Carter glanced at Neil and then Blake. "I'm glad. So, Dad, what did you find out?"

Cash's easygoing smile dropped. "Before I tell you what I learned, first you need to tell me your connection to this scumbag Sanchez."

That didn't sound good. Already, there was fight in his father's voice.

"It's not me as much as it is Eliza. Her parents…"

Cash swallowed hard and dropped back in his seat. "Eliza's last name wasn't Havens, was it?"

"No."

"I was afraid of that."

"What is it, Dad?" Carter sat forward, rubbed his hands together. From the gray look on his father's face, he knew it wasn't good. Even for a seasoned veteran of the force.

Cash pushed a few papers around on his desk and perched a pair of reading glasses on the end of his nose. "Ricardo Sanchez is doing two life sentences at San Quentin. He doesn't care who he pisses off in prison, spends plenty of time in solitary. Though, of late, he's backed off. The guards say it's normal for a man in his forties to lay low."

"Why is he there?" Carter knew Eliza's parents were murdered, but had Ricardo personally ended their lives? Or had he called in the hit?

"Sanchez ran a well-organized sex trade operation. Anytime sex is involved, you'll find drugs. And he had a hand in that as well. His reach covered a dozen states and three countries. Some of the testimony that I found indicated that he was a modern-day mob boss. He had a family, kids, even a dog—if you can call a vicious pit bull trained to eat small children a dog. Still, he was respected and feared. He evaded arrest—and notice, for that matter—for years because of the legit business he used to cover up his criminal activities. That's where Kenneth Ashe comes in. Name mean anything to you?"

It should have. Something told Carter he should have known that name. He shook his head.

"Mr. Ashe drove a shipping truck at night for Sanchez's models." Cash air-quoted the word *models*. "You see, Sanchez disguised his sex slaves as runway models for second-class fashion shows. Sanchez didn't keep the same legit men on the jobs for more than few weeks before swapping them out. He had oblivious drivers drop off and set up runways. Later he'd have his boys come with the mostly underage girls to entertain an exclusive group of men. The men at the front of the caravan never knew what was happening on the other end. According to the testimony, Ashe was on his second week as a driver and had lost something at work. Unfortunately, he returned later that night for it.

"Ashe slipped into the back room of the 'fashion show' and found Sanchez in the act of raping and beating a minor. Ashe was a family man. Had a kid of his own—a daughter. He hid, but was trapped, unable to leave until after Sanchez was done."

"He didn't try and stop him?" Neil asked.

"The room was filled with women, girls, and several of Sanchez's men. All armed. If Ashe had tried, he would have died."

Carter swallowed a mouthful of bile. Ashe must have been Eliza's father.

"Sanchez killed the girl, as an example of what would happen if the others didn't cooperate. He boasted that every time a new batch of girls came in, he personally sacrificed one."

"Jesus."

"No, I don't think Jesus was invited to this party. When Ashe managed to get away, he went to the authorities. An investigation was launched, and Sanchez was taken into custody. Within a week, every girl had been murdered and found in the most horrendous of places, all violated, thrown away like garbage."

"What happened to Ashe?"

Cash removed his glasses and looked at Carter through the video camera. "He, his wife, and their young daughter were taken into protective custody. After the trial, Sanchez was sentenced, and the Ashe family disappeared into the Witness Protection Program."

Carter dropped his head into his palms. Blake placed a hand on his back.

"Do you want to hear the rest?"

Carter nodded, but he didn't look at his father.

"Kenneth and his wife, Mary, attempted to live life within the system. But like I said, Sanchez had a reach. A year or so later, the authorities found Mary, much like the girls from the sex ring, dead, violated, and her husband bound so he could watch. His throat slit. A note was pinned to the skin of his forehead letting whoever found them know that their daughter was next. Luckily, the girl had been in school that day."

Carter felt his lunch in his throat. Thank God Lisa hadn't been there. Did she know all of these details? She couldn't, he decided, or she would have run with the first threat to her safety. No wonder Dean and Jim were so persistent about placing her in a bunker.

"Where is your wife, son?"

"Packing."

Neil stood and started to pace. "There are two California Highway Patrol on her twenty-four/seven, and I have another private man on the house."

"Do we know if Sanchez still runs his business from the inside?"

"I'm working on that now. He still has contact with his wife and kids."

"How fucking fair is that?" Carter exploded. "He destroys Eliza's life and then goes on with his own?"

Blake clasped his shoulder. "We won't let him get to her."

"I knew it would be bad, but this? Dammit, Blake."

"It's OK. Eliza is fine, guarded."

Carter's skin boiled, and his blood threatened to blow like the top of a volcano. Eliza was fine—but for how long?

Eliza ran out of words explaining her honeymoon and everything "Carter" to Sam and Gwen. Miss Prim-and-Proper fanned herself with a magazine, and Sam sat forward, leaning over her knees with her chin in her palm.

"You look happy," Sam said.

Eliza's cheeks ached from smiling. "I am."

Gwen patted her knee and stood. "We might want to begin packing. I'm certain Carter will be worried if we delay."

Eliza glanced around the living room, her home for the past couple of years, and sighed. Deep in her heart, she knew she wouldn't be returning to this small Tarzana home. Even if the day came when she and Carter separated, the chances of her living there again would be slim.

The three of them filed into her bedroom and moved in separate directions to pack her personal things. "This shouldn't take long," she told the women. "Carter's home is filled with furniture. Besides, most of this is yours anyway, Sam."

Sam pushed at her unruly red curls until they were tucked into a band and out of her face. "It seems like yesterday that Blake and I were here packing my clothes. Maybe the bed is blessed and those who sleep in it are marriage-bound."

Gwen tilted her head and considered the mattress with renewed interest. "If that's the case, perhaps I should move in here." She placed both palms on the covers and gave it a tiny shove.

"You want to get married?"

"I've wanted to marry for years, but the men I've dated simply didn't suit me for the long term."

Eliza laughed. "You might have to give them more than a week of your time." During several of their late-night conversations, Eliza had discovered a lot about Gwen's dating life. As a daughter of a wealthy duke, her family expected her to have a very discreet private life. That translated into boring dates and forgetful sex. Many of the royals who'd lost their money, but not their titles, didn't fall into the public eye. The Harrisons were different. Their faces were splattered among the British tabloids as often as any starlet in Hollywood would be in the States.

"It's not my fault the men I've met bore me to tears. There needs to be interest inside the bedroom and out, wouldn't you agree?"

"You're talking to two women who married their husbands before they slept with them. I don't think you have the right audience for that argument."

Gwen's eyes grew wide, and her mouth dropped. "I can't imagine. What if Carter made love like a wet fish?"

"I think you're selling yourself short, Gwen. If a man warms your blood before your first kiss, the chances of that kiss being cold are slim. Carter can make me blush from across the room. And don't you dare tell him I said that." Eliza didn't want all her secrets revealed to her husband. Not yet, anyway.

"I knew Blake would be a fantastic lover the first time he touched my hand." Samantha licked her lips as she spoke.

"Truly?"

"Call it chemistry, energy, desire…I knew. If you had told me a year before we married that I wouldn't sleep with my husband before the wedding day, I would have reacted like you."

Gwen leaned on one arm as she listened. "You met my brother only days before you married."

Sam rolled her eyes. "Details, details."

"You can't say that about me and Carter."

"No, I guess not. Surely there was some contact before the wedding, wasn't there?"

The memory of their encounter in the kitchen surfaced in Eliza's mind. Her face grew hot, and Gwen and Samantha started laughing.

"Busted."

"We didn't have sex. Heavy petting and hot, sultry kissing."

Gwen tossed a pillow in Eliza's direction.

They all laughed until their sides hurt.

"I'll miss this terribly. I've never had girlfriends as close as the two of you," Gwen said.

"I'm moving out, not away," Eliza reminded her.

"We should initiate a girls' night out once a month—maybe twice."

"That sounds delightful." Gwen scurried off the bed and picked up a box from the floor.

"No talk of work. Just girl talk."

"Sex talk."

"You'll have to find a boyfriend if you're going to entertain us," Eliza chided.

"I might just do that."

Sam turned toward her sister-in-law. "Have anyone in mind?"

Gwen hesitated and then shook her head. "No."

"Liar."

Gwen's jaw dropped. "I'm not lying."

Eliza folded her arms over her chest. "Are you telling me there isn't anyone who makes your insides boil…that makes you spark just thinking about him?"

Again, she hesitated. "No."

Sam shook her head. "Liar."

Gwen let a tiny smile cover her face as she turned away. "Believe what you must."

Sam glanced up at Eliza with a questioning stare.

They both watched as Gwen looked into the lens of the camera mounted in the doorway.

Gwen was keeping secrets from those who monitored the house.

Probably Neil.

It took every effort of control for Eliza not to call Gwen out.

The doorbell rang and distracted them away from the conversation. Eliza moved from the room, waving a finger in Gwen's direction. "This isn't over with, Miss Prim-and-Proper."

Zod stood by the front door while Eliza opened it. Russell, one of the bodyguards, waited on the other side. "Sorry to disturb you, Mrs. Billings, but your husband has asked that we keep you in sight or hearing range at all times."

Reality slammed into her chest. All the girl talk and ease of the day shot away faster than the bullet leaving the chamber of a .357. "Why? Has something happened?"

"Not that I know of, ma'am. He directed me to step into the house."

A shiver fluttered up her spine. She opened the door wider and let him in.

Samantha walked up beside her and laid a hand on her shoulder. "It's OK, Eliza. You'll hardly notice him after a while."

I wouldn't bet money on that.

Packing went quickly, and Eliza was taking another trip to the car when Mrs. Sweeny, the neighbor from next door, walked around the hedge with a pot in her arms. "Eliza? Eliza, dear?"

Zod snarled at the older woman wearing an apron who smelled like fish.

Eliza called him down. Her bodyguard watched from inside the house.

"There you are. I never knew you were dating our future governor, and here I saw a picture of you in a wedding dress standing next to that handsome husband of yours." Mrs. Sweeny liked to talk, and she never put on airs.

"We didn't announce it to the world until after the ceremony. You're not the only one surprised by our union."

Mrs. Sweeny bobbed her head until her gray hair started to tumble into her eyes. "I should be grateful you didn't attract many of those men with cameras like Samantha did."

"I tried."

Mrs. Sweeny struggled with the pot in her arms and shifted on her feet. "They've been here, but not many of them are hiding in the bushes. I've only had one broken rosebush this time."

Samantha and Blake's marriage had brought on a circus of paparazzi attempting to capture the new duchess doing something naughty. Poor Mrs. Sweeny lost many buds that year.

"I'll pay for any damage, Mrs. Sweeny."

"I know, I know. I'm just so happy for you. Here." She lifted the pot higher, and Eliza reached for the smelly stew.

"It's my famous linguine-and-clam sauce. I know how much you like it. Being newly married and all, you probably won't be in the kitchen very much." The older woman winked, leaving Eliza a little baffled. Who knew Mrs. Sweeny carried such wicked thoughts?

"Thank you." Eliza took the pot from her neighbor and ignored the nauseous smell of the attempt at fishy pasta. Poor Mr. Sweeny must not have any taste buds left. None of the neighbors escaped a homecoming, welcome baby, happy bride pot of gritty clams in a sauce that might be white, but wasn't creamy, covering cheap linguine. But the thought was always welcome, and no one told Mrs.

Sweeny that the contents made their way directly into the garbage disposal in the sink.

"No problem at all, and congratulations, dear. You let your husband know he has my vote."

Mrs. Sweeny waved as she walked away.

Inside the house, Samantha and Gwen were already running the water in the sink.

Gwen held her nose, and Sam turned away as the food went down the drain. "We saw her talking to you and smelled this from upstairs."

"How can she eat this stuff?"

"Have you ever seen her eat it? Seems she is always giving it away."

The noise from the compactor filled the kitchen until all of the odiferous food was gone. "You're going to have to burn a scented candle to get the smell out of here," Eliza told Gwen.

"I'm ahead of you. One is burning in the living room already."

"Smart girl."

Eliza washed her hands and prayed she didn't smell like fish. "Well, I think that's it."

Eliza gave Gwen a hug and turned to Samantha. "Thanks for helping me pack. Carter and I are going to work out a schedule between his campaign and Alliance. I'll be back to work next Monday."

"Take some time off, get settled."

"I'd go crazy doing nothing. I'll be back on Monday."

Samantha knew better than to argue and dropped her concerns. As they walked out the door, Mrs. Sweeny's conversation about broken roses rang in her ears.

"Gwen, have you seen any paparazzi outside the house?"

"No, why?"

"Mrs. Sweeny said something about her roses. Maybe it was Zod."

"I know how to handle the media. Don't worry."

"Be careful. And call if you need anything."

Gwen hugged her again. "I'm not a child."

"I know."

"I'll walk you out. I need to get home myself," Sam said.

Eliza took one last look at the house as she waved good-bye. "There goes a chapter of my life," she whispered to herself.

"What was that, Mrs. Billings?"

Eliza turned to her bodyguard and called Zod to her side. "Nothing."

Chapter Twenty-Two

"Hey, Harry! You have a visitor."

Harry looked at the face of the guard and considered the man's words. *A visitor? Who?* he wanted to ask but kept his mouth shut. Visitors had been limited since his incarceration. Funny how when you swindle your friends and destroy your family people have no use for you. He'd made his bed and slept on the lumpy mattress every night of his pathetic life.

Harry pushed himself off the bench where he had been reading a paper and followed the guard to the visitors' room.

The space was vacant. Only he and the guard stood on the inmate side of the protective glass. Halfway down the flank of chairs sat a man dressed in a tailored business suit Harry would have worn on the outside. He recognized the man, though they had never met. Harry's heart sped in his chest, and for the first time in years, his palms grew moist. He shoved down the drop of hope that threatened to take hold and spread into a lake of want. Wanting what he could never have would only breed discord and pain. Though he deserved it, he avoided emotional pain as much as possible.

Harry sat in the government-issue chair and considered the man in front of him.

He picked up the phone and patiently waited for the other man's move.

"Mr. Elliot."

Harry tilted his head to the side. "Mr. Harrison."

"You know who I am?"

"You're married to my daughter. Of course I know who you are."

Blake Harrison, the duke of Albany, stared at him through the glass.

"You look nothing like your photos," Blake told him.

"Prison has a way of kicking the life out of you. Is Samantha OK? Jordan?" Hearing his daughters' names roll off his tongue shocked even him. Regret choked him hard.

"They're fine."

"The baby?"

"Fine."

Reading about your child in the papers wasn't the same as hearing the words said aloud by someone who had contact with them. Some weight of Harry's concern lifted. "Does Samantha know you're here?"

"No. Not yet."

"Then why are you here?"

Blake assessed him with a deep, penetrating stare that ran through Harry's body with a rush of power. There was a time in his life when he could make a man squirm with a look, but that wasn't easy wearing jailhouse blues. He sat taller, however, and did his best not to look away.

"Why did you do it?" Blake asked. "You had to know you'd get caught sooner or later."

Harry blinked. Blake wasn't there to ask about his past crimes, but something told him his answer would either gain Blake's trust or dispel it. Having the trust of his daughter's husband might mean catching a glimpse of his grandchild or daughter outside of a newspaper article.

"You're a businessman. You understand the power of money."

"Money-induced power can be a curse."

Harry nodded. "Precisely." Money was Harry's addiction. It didn't matter that he had more than he could ever spend. Each week his portfolio would grow. He had acquired everything a man could want and lost his family, his freedom, in return.

They both sat for a moment and said nothing. Again, Blake stared, and Harry felt his heart kick higher.

"Do you think of your daughters?"

He thought of the only items in his cell he might consider isolation time to keep safe. "Every day."

"How come you've never tried to call Samantha?"

Harry looked away. "I don't deserve her. I've only brought her pain." His throat tightened, and he swallowed hard.

Blake shook his head, clearly struggling with what he wanted to say. "I need you to do something for me, Mr. Elliot."

"What can I possibly do for you?"

Their eyes met. "I need you to destroy every picture, every article, every anything in your possession about us."

His palm ached with the death grip he had on the phone. "Why?"

"There is someone inside who doesn't need to know about us or our friends."

Harry considered his son-in-law with narrowed eyes. "Are you going to tell me who this man is?"

"I'm not at liberty. But for the sake of your daughters, and the people they love, you need to do this."

"One more minute, Harry," the guard informed him.

He contemplated Blake's request and affirmed it with a nod. "Take care of them."

"I will."

Harry replaced the phone on the hook and took one last look at Blake before he walked away.

"The press wants to see both of you, onstage, in full color." Jay tapped his pen against the legal pad sitting on his lap and stared at both of them. "If you don't hold a press conference about your marriage, you'll be hounded until you forget what it was like to go into a public bathroom without a camera in the next stall."

Carter closed his eyes and shook his head. When had life become so damn complicated? Eliza ran a finger along his forearm, and he tried to smile.

Now that he knew the truth behind why she hid, he understood the need to keep her beyond reach and out of the spotlight. Dean had been right. Eliza should have run. Carter felt selfish knowing she stayed because he asked her to marry him. The image of innocent women murdered at the hands of Sanchez threatened to surface, but he pushed them back.

"Carter?"

He blinked a couple of times until Eliza's chocolate eyes met his. "Yeah?"

"I think we need to let Jay in on what's going on."

"Let Jay know what?" Jay asked. The smaller man kept tapping his pen and switching his gaze from one of them to the other.

Carter ran a hand through his already tousled hair. To tell Jay anything was risky. But then, marrying Eliza and showing her off to the world had been ludicrous. He knew that now.

Eliza's fingers rolled in small circles over his, as if coaxing him into submission. If anything ever happened to her, it would be his fault. Had he listened to Dean and pushed, maybe she would have been safe. Secluded from her friends, but safe.

"Let Jay know what?" Jay bit out.

There was already speculation on the news about Eliza's background. It appeared his rival in the gubernatorial race wanted a full background check and immigration status of Eliza Havens Billings. With illegal immigration at the top of California's hot topics, having a possible illegal as the first lady of the state was Carter's ticket to second place.

He couldn't bring himself to care.

Yet being the governor, or running for office, afforded him some insight and protection that Carter Billings the judge or lawyer didn't have.

No. He needed to see this through.

And he needed to call in a few favors.

He turned his palm over and laced his fingers with hers. "Eliza has been part of the Witness Protection Program. Her name was changed to protect her."

Jay's pen stopped tapping, and his gaze swiveled to Eliza. "Really?"

She lifted her eyebrows and nodded. "Yeah."

Jay stood and started to pace like a man who had drunk six cups of coffee before his first union break. "So that's why the extra security? Someone is after you?"

"It's possible."

"Who else knows this?"

"Close friends, close family…Why?"

Jay rubbed his chin in thought. "Now that you're married, this is going to come out. You know that, right?"

Eliza's slow nod let him know she wasn't completely prepared for what would come next.

"What about your uncle?"

"Max?"

"Yeah, him."

"We're not close."

"But he's family. The voting public is aware of that. I've said all along you needed to tap into his connections, and now it seems you have no choice."

"Max can't be relied upon."

"He's up for reelection in two years. He'll obtain votes however he can."

"What are you suggesting, Jay?" Carter leaned forward and listened.

"That we blow the lid off this before anyone else. And we do it with your uncle at your side. Hell, he doesn't even need to know why he's there. We can tell him the media wants photos of you both."

"Max is vain, but not so much that he'd fly out for a photo op."

"What about the fund-raising dinner scheduled for Saturday?" Eliza suggested.

Carter wasn't convinced. Making a deal with the devil might prove a better risk than his uncle. "What exactly do you think my uncle can do for us?"

"Like it or not, Carter, Max is respected and probably feared by his peers. As you already know, politicians might sit on opposing sides of the fence on how to pass bills and run this country, but all of you have one common bond: protect your families. What you do will reflect on Max and him on you. It would be in his best interest to stand united with you and Eliza as you move forward with this information. Max didn't earn a senate seat being stupid."

Max was anything but stupid. Max was dangerous. The thought of owing him a favor rankled in Carter's stomach like acid.

"What's going through your mind?" Eliza asked quietly.

He brought her hand to his lips and kissed her knuckles. "I don't know if we can trust him. In fact, I know I can't."

"Could he make things harder for us?"

"In the short term, probably not." But the devil always manages to get paid in the long run.

Jay stood to the side and fiddled with the pen he held between his fingers.

"Why don't we ask your mother? She knows Max better than all of us."

Carter forced a smile he didn't feel. "Yeah…OK."

Eliza squeezed his hand and turned to Jay. "Make sure we have extra space at our table at the dinner. We'll let you know what names need to be added to the guest list."

"Great." Jay started to leave the room to carry out their requests. "Remember what they say, Carter. Keep your enemies close and all that…"

Once again, Eliza used Gwen's fashion expertise to dress her as a political wife. Carter opened his accounts for Eliza to use. As an independent woman, the thought of spending someone else's money felt wrong. Wrong or not, Eliza's personal bank account wouldn't hold up long under the strain of Gwen's taste.

It wasn't until Carter asked her opinion on the size of a private jet that the magnitude of his wealth sunk in.

"You're serious?" she asked him.

"Like I said, I can't keep using Blake's. He has his own business to run." Carter pointed to the sleeping quarters within the plane. "It sleeps two. Even the chairs fully recline."

"It's a plane. A jet plane."

"Yeah, so?"

"Can you fly it?"

"That's what pilots are for."

"You're seriously considering buying an airplane?"

He leaned forward in his chair to peer deeper into the monitor that covered one-third the size of his desk. "I'm not sure about the interior," he mused aloud. "I think darker colors would feel more modern."

Eliza closed her eyes and shook her head. "Have you seen the amount of zeros behind the first two numbers? How big is that coffee can buried in your backyard?"

"I've been saving." He clicked on another page and grinned. "Oh, I like that better. What do you think? It seats twelve."

"You're crazy."

"I like the dark wood."

"You're talking millions, Carter. You can't be serious."

He clicked another page, and his eyes lit up. "Now we're talking. This has a range of over five thousand miles, and it seats eighteen. Perfect."

Eliza grabbed his shoulders and forced him to look in her direction. "What are you doing?"

"I'm buying a plane. What does it look like I'm doing?"

"Why?"

"Because we need it. I fly damn near every week, and I'm sure as hell not going to put you on a domestic flight. Blake encouraged me to invest in this years ago, but I didn't see the need. Now I do."

"Blake's a duke. He can wipe his ass with hundred-dollar bills if he wants. You don't have to keep up with your best friend."

Carter cocked his head to the side and offered her a coy smile. "I'm not keeping up with the Joneses, Eliza. I've considered this for a while."

"Why now?"

He pulled her down into his lap and perched her on his knee. His arms circled her waist, and the pure masculine scent of him surrounded her in a familiar warmth.

"It's time," he said. "Time to stop pretending I don't have the means to afford this…to take care of you."

Eliza lifted her hands to his broad shoulders and kneaded the muscles behind his dress shirt. "I don't need a plane."

He leaned forward and kissed the tip of her nose. "I disagree."

"You're crazy," she told him again.

He laughed and swiveled in the chair, with her in his lap, until they were both facing the monitor filled with luxury jets. "Which one do you like?"

"Crazy."

"Dark wood or a light pine?"

Eliza's gaze found the monitor. "The light looks dated."

Carter's fingers squeezed her side. "So dark it is. And we want to make it across the country without refueling, so we need one of these larger models."

It was hard not getting caught up in the shopping experience. But good Lord, they were looking at jet planes. "If we're going all out, it has to have a bedroom." Her thoughts returned to the short time they had on the return trip from Hawaii. Her cheeks grew warm.

Carter snuggled closer and clicked the mouse on the two most expensive models on the screen. The lush interior of the jet sparkled through recessed lighting and leather reclining chairs. A bar area with a small kitchenette took up a small corner. The full bathroom contained everything a traveler could need.

"The bed isn't that big."

Carter kissed her shoulder and nuzzled her neck. "We don't need a lot of room."

Eliza turned her head and found his lips. Thoughts of airplanes and bedrooms disappeared as Carter reminded her of how very little room the two of them took up on a bed.

Abigail agreed with Jay. Though she didn't completely trust her brother, she knew he would avoid scandal to preserve the family name.

Jay altered the guest list for the fund-raiser by adding members of Carter's family and members of the press. Neil's team would handle security and the government-issued bodyguards.

The formal dinner meant wearing a floor-length gown that hugged Eliza's waist and enhanced her cleavage. Eliza scoffed at the gown at first, and then Gwen reminded her that the fashions she wore would be mimicked. Suddenly, her wardrobe needed an overhaul. Assuming the role of Carter's wife held more responsibility than she ever thought possible.

Even in a room full of gun-toting security, Eliza felt naked without her firearm close by. The dress she wore didn't allow it.

The two of them sat in the back of a limousine en route to the hotel where the fund-raising event was being held. The opulence inside the luxury car matched that of the private jet. Neither of which she thought she'd get used to, ever. Carter sat beside her texting Jay and confirming everything was ready for their arrival. The city lights of Los Angeles whizzed past as the driver cut through traffic. Outside the shaded glass, other drivers craned their necks to see if they could catch a glimpse at who was inside the oversized car. In the deep recesses of her memories, Eliza fantasized about living the life of someone who used a limo. That childhood dream always came equipped with a handsome prince who took care of her every whim. Now, here she was, sitting next to arguably the most handsome man she'd ever met, wearing his ring—the one he refused to reveal the cost of—and calling herself his wife.

A fluttering spark of happiness took hold inside her heart and spread through her soul. Carter had managed to wriggle deep into her system, so deep it scared her. Maybe their marriage could last. Discussing this subject was off-limits. At night, when they made love and murmured sexy things to each other, they didn't utter a word about love. Eliza couldn't help wondering if there was something else other than the election fueling Carter's insistence for marrying her. Then again, according to the polls, he needed a wife. Outside of a divorce, while a man held the governor's office, there hadn't been a bachelor voted into the seat.

He was as noble as any knight. Since he felt responsible for her past exploding around her and her cover being blown, he wouldn't be the kind of man to walk away, not without a reason. And as long as her past sought to catch up with her, he would be there. As much as she wanted to feel guilty for holding him hostage in this marriage, she couldn't. Not after the passion they'd shared since they married. Yet she couldn't help worrying. *What happens when the honeymoon is over?* She winced at the thought.

Maybe the honeymoon won't end. The last time she'd been this optimistic, her parents had been alive. *Everything good in life comes to an end.* She hated how her fears tried to push the good thoughts away.

Carter had stopped clicking away on his phone and captured her hand. "Are you OK?" he asked.

"I'm fine," she said a little too quickly.

"Are you sure? One minute, you were smiling; the next, you looked upset."

She squeezed his hand as the limo rounded the corner to the bright lights of the hotel. "I'm wondering how all of this is going to unfold."

"So, you're nervous?"

"A little."

The car stopped and the driver jumped out to open their door.

"I'm right here."

She offered him a smile as he stepped out of the car and helped her to her feet.

Half a dozen cameras snapped pictures as they walked into the reception hall of the hotel. Neil stood to the side of the hall, and a guard walked behind them. Everyone wearing a suit and standing alone appeared to be some kind of security. Soon those security guards faded into the background as their hosts approached her and Carter.

The Hollywood power couple shook Carter's hand as he introduced Eliza. The starlet greeted her as if they were old friends, which helped Eliza avoid being starstruck. After kissing both her cheeks, Marilyn offered a million-dollar smile Hollywood paid dearly for. "We had to add four extra tables after the announcement of your marriage made the papers. Tom and I are delighted that you've made this your first public appearance."

"We appreciate your hosting us."

Marilyn was even tinier in person. Even with her four-inch heels, the petite woman barely made it to Eliza's shoulders. "It's an absolute thrill."

Carter shook Tom's hand and echoed Eliza's sentiment. "I hope the extra security wasn't a hassle."

"Not at all. Once we heard your uncle was joining us, we understood the need."

Eliza held back a chuckle.

Tom and Marilyn led them into the dining hall, where the party had already begun. Eliza scanned the room for a familiar face and didn't realize she had latched on to Carter's arm until he patted her hand. She instantly relaxed her hold. When had she become so needy? Showing any fear in this environment could prove lethal, yet as they passed a mirror, she noticed the doubt in her eyes.

Suck it up, Lisa.

Carter stopped a waiter with a platter of champagne and handed her a glass. He leaned in and whispered in her ear. "You look like you could use this."

She did. A couple of cool sips of liquid courage and her body relaxed.

"Mrs. Billings?"

She hesitated and then realized that someone was addressing her. "I'm Jade Lee, and this is my partner, Randal." Jade Lee, as in the most-sought-after fashion designer in Hollywood and probably a perfect size zero. *Man, doesn't anyone eat around here?*

"Pleased to meet you."

Jade complimented Eliza on her dress and asked who'd made it. Eliza hadn't a clue. That was the kind of thing Gwen would have remembered. Jade laughed off Eliza's lack of knowledge and suggested she stop by her studio sometime for a private showing.

They talked a little about fashion and even the weather. It wasn't long before Eliza found herself a few feet away from her husband. Everyone knew her name, and because movie stars hosted the party, Eliza knew some of theirs. In a short time, she'd forgotten about the security watching over them and played at being the perfect political wife.

On occasion, someone would ask where her husband stood on the hot political buttons that fueled the election. Jay had already coached her on what to avoid. Instead of offering Carter's views, she told them something far nobler. "Carter will represent what the voting public wants. Isn't it the governor's job to represent his people and not dictate to them?"

Her simple statement met with approval to most who asked. Others pushed, but not to the point of annoyance. Many of the guests wore sugary-sweet facades. The popular designer wanted her to wear her dresses because that would equate to sales. The producers wanted a friendly face in the governor's seat so they could cut through the political red tape and film productions could stay on time. Everyone had his or her own agenda.

The room held many powerful people. She searched the crowd for a friend. Eliza found Carter across the room and waited until the weight of her stare made him turn around. When he did, he smiled in her direction and then questioned her with a look.

She shook her head to indicate she was fine and continued to talk to the woman by her side. Only when Samantha arrived and found her way to her side did Eliza truly relax.

Chapter Twenty-Three

Carter drank his water and washed down the filet. Eliza sat by his side and charmed their hosts. Max and Sally sat at a nearby table, Blake and Samantha at another. Over three hundred guests finished their dinners that cost them anywhere from five thousand to fifteen thousand a plate. Only Hollywood could demand such a price. Every one of them would use their dinner as a write-off on their taxes and several more would find critical connections to make them more money. Attending dinners like this secured votes and paid for commercials. His hosts expected that. What they didn't expect was how Carter and Eliza were going to manipulate the spotlight to rally allies for Eliza's safety.

Jay walked through the tables and whispered in Carter's ear. "Are you ready?"

Carter cast a glance over his shoulder to Eliza. She nodded and dropped her napkin on the table.

Tom and Marilyn led the two of them to the podium on the small stage. Behind them, Max and Sally followed, and in their wake, Blake and Samantha.

Carter nodded at Neil, who spoke into a small microphone dangling from an earpiece. Beyond the tables of people, Dean and James stood at opposite corners of the room.

A hush fell over the room as Tom and Marilyn stood together to introduce their guests of honor.

There were several invited reporters at the dinner and two camera crews. There wasn't a live feed, but that didn't mean every word Carter said wouldn't be heard. There were times when he needed Jay to help him with some of his speeches, but this wasn't one of those times.

"Thank you all for coming tonight," Tom began. "Your generous contribution to Mr. Billings's campaign will go a long way to helping him win this election."

The crowd applauded, and Carter felt Eliza lift her hand from his to clap along with them.

He kept her hand clasped in his and lifted it to his lips to kiss. At least one bulb flashed and captured his gesture. Her thumb rubbing the backside of his hand was the only outward indication of her nerves. She did well under pressure, he realized. He just wished she didn't need to be so strong.

Tom dropped a few names within the crowd and bantered with Marilyn about their choices in the menu. After a few laughs, Tom released the microphone to Carter.

The guests remained seated, and Carter stepped forward to give the attendees his attention.

"Thank you, Tom and Marilyn. Everything about tonight has been perfect."

Again, the crowd clapped.

"I've had a very tight schedule in the past few months, but it always feels great to drive to the event instead of flying."

"It's a long drive from Sacramento," someone called out.

Carter laughed and nodded. "It is. But in order to make positive changes for this state, I'm willing to make that drive. So many of our jobs—*your* jobs—are being shipped elsewhere. It's time to work through some of the bureaucracy and return our jobs here."

He paused for applause.

"Shipping our families out of state to put bread on the table shouldn't be the default suggestion for Southern California's second-largest economic contributor. If all of you, Hollywood's elite, left Hollywood, then our number one largest employer, tourism, would drop. Our state parks are some of the finest in the world, and yet we close them because of budget cuts. We have cuts because state revenue is spent elsewhere to produce movies and television shows."

The guests murmured in agreement.

"I understand our problems, and if elected, I'll do everything within my power to shift our jobs back here, where they belong."

Again, the crowd applauded.

"Unlike any other time in my personal life, I'm more vested in making California a home for my family." He glanced over his shoulder. Eliza's cheeks grew red. "In case you didn't know, I signed a pretty big deal last weekend." While the audience laughed, Carter extended his hand to Eliza. "I'd like to introduce you to my lovely wife, Eliza Billings."

Eliza turned to the lights and offered a wave.

"I think she'd make a great first lady of the state, don't you?"

He paused for a moment and waited for the planted questions to come from the media. It was time for the real show to begin.

"Your opponent suggested that your wife isn't a legal immigrant."

A few people gasped at the comment. Some hushed the reporter.

"It's OK," Carter told the crowd. "Eliza and I knew questions would be raised about her past."

"According to my research, Eliza Havens wasn't born here."

Carter lifted his hands to the crowd to settle them. "My father was part of the police force for over thirty years. His motto on the job was simply this: 'Believe none of what you hear and half of what you see.' Your research, and that of my opponent, has found a dry trail in relation to Eliza's birth and background. Of course you'd assume she immigrated to this country. With immigration topping the political forum, it's easy to point fingers and cry foul." Carter lifted his eyes to the audience.

"There are reasons beyond immigration for which people have a need to hide, to change their names. Eliza's story would make a blockbuster film if it weren't so painful."

The room went quiet as everyone listened.

"Up until a month ago, Eliza hid herself from the public eye because she has lived the majority of her life under the Witness Protection Program."

The eyes in the room shifted to her. Flashes snapped in rapid-fire, and Carter grasped Eliza's hand hard.

"Is that true, Mrs. Billings?"

Eliza leaned forward and spoke into the mike. "It is."

"What happened?"

"Who are you hiding from?"

"Why reveal your identity now?"

Questions flew at her from everywhere at once.

Everything blurred. Eliza felt her breath coming in short pants, and her palm grew moist in Carter's. She knew the spotlight was on her, and she alone needed to ask for the public's help.

Carter pulled her beside him and let her address the audience.

"My father was a hardworking American man. He and my mother had the kind of family values we all want to project to our children. After my dad witnessed an unmentionable crime, he did what so many people would not. He stepped forward to do what was right. He wouldn't have been able to live with himself if he hid the truth."

She thought of her dad, his smile, his robust laugh. "We were taken away, our identities changed. But it wasn't far enough."

Emotion clogged the back of her throat. "He and my mother paid for his testimony with their lives."

She found Dean in the back of the room and spoke to him. "I was taken away, given a new identity, and have stayed hidden since I was a child."

"Is the threat behind you, Mrs. Billings?"

She shook her head. "No. But I couldn't stay hidden any longer. Carter entered my life, and the people I cared about wouldn't let me run any longer."

"So there's someone still after you?"

She shrugged. "There is no reason to believe the man responsible for my parents' early death doesn't still have a vendetta against me."

"Who is it?"

Eliza shook her head, and Carter stood up to the mike. "We cannot disclose that at this time."

"Why protect him?"

"We're not. But the man has a family, children of his own," Eliza protested. "Is it fair to condemn them the way I've been condemned? Believe me, I want nothing more than to think the past is behind me so I can look to my future without a roomful of bodyguards."

The reporter turned in a circle, as did many others, and the physical presence of guards became abundantly clear.

Behind her, Samantha's arm rested on her shoulder. Then Max and Sally approached Carter's side. "I stand in support of my wife and will do everything in my power to keep her from harm," Carter pledged. "I'm in awe of her courage to stand before you and tell her story. I hope you will support me in keeping her safe."

The room was utterly silent until one lone clap sounded from the back of the room. Eliza's eyes misted as she saw Dean clapping. Soon the room responded until everyone was on their feet.

"Nice speech."

Carter turned toward his uncle's flat voice. "She did well."

Max rocked back on his heels and watched Eliza over the rim of his cocktail glass. "Convincing. Even to me."

"The truth has the unique ability to carry weight." Carter nodded toward a couple who passed them without interrupting.

Max lifted his drink to his lips and murmured his next words. "It's not enough."

"What isn't enough?"

"Playing the martyr. The past has a way of catching up with you. You should know that, Counselor."

"What are you saying?"

Max leaned forward so only Carter could hear him. "People like us don't *hope*. We make things happen." Max brushed off the edge of Carter's dress coat. "I'll be in touch." Max set his empty glass on a waiter's tray before walking away.

An uncomfortable ball of lead threatened to settle deep in Carter's stomach. Why did he feel his uncle's words were more threat than a legitimate call to action?

Probably because they were. Carter knew that asking favors from his uncle would haunt him. Carter couldn't bring himself to stop Max from whatever he had planned. Keeping Eliza safe was paramount. Nothing else mattered.

Their return trip from the dinner sped by. Eliza spoke of the actors she'd met, the producers. She didn't mention the unveiling of her darkest secret to the world. It wouldn't be long before the media dug and found the name of the man responsible. Carter knew this. And as he watched her nibble on a fingernail, he knew she thought about it too.

She was worried.

Instead of addressing the problem, Carter kept the conversation light.

Still, when they drove up to the front doors of their home, he peered into the darkness, listening to the sounds of the night for anything out of place. All he heard were crickets and the rustling of leaves in the trees above their heads.

One of the bodyguards had preceded their arrival and made certain no one lurked inside. When Carter waved the armed guard away, he captured Eliza's hand in his and kissed her battered nails.

She sent him a bashful smile. One he didn't see often. "We're going to be OK," he promised.

She opened her eyes wider, and he saw the mist gathering behind her lashes. "I…I'm scared, Carter."

Her admission slammed into his soul. Carter took her face in his hands and did what he could to drive away her fears. He lowered his lips to hers and willed her to forget her fears with his kiss. He stifled her whimper by deepening their kiss. The tip of his tongue coaxed hers open to allow him inside.

She opened and melted against him in the same instant. Her timid hands flattened on his chest and burned a path straight to his heart. He moaned, or maybe it was she, and he wove his fingers alongside her neck and laced them into her soft tresses. Pins scattered onto the floor of the foyer. The length of her body meshed with his from lips to toes.

The tip of her tongue teased his until he responded with indecent kisses. Eliza sucked in a desperate breath and released a nervous laugh. Carter smiled as he kept her lips occupied. He'd managed to make her forget.

He bent down and swung her into his arms.

She chuckled low in her throat and nuzzled his neck as he carried her to their bedroom. "You don't have to carry me," she told him.

"Having to doesn't play into my thoughts."

She used the hand she wasn't using to keep from falling to loosen the tie around his neck and unbutton his dress shirt. "You smell so good. Spicy, masculine…desirable."

His already aroused state burned with need from her words. Carter kicked their bedroom door closed behind them. "What does *desirable* smell like?"

Eliza slid alongside him until her feet touched the ground. She slowly removed his tie and tossed it to the floor. "Mmm. Sexy. I think I understand what pheromones are now."

"Pheromones? As in what animals emit when they're ready to mate?"

Her dark eyes rounded with passion as her fingers loosened every button on his shirt. The cooler air of the room did nothing to ease the fire burning in his veins. "Exactly. I've heard that females have a unique scent, but I think it's men who draw women in." She ran her hand down his arms and fiddled with his cuff links until they also fell to the floor.

"All men?"

Soft lips pressed against his chest. She pushed his shirt from his shoulders and held him captive with her words. He might have been the one who'd started this seduction, to make her forget, but he was being thoroughly seduced. "I've never smelled a man's need like I do yours."

Her tiny tongue shot out and tasted his nipple.

He shivered. "Be careful, Lisa…My ego is growing."

She giggled and lifted her eyes to his while her hand slid below the waist of his pants. She cupped him fully. "That's not the only thing growing."

He pounced, dragging her lips to his while spinning her back to the door. The taste of her, his need for her, surged into him like an arc of fire shooting from a comet. If she sensed his desire before, she must be suffocating with it now. He pressed his arousal against the soft folds of her skin through their clothes. With the door at her back, she arched toward him, increasing the contact and his need.

The slender span of her waist filled his palm. Then he tried to touch her everywhere at once. They kissed until they both needed air. Only when she was panting hard did he move his mouth to her neck, her shoulder. He clawed at the length of her dress until he touched the tantalizing hot skin at her hip. When his fingers came in contact with a strap, he opened his eyes wide. He followed the elastic strap with his fingertips. Eliza watched his reaction with a hooded gaze.

"Lingerie?"

She caught her lower lip between her teeth and rested her head against the door.

The image of her wrapped in straps and silk undid him. Unable to control himself, he spun Eliza until her breasts pushed against the door, and he found the long zipper of her dress. He eased it down by slow degrees. He kissed her neck and the hidden space between her shoulder blades. As the gown slid to the floor, his chin dropped.

Tiny scraps of ivory lace covered only the most intimate places on her perfect body. Stockings made their way midthigh, held up with dainty clasps. Carter ran his hand down her spine. Eliza struggled to breathe and watched him over her shoulder.

He could keep her dressed in lingerie every day and never get used to this view. "Lovely," he whispered.

"Can I turn around?"

He held her in place. "Not yet…I'm not done."

Gooseflesh rose on her exposed skin. He liked how his words made her squirm. He traced his hand down her spine and kissed her in its wake. She tasted like spring, fresh and inviting. He fed from her like a starving man. When her hips lifted as his tongue traced the sensitive flesh under her lace panties, he smiled. He knelt behind her and molded his hands down her shapely thighs. Even the silk of her stockings felt like sin. He nibbled at her hips and lowered the fabric of her panties without disturbing the garter holding up her stockings. He helped her lift one foot at a time and tossed the garment aside.

"You're killing me, Carter."

He touched the soft globes of her bare bottom and between her thighs. She was molten and pliant to his touch. He sought her most delicate places, and when her breath hitched, he dropped his forehead to the small of her back.

"Please," she begged.

Twisting her around, he licked and kissed his way to her core. When there, her knees buckled as he drank his fill. She squirmed against him and mumbled equal desires for him to stop and to continue. Her hands held him closer and kneaded his flesh, leaving indents with her nails. Her breath hitched, and then he pulled away.

"You'll pay for this," she promised.

He couldn't wait.

He released her from the door and backed her to the bed. She crawled into the center with stockings and heels still intact. Damn, she was sexy. The pins in her hair scattered. Her hair tumbled, cascading loose, and draped over her shoulders. After kicking off his shoes and hastily removing his clothes, he joined her on the bed and pulled them both to the middle of the mattress. Her high heel scraped the back of his thigh. His erection throbbed.

When the lace of her bra soon became too much of a hindrance, he removed it for better access and tasted one pert nipple before turning to the other.

Soft hands clawed at his back and pulled him closer. The heat of her sex beckoned, and Eliza enticed him with her scent. Slim fingers wrapped around him, stroking him and destroying any ability to think.

When had he ever wanted a woman this much? Had he ever? With Eliza, it was more than want. More than sexual need. She nudged him between her thighs and opened for him to take.

As he seated himself and sheathed his body within hers, his heart opened wide.

"Oh, Carter." She tilted her hips toward his, and he moved within her. Each stroke, every quiver, brought him close to spilling inside her. As he took her, claimed her in the most primal of ways, he knew his heart was lost. She owned every ounce of it.

Their movements increased. He drove into her hard, but kissed her with all the tenderness he could manage. When she broke away and her slick channel clutched him tight with her release, he allowed himself to join her.

They caught their collective breath together. Their damp skin mingled and scented the sheets with a unique, pleasant aroma. "I could stay like this, with you, forever," he admitted against the side of her neck.

She wrapped her legs around his waist and tightened her womb. "It's the shoes, isn't it? I've never made love with my shoes on before."

"That's not it."

"The garter belt? I thought you'd like it…But I thought it would eventually make its way to the floor."

"It's not your sexy lingerie. But I do like it."

"Then it must be my sunny disposition," she teased.

Carter removed some of his weight from her frame and gazed into her big brown eyes. "It's you. Your courage, your strength… your ability to make me boil from the inside. I'm lying here and wondering why it took us so long to connect."

She intently watched him, her eyes unwavering. "Because you battled with me about everything, from football teams to the temperature of tea. That's why."

He laughed then, remembering some of their earlier arguments. “Sexual tension.”

Her eyes narrowed. “Seriously?”

“Yeah.” He moved to her side but gathered her close. “I remember when we first met. Samantha and Blake had just married, and we were both invited to their reception in Europe. I think you flirted with every man there.”

“I did?”

“Except me. You avoided me like the black plague. I knew then…”

“You knew what?”

He kissed her nose, sensing she was reading something inappropriate into his words. “I knew we’d match. No two people could repel that much and not be so very good together.”

Her smile fell. “You’re full of shit. You hated me back then.”

“Hate? I never hated anything about you. You sparked my curiosity, made me want…But hate was never an adjective to describe my feelings toward you.”

“Then why did you argue with everything I said?”

He played with her hip and pulled the covers over them. “You should see the spark in your eyes when someone gets under your skin. The passion when you know you’re right and someone begs to differ. You, my little fireball, are fresh air on a stale day. I fear for anyone who truly stands in the way of you getting what you want.”

Eliza lifted her knee high on his hip. “Are you telling me you argued with me just to get a rise out of me?”

He cocked his head to the side and remained silent.

She let loose a playful fist on his chest. “You’re awful.”

“C’mon. You can’t say you didn’t enjoy it.”

“I didn’t.”

“Liar.”

She attempted to keep a straight face and failed. Her lips slid into an infectious grin as she giggled.

"Who's the liar now?"

"I'll take it to the grave," she told him.

And as quick as her words, his mind shot to a vision of her still and lifeless. He sat motionless and knew his grin faded. She noticed his unease but didn't call attention to it. Instead, she burrowed her head into his chest.

"We did the right thing tonight, right?" she finally asked.

He brushed the back of her hair with his hand. God, he hoped so. "We did."

Yet, as she slipped into slumber and he lay awake, he wasn't so sure.

Chapter Twenty-Four

Eliza languished around the house for two full days following the Hollywood dinner. The news of her past didn't stop with the local broadcasts. It went national. Eliza's cell phone rang continuously with offers for exclusive interviews—all of which she ignored.

The magnitude of what she'd done, by telling the world, was driven home when Jay arrived early Tuesday morning with an armful of mail. "This is for you," he said as he dropped dozens of letters on the kitchen counter.

"For me?" She eyed the mail with a frown.

Jay's magnetic smile lit his face. "The sympathetic public has a big soft spot for you and your plight. The mail started arriving at the local campaign office, and I'm told there is more at the headquarters in Sacramento and San Francisco."

Eliza picked an envelope at random and tore it open. Inside was a handwritten letter from a woman who lived in the desert community of Lancaster. She applauded Eliza's courage to come forward and then went on to ask if there was a way she could get in touch with her son who'd also entered the Witness Protection Program years ago. Not knowing if he was dead or alive had killed a small piece of her spirit. Anything Eliza could do to help would be appreciated.

"What does it say?" Carter scooted closer and read the mail over her shoulder. "Oh, wow."

"Yeah."

She opened another, this one from a father who'd lost his wife to a drive-by shooting. He told her how he wished more people would report crimes so criminals could be taken off the streets. Apparently, the authorities had never caught his wife's murderer.

"I took the liberty of opening up an e-mail address under your name. Carter's box filled up overnight," Jay told them.

"What am I supposed to do with these?"

Carter shrugged his shoulders. "Ignore them. Write them back. What do you want to do with them?"

She didn't know.

"While you figure that out, I have other news to share." Jay took the liberty of pouring himself a cup of coffee. He'd obviously spent a lot of time in Carter's home and knew where everything was. "Your standings in the polls shot up over the weekend. Not only did your marriage add to the percentage of voters checking your name, but Eliza's compassion swayed the swing votes too. If there was ever a political power couple, it's the two of you."

"Political power couple? I didn't see that coming," Eliza said.

Carter patted her on the back. "If I'm going to be a political anything, I'm going to have to get back to work."

Apparently, the honeymoon was over. "You're such a slacker," she teased.

"Are you going to be OK here?"

She rolled her eyes. "I'm fine. I have bodyguards and Zod. I was thinking of going in to Alliance, but I might put that off for a few days. See what I can do with these letters."

"Alliance? Doesn't Gwen have that covered?"

"Gwen still has a lot to learn."

Carter frowned.

"What?"

He glanced over to Jay and said, "Can you excuse us for a minute?"

Jay took the hint and walked out of the room with his coffee.

"What's on your mind, Hollywood?"

"It's Alliance. Sam would understand if you needed to step back from that for a while."

"What do you mean?"

"Step back, take some time off."

"I've already taken almost two weeks." What was he getting at? Did he want her to be a housewife? That was so not going to happen.

He ran a hand through his sandy-blond hair and struggled with his next words. "Every time you leave the house is risky. We don't know what Sanchez is going to do."

"So I'm supposed to do what, exactly? Stay here as a prisoner?"

"Don't be ridiculous."

"It's you who's cornered 'ridiculous.' If secluding myself from the world was the only option, I wouldn't have gone through all this trouble to begin with." Her skin started to heat, and her temper flared. "I'm not hiding, Carter."

"Not hide. Just move with caution."

"That's not what you're suggesting. What you said was to take some time off and stay in the house."

She stood and started to pace.

"I didn't say stay in the house."

"You alluded to it."

Carter stepped behind her and caught her shoulders. She twisted out of his reach. "You're a smart woman. I know you can see my logic."

She turned to glare at him with her hands perched on her hips in defiance. "I see your logic; I simply don't agree with it. I'm going to live my life. And for the record, being condescending isn't going to go far with me."

"Dammit, Eliza. I can't let anything happen to you," he barked.

His outburst shocked her silent. His request stemmed from fear. The panic sitting behind his eyes wasn't something she'd seen before, and she wasn't sure if it made her feel better knowing he cared or frightened because he looked so scared.

He stepped into her personal space and grasped her face with the palms of his hands. "I won't let anything happen to you." His voice dropped into a rough whisper.

"One week. I'll have Gwen meet me here for now, but I can't be held prisoner, Carter."

"I know. We'll work something out." He kissed her then, as if sealing his words with a promise.

As it turned out, staying in Carter's home wasn't a chore. Gwen spent nearly as much time in Eliza's new home as she did in Tarzana. It helped that Eliza's attention shifted to the nonstop flow of letters, which arrived daily from all over the States. There were a slew of people searching for loved ones who had testified against someone and then disappeared. The lack of closure for these families was heartbreaking. Some didn't know if their loved ones were alive and safe or had met with foul play.

Each story tugged at Eliza's heart and demanded an answer.

"There is a serious flaw in the system," Eliza told Gwen one afternoon. "My parents were on their own—my grandparents were gone shortly after I was born. But these people, they left mothers and fathers, aunts, uncles. I can't imagine not knowing."

"Surely there is something in place to aid these families."

"If there is, I don't know about it." Eliza stacked the letters into categories—one pile, parents searching for their children who knew they were placed in a witness program, another for friends who didn't know why or where a friend had disappeared.

There was even a pile of letters from family members of criminals suggesting that the witness in their particular case no longer needed to hide, because the criminal had died or was otherwise no longer a threat.

"What about the peace officer friend of yours? Can he help?"

"You mean Dean?"

"Yes."

"I don't know. He was always there for me, but I don't remember him talking about extended family of witnesses."

"It can't hurt to ask what he knows or to see if he can assist you in some way."

Eliza sat back in her chair. "Assist me, how? I don't know what to do with all this. These stories might make for a great novel, but I don't know how I can help."

"Oh, I'm certain you'll think of something. It's what those of us with money do when we don't need to work to earn it." Gwen tossed a lock of hair behind her back with a smile.

"I'm not that girl. I still need to earn a living."

Gwen laughed and then covered her smiling lips with a hand. "I'm sorry."

"What's so funny?"

"Eliza, dear, you are that woman. You're married to arguably the most influential man in this province—er, state—and you no longer need to concern yourself with making a buck."

Eliza didn't want to admit Gwen was right. "You understand more than most that Carter and I married for reasons beyond love and forever. There's no guarantee we'll last."

"You worry too much."

"I have to be able to take care of myself. No one knows better than I that guarantees in life are nonexistent."

"Poppycock. Carter cares for you deeply, and you've nothing to worry about."

"Poppycock? Did you just say poppycock?"

Gwen rolled her eyes. "Don't make fun of my expressions. You know what I say is true."

No, she didn't. Eliza had no idea where Carter's head was when it came to tomorrow. Sure, their immediate future was stable, but who knew what next month or next year would bring?

"Why the secrecy?" Carter sat opposite Blake in Blake's office and crossed his ankle over his knee.

Blake lifted up a finger and picked up his phone. "I need you to hold my calls," he told his secretary. He returned the receiver and focused his attention on Carter. "I think this office is the only place another set of eyes isn't watching you."

"OK." Obviously, what Blake was going to say was private.

"I met Sam's dad last week...before the dinner."

Carter held his breath. Although he and Blake had never discussed Harris Elliot, Carter knew of the man, of his past crimes. He also knew that Harris and Sanchez were housed in the same prison. Carter would never have asked Blake to contact the man on his behalf. It appeared he didn't have to.

"Does Sam know?"

Blake nodded once. "I told her after I returned."

"How did that go?"

"She was resolved with it. She'd do anything for Eliza."

"Even connecting with her dad, who screwed up her life?"

Blake sat back in his chair and laced his fingers together. "It's strange how when things brighten in your life, it's hard to blame others for theirs. It helped that Harris appeared truly sorry for the pain he'd put his daughters through."

"I assume you want to tell me something more than a recap of a family meet and greet."

"Right. I asked him to destroy all photos of Sam, of anything that could lead Sanchez to Eliza."

Carter wanted to think that was all they would need. "Thank you."

"It might not make a difference." Blake voiced what Carter thought.

"Then again, it might."

They sat in silence for a moment, neither voicing their concerns.

"What else can I do, Carter?"

"My father is checking on Sanchez. Trying to determine if he is still working his criminal ring from the inside. According to Dean, he did when he first went to prison, but it's been a few years since any direct criminal activity has pointed his way. My guess is there is nothing new to report, or Dean would have said something. No news isn't always a good thing."

"I have a two-year-old. I understand that."

Carter laughed and some of the tension eased from his shoulders.

"Didn't you say Sanchez had contacts in Mexico?"

"Yeah."

"I can have someone look into his old activities there—see if anything new is worth mentioning."

Blake had shipping hubs all over the globe, which equated to connections. Sure, Carter had connections too, but exercising them while running for office could mean political suicide.

"Gathering information can't hurt," Carter said.

"Consider it done. How is everything else going? Samantha told me that Eliza receives mail every day asking for her help."

"Every day? More like every hour. She's on a mission to reunite families and fix issues within the Witness Protection Program."

"If there is anyone who can, it would be someone who has lived it."

Carter agreed. "The letters have taken her mind off the fact that she's somewhat secluded."

"What do you mean?"

"I asked her to avoid going out—to stay home where she's safe."

Blake rubbed his jaw and frowned. "That doesn't sound like Eliza."

"It isn't. Hopefully, we'll know more about Sanchez soon and be able to neutralize his threat."

"If that were possible, don't you think the police would have done that early on and avoided placing Eliza in the program?"

Carter felt his jaw tighten and his shoulders tense. "I have to believe there is something more I can do, Blake. Otherwise, I've put my wife in harm's way instead of saving her."

The muscles on Blake's face softened, and he attempted a grin. The attempt was lame, however, and Carter didn't want to see the sympathy. He stood abruptly and said, "I'm needed across town."

Blake walked him to the door. "I'll be in touch."

Carter punched his steering wheel once he was alone. What the hell was he going to do?

Dean sucked in the nicotine and felt his nerves instantly calm. He'd been reduced to leaning against a black-and-white in the yard to take his cigarette fix. Even the sanctity of the station, which used to sport a gray hue of smoke like a badge of honor, had been poisoned by the nonsmokers. *Don't smoke close to the door! Don't smoke in the cars! Just quit, you're better off!* As if the warning label on the damn pack wasn't enough of a threat, it seemed everyone scowled at the smoker. He drew in another breath and blew the smoke out through pursed lips.

The world could bite him. His attempts at stopping never worked, and the gum tasted like shit.

"I knew I'd find you out here."

Jim strode toward him with determined steps. In his hands were papers that he was currently tapping against his thigh. He eyed the cigarette but didn't comment.

"Just taking a break."

Jim leaned against the car beside him. "Better off talking out here, anyway."

That didn't sound good. "What's up?"

He tapped the papers against his palm before handing them to Dean.

Dean took one last drag and tossed the butt to the ground next to plenty more left by other cops. He took the papers and glanced at a cheap printed picture.

"Carter's friend Blake visited his father-in-law."

"Do we know what they talked about?"

"We can guess."

He flipped through the pages of pictures taken by the cameras at the prison. It didn't appear that Blake had arrived with anyone.

"Any word on the inside?"

Jim shook his head. "It's quiet. Too quiet."

Dean hated that word. Nothing good ever came from it, and it never lasted long.

"Have you heard from Eliza?"

"Only a steady stream of her shoe bills."

Jim laughed and crossed his arms over his chest. "Could it be that Sanchez isn't interested anymore? That he's moved on?"

Criminals didn't move on. And they never forgot. "Remember the picture of Eliza's mom?" Dean didn't have to remind Jim of which picture he referred to. Jim's smile faded.

The sun that always managed to shine in Southern California slipped behind a cloud and Dean felt a chill. "We keep vigilant.

Sanchez has time on his side and won't be in a hurry. It isn't as if Eliza will slide off his radar anytime soon."

The stress of Eliza's case would ensure Dean's cigarette habit for years to come. He thought of his own daughter and how much she looked like Eliza.

"Thanks for doing this here." Samantha tucked her legs under her bottom and made herself comfortable on the couch. Eliza, Gwen, and Karen made themselves comfortable around the formal living room. "Eddie hardly naps any longer, and I'm exhausted by the end of my day."

Eliza had slipped into Eddie's room before joining the other women. He looked like he was napping fine today. She couldn't help wondering if maybe Samantha used him as an excuse to keep Eliza from going to Tarzana.

Gwen added sugar to her tea and made small chiming noises with the cup. "Eddie is adorable."

"Thanks."

"How is everything at the house?" Eliza asked Gwen.

"At first, it was quite hectic. The phone rang relentlessly. Nothing legitimate. Things seem to be calming down now."

Samantha and Eliza had prepared statements for Gwen to recite to the callers. Eliza remembered well what it was like after Sam and Blake were wed. The media had made every conceivable effort to find something seedy about Alliance.

They'd failed.

"Have we lost any clients?"

"Candice asked to have her portfolio put on hold. She met someone on holiday, and things are working out well."

"Good for her," Samantha said.

"That's all?" Eliza took a cookie off the serving plate on the coffee table and broke it in two.

"Yes."

Karen cleared her throat. "You might want to take Sedgwick off your list."

"Oh?"

"He and my aunt have a weekly date, though neither of them call it that."

An uncontrollable grin met Eliza's lips. "That's awesome."

"It is. I didn't think my aunt knew what blush and lip gloss were, but I noticed her wearing it the last time he came over. It's too damn cute."

"Are you still escorting him?"

Karen nodded. "He picks me up, or sometimes I pick him up. It's hysterical watching the grandkids crane their necks to see me and scowl every time I'm there. His children are more subtle, but just as unhappy."

"So they still think the two of you are seeing each other?" Eliza nibbled on her cookie and wished she could see a video of Sedgwick's greedy grandchildren.

"Yes. Stanly is having a grand time duping his heirs. And my aunt is coaching him on what to say to get under their skin." Humor filled Karen's eyes as she spoke. She obviously got as much out of this crazy arrangement as the older couple did.

"How long do you think you can keep this up?"

Karen shrugged. "A little while. I make a point of leaving the two of them alone. My guess is Stanly will eventually relieve his kids and grandchildren of their worry. Although him having a young woman in his life might seem the bigger evil, they haven't met Aunt Edie."

"I want an invitation to the wedding," Eliza said.

"It's a little soon for that, but don't worry."

After a few minutes of wedding talk and how to throw a bachelorette party for Edie, Karen changed the subject.

"Other than the update on the happy couple, why did you ask me to what I assume is a business lunch?"

Eliza glanced at Samantha and Gwen. "Sam and I have been talking. I'm at a crossroads right now, and we think I need to back away from the daily running of Alliance."

Gwen sighed. "Are you sure?"

"It wasn't like when Blake and I married," said Sam. "A wealthy businessman here in the States is expected to go through whatever it takes to find the right bride. But Carter's life, and Eliza's, is being scrutinized, and anything will be used against them. If, by chance, Carter isn't elected, then maybe that will fade."

Eliza interrupted Samantha. "But if that doesn't happen and a tabloid finds I'm still running a bride-for-hire service, it wouldn't reflect well. Especially with the institution of marriage up for debate at nearly every election."

"I'm sure that's true," Karen said. "But it doesn't answer the question of why I'm here."

"We need help." Eliza smiled at Karen as she spoke. "Gwen has done a great job keeping it all together. Samantha helps where she can. But between Eddie and her responsibilities here and in Europe, time isn't plentiful. We wanted to know if you'd be interested in a job."

Karen fiddled with her necklace. "I have a job."

"But this one would be more flexible. You'd have more time to help the kids." Karen spent her off time volunteering at local youth groups mentoring needy kids. "You already understand what we do, and most important for us, we trust you. We can easily match your salary with a raise."

Samantha paused, and Eliza waited for a reaction from Karen.

"I'm listening."

Eliza relaxed in her chair and let Samantha explain what they needed and would expect. By the time she finished, Karen was nodding and trying to hide a smile.

"Well, what do you think?"

Karen sighed and didn't hesitate. "I need to give notice at the nursing home."

Gwen clapped her hands together two times. "Oh, super. You'll adore working at Alliance."

Part of Eliza regretted having to step away from her job. She'd still be around to help, but all paper ties would sever.

They spent the next hour bringing Karen up to date on a few of the active clients, those for whom they still needed to find the perfect companion. Of course, Karen happened to be one of them, and she made a point of insisting she wanted first dibs on the perfect groom.

Chapter Twenty-Five

Carter arrived home before Eliza with takeout from the Villa. The tucked-away Tuscan restaurant had been a hit with Eliza when he introduced it to her shortly after they married. If it weren't for takeout, Carter would have died of hunger years ago.

He slid around Zod, who sniffed the aromatic bag and barked in welcome. "What are you barking at? You won't eat it anyway." *Stupid dog.* As much as he tried to get the dog to cheat, the four-legged K-9 wanted nothing to do with table scraps.

Carter clicked on the kitchen light and set the bags on the counter. He wanted to make the night special for Eliza. She'd resigned from Alliance today, and he knew she wouldn't be happy about it.

He walked into the den and turned on the radio. En route back to the kitchen, he found a half-eaten stiletto at the side of the couch. "Zod!" he yelled for the dog.

Zod ran to his side and barked, oblivious to the trouble he was in.

Carter waved the shoe in the air and scolded the animal. "I'm tempted to beat you with this. Bad dog!"

Zod barked twice more.

"How am I going to advocate that you stay with us if you keep dining on her shoes?"

The animal sat and rolled his tongue out of his mouth. Carter swore the dog smiled behind his elongated chin and sharp teeth.

"Bad dog," he said one more time before walking away.

Carter took the shoe to the side yard and buried it in the trash can. He didn't want Eliza to see it. Maybe she'd forget about the shoes and think Zod had kicked the habit. As it was, Eliza had been pretty good about using the high rack in the closet for her footwear. This one must have slipped her mind. Or maybe she'd been in a rush when she left. Either way, Carter wasn't going to announce the dog's obstinate behavior.

He managed to set the table and light a candle before he heard the chime indicating that a car was coming up the drive. A security monitor in the kitchen kicked on, and Carter recognized the car as theirs.

Shortly after Eliza's car, the second security guard drove behind them. He heard the front door open and voices.

Russell, the security guard who escorted Eliza more often than not, bid her good night in the hall. By the time she walked into the kitchen, the guard had slipped away. Carter never forgot they were there, but they did a great job of staying in the background.

"What smells so good?" Eliza asked as she walked into the room.

"That would be the spicy chicken pasta, light on the sauce."

Carter finished pouring the sparkling wine into a glass while she set her purse on the counter. "What's the occasion?" she asked as he handed her the tall flute and clicked it together with his.

"Do we need an occasion?" He gave her a brief kiss before she could answer. He liked this, the domestic bliss between them. He kissed her when he came home and before he left. They would text each other a few times during the day, and those small things felt perfectly right. There was nothing clingy about Eliza, nothing that pulled on his nerves. She'd adjusted to her new life better than he'd thought she would.

And that made him smile.

"The wine, the music…the food? If I didn't know better, I swear you were trying to get laid."

Carter slapped a hand to his chest. "I'm crushed."

Eliza sipped her wine. "Yeah, right. Sure! What's up?"

He pulled out a chair and encouraged her to sit. "You were at Sam's, right?"

"Uh-huh."

"Did Karen take the job?"

"She did. Oh, that's it." Understanding filled her features. She sat the glass down, reached over the table, and took his hand. "You worried about me quitting my job."

"I know you didn't want to."

"Dang, Carter, that's downright sweet of you. Where have you hidden all this charm?"

"In the closet…" *With your chewed-up shoes.* He glanced down at her feet and noticed her sensible heels. "Let me roll out some of that charm and help you relax." He reached down and slid them off her feet. He shot Zod a look before taking them to the mudroom in the back of the house and placing them on a top shelf.

Eliza wore a playful smile when he returned. "You put them up, right?"

"Always."

They talked a little about her day as Carter divided the meal onto their plates. Eliza drizzled dressing onto the salads, and within minutes, they were both eating.

"I need to learn how to make this," she said between bites.

"You know what would make it better?"

"Can it get any better?"

"Mushrooms." Carter filled his mouth and savored the garlic white sauce and a chunk of grilled chicken.

"Now, that sounds perfect. Not a lot of mushrooms, just a few. Maybe I should ask the chef to add them."

"Chefs can be more temperamental than a basketball player after a foul is called. Next time we order out, we can add them ourselves."

Eliza pointed at him with her fork. "Now you're thinking."

"So how are you…really?" There wasn't a hint of sadness in her face, but he needed to ask.

"I'm OK. I thought it would be harder than it was."

Either she was an Oscar-worthy actress, or she really wasn't upset. If it weren't for the constant flow of letters arriving daily, Carter thought she would have a bigger issue.

He wanted to point out that she didn't have to worry about money, that he would take care of her. Somehow she probably wouldn't see that the way he did.

"Excuse me." Russell interrupted their conversation with an uncharacteristic visit to the kitchen. "I'm sorry to bother you."

The man glanced at Zod and walked into the room. "We know you want to be alerted to anything out of the ordinary we catch on the monitors."

Eliza stopped chewing her food and slowly placed her fork on her plate.

"What was it?"

"Probably nothing. Shortly after we left this afternoon, Zod bolted out of his door barking. The cameras didn't pick up anything. Could have been an animal, or anything. The off-site surveillance team didn't warrant a drive-by, but I thought it better to tell you."

Eliza's smile fell. So much for their quiet dinner.

"Pete and I searched the yard. There's no evidence of anything out of place."

"How long did Zod bark?" Eliza asked.

"Not long. The motion detectors caught him searching the bushes in the side yard before he moved on. He barked a couple more times and then returned to the house."

Carter thanked the man, and Russell walked away.

"Trained police dogs don't bark at neighborhood cats," Eliza told him when they were alone.

That didn't sound good.

She moved food around her plate a couple times and gave up. "I need to see the video."

He shoved his chair back and followed her up the stairs.

They invaded the small security room where Russell took watch. Pete followed behind them.

Russell moved the control on the computer. They all watched Zod sense something and run out the dog door. The leather flap on the small opening had a magnetic key lock attached to Zod's collar. Only he could open the thing, or a criminal would have to pry the collar off the deadly dog's neck to gain access. That wasn't likely.

Even though Carter had expected it, Zod's obsessive barking on the screen brought a wave of panic over him.

"The stationary camera catches him here, and then the sensory camera turns on and catches him here." Russell pointed out each camera angle.

Zod scurried into the bushes and the barking stopped. When he emerged, he held something in his teeth.

"What's that?"

Russell sent them a wry smile. "One of Mrs. Billings's shoes, I'm afraid."

Carter peered closer. Sure enough, the shoe he'd tossed in the trash sat happily between Zod's teeth.

"Most dogs bury bones," Eliza murmured.

"Maybe he thought someone had found his hiding place."

Eliza shook her head and turned for the door. "I knew he wouldn't have run after a cat. Unless the cat found a hidden shoe, then maybe. Damn dog."

Carter patted Russell's back and walked with Eliza back to the kitchen.

Zod met them at the door and cocked his head to the side before giving a happy bark.

"Bad dog."

Zod's eyebrows shot up, and he looked between the two of them. Damn dog looked like he wanted a Scooby snack or some damn thing.

Harry hadn't made it to jail because he was a stupid man. In fact, his intelligence had paved his way to the big house with other people's money. There was one thing that Harry wasn't. Violent. He'd taken a few hits when he first arrived at the state penitentiary, but that had been years ago and the pain long forgotten.

At Blake's request, he'd quietly ripped up every newspaper clipping, every picture, and flushed them down the toilet. He kept only one. A snapshot of his life when it was whole. His wife and daughters sat beside him on a yacht he once owned, they smiled for the camera, and he stood there wearing a pompous smile.

Everyone in the jail became a suspect. Whom had Blake warned him about? It wasn't until Harry was told he had a phone call that he knew the name of the man. The caller didn't identify himself, and his voice wasn't familiar. Betting man that he was, Harry would put money on the voice being disguised. His words, however, were clear as ever.

"Ricardo Sanchez," the caller said. Followed quickly by, "Solitary."

Harry couldn't decide if the caller was making a request or sending a warning. For two days, Harry watched. He quickly determined that more than one set of eyes followed his burly roommate around.

"How you doing, Harry?" one of the block guards asked in passing.

"Fine, fine." Harry's gaze found its way across the communal area to where Sanchez stood alongside his "friends."

"You let me know if you have any trouble."

As if. The code of prison conduct was to take care of trouble on your own. Telling the guards would land you in the hospital ward or worse. Eventually, the inmates who'd put you there would return from solitary.

Harry swallowed hard and realized he was staring at Sanchez when the man turned his way and scowled back.

Thoughts circled in Harry's mind. Sadly, every one of them had him bloody and broken.

"Come with me."

They'd been over this before. "You have work to do. And I'm meeting with Agent Anderson tomorrow." Agent Anderson was the FBI liaison working with marshals and occasional detectives like Dean and Jim in regard to the Witness Protection Program in the State of California. Fewer and fewer people were coming forward to turn in hardened criminals because of the reach so many criminals had from prison. Eliza found sanity in her cause to make the system better. To keep witnesses protected while giving them their lives back became her mantra.

Carter had been at Eliza's side every night since Zod's little scare session in the yard. The fact that he wanted to force her to go on his trip to Northern California proved he wasn't ready to let loose his hold. The attention was nice at first. But his constant surveillance was interfering with his campaign.

"Postpone it."

Eliza cocked her head to the side and sent him a wry look. "No. Please, Carter, this has to stop."

"What has to stop?" He feigned innocence with his sad eyes and tousled hair, but she wasn't fooled.

"Please. You know what I'm talking about. You're neglecting your campaign. People depend on you. You can't let them down because you're worried about me."

"But—"

"No buts. We got married to provide me with protection. You've done that. If I thought for a minute you were going to neglect your own life for mine, I wouldn't have said yes."

Although she knew her words were true about her past, she neglected to tell Carter how much she loved her life with him. How much she loved him. Even with his concern and suffocating hold, she wouldn't change their marriage for the world. Telling him her feelings now might make him hold tighter. And if there was one thing Eliza didn't want to be responsible for, it was Carter's career taking a dive. He was a born ruler, and she very much wanted him to achieve his goals. Even if that meant keeping some of her deeper feelings to herself. At least for now. Besides, it wasn't as if Carter was free with words of love and forever. Perhaps she'd feel differently if he were.

"Are you saying you *only* married me for my protection?"

Oh, damn. He actually looked hurt.

"Your skills in bed don't suck," she teased, attempting to bring a smile to his lips.

"You didn't know about those skills when you said 'I do.'"

"Your lip-locks made my knees buckle, Hollywood. I knew."

He smiled then, reached out, and grabbed her around the waist. She settled between his thighs as he leaned against the counter in the kitchen. "Buckle, huh?"

Eliza rolled her eyes with as much drama as she could. "I knew you'd run with that."

He kissed her then, until her heart sped and her knees went weak.

They drew apart, breathless. "Are you sure?" he asked one more time.

"I'm sure."

Later that night, although Eliza decided she'd never admit it, sleeping in their big bed all alone was impossible. Apparently, her husband wasn't the only needy one in their relationship.

Agent Anderson was a petite woman in her midforties. She talked a hundred miles an hour, but when she listened, you knew everything was being downloaded and stored for later use.

Eliza felt a genuine compassion from the woman when they spoke on the phone. Face-to-face, that feeling grew. Thirty minutes into their meeting, Eliza stopped talking about her case and about the letters, and pushed forward with solutions. "We agree things need to change."

"Yes. With government funding, or the lack of funds driving many of the decisions we make, I'm not sure how to work toward making the system better."

"Sometimes the easiest answers are right in front of us. If the criminals have committed a crime so heinous that they're a threat to those who testify, why not sever their ability to contact the outside world entirely? Why segregate the good guy and let the bad guy hold all the rights?"

Anderson shook her head. "There are more inmate rights groups than witness protection rights groups."

"Maybe that's the problem. It costs the state, the Feds, a hell of a lot of money setting up long-term protection."

"Actually, the short term is where the money is spent. If your parents had survived, they would have been dropped from the system within a few years. You stayed in the system because of your parents. That, and I think Dean has a soft spot for you. But you're right—the criminals hold too many rights in these cases. The only way to change that is to rally witnesses, their families. Changing the law takes time."

"Time well spent, if you ask me."

"You have a friend in me, Mrs. Billings. You have people talking in Washington, and that's a start. It doesn't hurt that you're now family to a senator."

Eliza lifted her eyebrows. "I'm not sure how much help he'll be."

Agent Anderson waved a hand in the air. "I find that the power behind movements of people lie in the wives and husbands. Most political wives don't hold down day jobs, which affords them the time to lobby for change."

Where had she heard that before? Maybe a phone call to Sally, Max's wife, was in order. Sally had to have connections. Years of them.

"If you were me, Agent Anderson, where would you start?"

"You have a gaggle of letters. Those people will be your army. Find your leaders among them, and put them to work. The ultimate goal of law enforcement is to encourage witnesses to come forward. Good Samaritans don't want to be victims, however. Placing a proverbial red target on one's back is the number one reason people stay silent. We need to remove that threat."

"Isolate the prisoner. Keep him from contacting the outside world."

Anderson shrugged. "For every rule, there is an exception. Maybe you can lobby for change there. I don't have the answers. For every step forward you make, there will be three back. I hope you're ready for that."

Eliza glanced at the stack of mail she'd brought with her. It would take an army of victims, of families. But it was the right thing to do. She thought of her father's words: *Do what's right, pumpkin, and you'll always sleep well.*

She stood and placed her palm out for the other woman to shake. "Looks like I have some work to do." That work would require help from her husband and his family.

Before Eliza committed herself to a cause that would involve hundreds, if not thousands, of other people, she needed to know her own life was secure. She twirled the chunk of diamond around her ring finger and smiled.

Please don't let me be wrong about Carter's intentions.

"What's that noise?" Carter asked while on the phone with Eliza. He had one more night away from home, and then he'd be tucked in bed with his wife. He couldn't wait.

"I'm at the back door waiting for this dog to do his thing, and the wind is blowing."

"Our pilot said something about Santa Ana winds." The hot wind that blew off the desert often reached tornado strength and was responsible for devastating fires throughout Southern California. They also delayed flights of smaller aircraft.

"For once, the weatherman was right." The wind beyond Eliza's voice shut off. "I hope you're done for the night, furry beast."

"Please tell me you're talking to the dog."

"I am. So when will you be home tomorrow?"

Carter stretched out on the hotel room sofa and kicked his feet up on the table. "I have that luncheon, and then I'll be outta here."

"By dinner, then?"

Carter smiled into the phone. "You sound excited to see me."

"Need to feed your ego much?"

His grin grew wider. "I missed you too."

There was a pause on the phone, and for a minute, he thought the line had gone dead.

"Call me from the airport," she said. "I'll order our pasta and chill the wine."

Our pasta from our place.

God, he loved this woman.

"Oh, damn."

"What is it?"

"The power went out." Her phone made a clicking noise. "And my cell is nearly dead."

Power outages in Southern California were rare. Outside of fallen trees and earthquakes, the power company didn't have to deal with many weather-related issues. "I'm sure it will kick on soon. Russell has a backup phone, and the alarm system will run for a few hours on battery backup. There's a flashlight in the pantry on the wall and another in my nightstand by the bed."

He heard Zod bark a couple of times.

"Oh, you big baby. How you ever passed police training is beyond me," he heard Eliza say. "Where do you keep the candles?"

"I only have the long ones we use on the dinner table. You sure you're OK?" The thought of her stumbling around in the dark made him itch. "I can call Blake, have you go there."

"It's just a power outage. I'm fine. Hey, Russell."

Carter listened to Eliza and Russell talking about candles, and reassured himself that she had protection in his absence. The phone beeped in his ear.

"I better go before the call drops. I'll see you tomorrow," she said.

He looked forward to it. "Sleep well."

"Dream of me."

Oh, he would.

Chapter Twenty-Six

According to the battery-operated scanner on Russell's desk, the power outage was due to a transformer blown a few blocks from the house. The battery backup ran low, and it appeared that they would be in the dark for a while. Pete, the second guard, said, "I'm not comfortable without another form of backup. If the batteries die, we're blind, surveillance is down, and we're screwed. I'm going by the office to pick up another unit before this one goes down."

Zod's special doggy door automatically stopped working in the event of a power outage, which put Eliza on alert for the dog's needs. She didn't mind. The eerie wind and dry air made her itch. She considered attempting to weed through the stack of letters to find the most articulate people to lead others, but concentrating on her work was difficult in the silent house. Strange how she'd become used to the hum of the refrigerator or the sound of one of the guards' radios upstairs.

The soft glow of the candle flickering off the walls of her bedroom blanketed the room with warmth.

She missed her husband. Power outages and candlelight would prove more romantic with her husband by her side instead of the dog. She made certain the door was open a crack so Zod could move about before curling up on her side of the bed with the second book in a series she'd been awaiting for months. She hoped the author hadn't been in the mood to write a passionate love scene within the first few pages. That would suck on this lonely, dark night.

Five minutes before the final bell tolled, signaling all inmates to return to their cells, Harry sat with his back against the wall pretending to read a book. One of the other inmates, Michael—or maybe it was Mitchell—hesitated as he walked by. He stopped long enough to make eye contact with Harry, dropped a piece of paper on the floor, and then walked away.

Harry bent down and retrieved the paper, hiding it between the pages of his book to open it. He glanced up several times, certain that someone was watching him.

On the wrinkled paper was a note: HE CALLED A HIT. HOPE YOUR KID ISN'T CAUGHT IN THE CROSS FIRE.

Everything inside Harry froze.

He'd waited too long.

The soothing sound of the heater turning on and off in the room finally filled Carter's noisy brain. He must have drifted off to sleep only moments before the shattering ring of the hotel phone shot him out of bed like lightning through a turbulent sky. Still, it took until the third ring for his mind to fully engage.

"Hello?"

"Carter?" It was his dad.

"Hey." He sat up in bed and turned on the bedside light. "Is everything OK?"

"Were you sleeping?"

Carter glanced at the glow of his cell phone clock—11:23. Yep, he was sleeping. "Not anymore. What's up?"

Cash hesitated.

Warning bells went off inside Carter's head.

"Dad?"

"I just heard from an old friend at San Quentin."

Eliza!

"What happened?"

"There was a disturbance tonight. Some information leaked out."

"What information, Dad?" Carter was wide awake now and kicking off the covers.

"My sources came across a note claiming Sanchez called out a hit. There weren't any names on the paper, but I have to assume he meant Eliza."

The air inside Carter's lungs escaped, and he grew dizzy. He knew the possibility of Sanchez making that call was there. Hearing it confirmed brought a sandpaper blanket of prickly dread over him. "How long ago was this?"

"An hour, maybe more."

Carter stretched the limits of the phone cord and retrieved his pants, yanked them on. "Did you call Eliza?"

"The line wasn't working. The power's out over half the city."

"Hold on." Carter unplugged his cell and dialed Eliza's cell. It went straight to voice mail.

"I've got to go."

"I'm on the first flight out," his father said.

"Yeah…OK."

No more words were necessary, and Cash hung up.

Carter called Blake's home number and met with a busy signal. The next call was to his pilot.

Thank God he'd bought the damn plane.

The door to Eliza's room slammed shut and jolted her out of her sleep.

Zod darted to his feet and whined.

The wind outside rattled the frame of the house—not a small feat considering the size of it. *Must be a window open somewhere.*

Eliza pushed off the covers and padded barefoot into the bathroom. She attempted the light switch, but nothing happened. Luckily, the glow from the nearly full moon illuminated the window, casting light inside.

Sure enough, the bathroom window was open by an inch. Just enough to make the bedroom door slam.

Eliza turned, nearly stumbling over Zod, who followed silently behind her.

She walked to the east window, made sure it was shut, and then walked to the north window and checked that one too.

Her eyes caught something moving in the backyard. One of the glass tables teetered on the edge of the swimming pool.

"Oh, man," she whispered. Shattered glass inside a body of water would be a nightmare to clean up.

With a flashlight in hand, Eliza donned her bathrobe and called Zod to her side. She passed her purse sitting on her dresser and quickly tucked her gun in the pocket of her bathrobe.

"Might as well let you out to pee while we're out there," she murmured to the dog. She walked by the security room down the hall from hers and poked her head in. "I'm taking Zod outside."

"Want me to do it?"

"No, I got it."

Russell pushed out of his chair to go with her.

"I can manage," she told him.

"The power's out, the wind is blowing, and the battery backup died twenty minutes ago. Pete isn't outside walking the yard. With all respect, Mrs. Billings, I'm going with you."

"Well, when you put it like that," she said with a little laugh. "Bring some muscles with you. The yard furniture is making its way into the pool."

Russell had to push against the back door to open it. The chimes that normally rang when the door opened didn't sound. She hoped the power company could get the juice back on soon. She'd grown used to all the security measures of late. Not having them left her feeling naked in some strange way. It didn't help that her husband was hundreds of miles away. Strange how quickly Carter had wriggled under her skin.

Zod braved the wind, and Eliza made sure the back door wasn't locking behind them when she closed it.

The wind was a typical warm Santa Ana. Her hair flew in all directions as she cast her light on the patio furniture in the yard. Sure enough, one of the glass side tables tipped close to the water's edge. She sat the flashlight on the ground and said, "Take the other side, and let's move it close to the house." After moving it safely beside the house, she retrieved one of the chairs, and Russell followed her lead with the others. *No use fishing anything out in the morning.*

Zod barked from behind them, his growl carried off by the wind. Then his bark changed, and the hair on Eliza's neck stood on end.

Oh God.

Zod's bark grew vicious.

"Get down!" Russell dropped the chair in his hand as he yelled.

Before Eliza could turn around and call a command, a flash of light and the sound of a gunshot filled the night.

"I need you to go get Eliza. Take her back to your house. Anything." Carter's words were as frantic as his stomach. He barked orders at Blake as if he had the right to.

"What's going on?"

"I heard from my dad. Sanchez called out a hit on Eliza." Carter was already in the air before he'd managed to connect with Blake via cell phone. "The power is off at the house, and I can't get ahold of anyone there. I called Dean. He's on his way there now."

"Son of a bitch. We're not there, Carter. Sam and I are headed toward you."

"You're what?"

"It's Harris. There was a fight. They rushed him to San Francisco General for surgery."

Carter clutched his fists as frustration filled his every cell.

"What about Neil?"

"He's with Eddie. Gwen's on her way to the house. I'll ask Neil to go get Eliza."

"Please." Carter would beg if he had to. "Jesus, Blake. It's all going to shit."

"Deep breath. You don't know if anything is wrong."

Yes, he did. Deep in his bones, he knew something wasn't right.

Zod tore into the shadows as Eliza grabbed her left arm and fell to the ground. Heat and searing pain followed warm, sticky blood oozing between her fingers.

A female scream lifted in the wind when Zod stopped barking and started growling.

Russell rushed to her side with his gun drawn. One look at her and he shielded her with his body and shoved her into the safety of the house.

Outside, the frantic screams of a woman yelled for Zod to stop.

Light-headed from the wound in her arm, Eliza removed her gun and turned off the safety.

"Go," Eliza told Russell. "Don't let them get away."

Russell swore under his breath, clearly torn with the decision to leave her side.

"I'll shoot anyone who walks through that door other than you."

Russell nodded and slid into the dark.

She curled up behind the center island and waited for Russell to return.

Her heart pounded in her chest as the reality that she'd just been shot washed through her.

She started to tremble and couldn't control the fear that followed. "Carter."

The wind settled long enough for the plane to land.

He broke every speeding law en route to his home, and as he rounded the corner of their street, his worst nightmare unfolded before his eyes.

Red-and-white flashing lights illuminated the night. Emergency vehicles filled the street and his driveway. The only thing missing was the coroner's van. *Eliza!*

He jumped from his car, engine still running, and barreled through the uniformed policemen on scene. "Eliza!"

"You can't go in there."

Carter shoved at the cop. "It's my house. My wife." Someone grabbed his arms and started to wrestle with him.

"Let him in."

The arms holding him let go, and Carter ran toward Dean. "Where is she?"

Dean glanced toward the gurney being wheeled from the house. "Oh, God."

He stumbled toward the paramedics and heard his name.

"Carter?"

Eliza? She can talk?

"Carter, it's OK. I'm OK."

Even with the light of the moon, he could see how pale she was, how frail. She lifted a hand with an intravenous tube running into it.

"Where are you hurt? How bad is it?"

Another gurney emerged from the house, this one bearing another woman Carter didn't recognize. *What the hell?* "What happened?"

"Sir, we need to get her to the hospital." The twentysomething paramedic pushed ahead toward the back of the waiting ambulance.

"I'm her husband. I'm coming with her."

The medic nodded. "You can ride in the back, but you need to give me room to work."

They loaded her into the van, and before the medic could shut the door behind them, Russell appeared. "The police have questions," he told Carter. "I'll be at the hospital as soon as they're done."

Carter glared at the man who had failed to keep his wife safe. He didn't trust himself to speak, so Carter gave one curt nod and then focused his attention on his wife.

The bright lights of the ambulance added a little color to her face. She forged a smile but winced when the van started to move.

"Hey, watch it," Carter yelled at the driver.

The medic frowned and turned to Eliza. "It's bumpy back here. We'll be at the hospital in ten minutes."

"It's only a flesh wound, Carter. I'm OK."

"Flesh wound?" His eyes scanned her torso and found a blood-soaked bandage on her left arm.

"The bullet went through. Nothing to worry about, right?" Eliza asked the medic.

"Bullet?"

"She was shot in the arm, Mr. Billings. The ER will take some X-rays, clean her up…She'll probably be able to go home tonight." The medic adjusted the IV as he spoke.

Some relief eased into Carter's bloodstream, but until Eliza was given a blessing from a doctor, he would hold his breath.

"What happened?"

"The wind blew the furniture around in the backyard. We went out to push it against the house. Zod started barking, and the next thing I knew, I was on the ground with this." Eliza glanced at her arm. "Russell tried to shield me, but the bullet traveled faster than he could run."

"A woman shot you?"

"It appears that way. Wait, how did you get here so fast?"

"I was told you were in danger. I tried calling…"

"The power was out."

He kissed the tip of her cold fingers. He had so much to say, so many more questions to ask. He tried to hide the tremor in his hand, but knew she felt him shaking. She'd been shot. His wife, the woman he'd sworn to protect, was lying on a gurney in pain, and he couldn't make that right.

A nurse and a doctor met them at the back door of the emergency room. Carter was whisked off to sign papers and check in Eliza. Less than ten minutes later, he was at her side while the doctor examined the hole in her arm.

He wasn't one of those people who melted when he saw blood, but when the doctor probed Eliza's arm, he felt light-headed and ill.

"An X-ray will let us know if the bullet hit bone. How bad is the pain?" Dr. Solomon asked.

"I've felt better." Eliza attempted a joke.

"I'll have the nurse bring you something. You're not allergic to anything?"

"No."

Carter sat to the side of her gurney and squeezed her good hand.

"She's going to be OK?" he asked the doctor.

"Your wife will be fine." Dr. Solomon left with the chart in his hand. Outside the door, several uniformed police were talking with the staff. He remembered the shooter on the gurney at the house.

"You're squeezing too tight," Eliza said.

Carter released her hand instantly. "I'm sorry." He offered a pained smile. "I'll go see what's taking that nurse so long with your pain meds."

"The doctor just left," Eliza said.

"I'll be right back."

He closed the door behind him and motioned to one of the cops. The officer broke off his conversation and addressed Carter.

"Do you know who I am?"

"Billings, right?"

"Right." Carter glanced around the department, wondering in what bed they'd placed the woman who'd attempted to murder his wife. He clenched his fists and sucked in a deep breath. "The person who shot my wife…She's here?"

The officer stepped in front of Carter and blocked his view. "Let us do our investigation. We don't want any trouble."

Carter shook off his retort. "A professional hit was put out on my wife tonight. Make sure your investigation checks that out. I want someone at this door."

The officer glanced over his shoulder to his partner. The other officer asked one of the nurses for a chair.

Once the officer stood guard at the door, Carter asked, "Where's Detective Brown?"

"He's on his way."

Carter nodded and followed the nurse back to Eliza's side.

Eliza forced a smile to her lips when Carter returned. She hoped the nurse had brought some happy juice of some kind. The pain in her arm was getting worse, not better.

Every time he opened his mouth to talk, he lowered his voice and spoke in calm, even strokes. His tone kept her calm, despite his shaking hands.

"I'm giving you morphine and something for nausea. You'll feel better in a few seconds." The nurse used the IV to administer the drug, and Eliza quickly felt the effects. Her limbs felt heavy, and the pain started to float away.

"Better?" the nurse asked.

The burning pain muted. "Much."

"X-ray should be here soon." The nurse left them alone in the room.

She needed to get her mind off what was happening. "Tell me again why you came home early?"

"Now's not the time."

"C'mon, Carter. No secrets."

He tilted his head to the side and gave her his Hollywood smile. "The medication is working?"

"It is. And you're changing the subject."

Carter ran a hand over her face and pushed a lock of her hair behind her ear. She attempted to sit up farther in the bed and shake some of the fog the medication produced in her brain.

"Not now."

"Carter…Someone shot me tonight. You keeping secrets is gonna piss me off."

The expression on his face told her he didn't like being put in a corner. "My dad called me. He heard from someone about a hit. I panicked when I couldn't get ahold of you."

The medication numbed the effect of his words. Still, something didn't feel right. "The woman who shot me was at point-blank range. If she was a professional, she sucked."

Carter released a nervous laugh. "You're joking. You were shot tonight, and you're joking."

Eliza lifted her bloody arm, surprised it didn't hurt. "Flesh wound." A warm trickle ran down her arm.

"Stop moving it. You're making it bleed again." Carter moved to the other side of the gurney and placed fresh gauze to her arm.

"My hero." He certainly was more gorgeous than any of the doctors who'd come in to help.

"A hero wouldn't have let anyone get close enough to hurt you."

Eliza opened her eyes, not aware that they had closed. "You couldn't have known. Don't blame yourself."

The door to the exam room opened and Dean walked in. Eliza remembered seeing him briefly before Carter arrived at the house. "Hey."

Dean winked. "How's the patient?"

"They have good drugs here. I don't know why people go to the street looking for them."

"She's feeling better," Carter said for her.

"I am."

"Your man Russell is outside. I told my uniform he could go."

"Tell me the shooter is dead," Carter said.

Eliza heard the venom in her husband's voice.

"Have a seat, Counselor."

Carter took Dean's advice and started asking rapid-fire questions. "Do we know who she is? Was she working for Sanchez?"

"We know who she is, and no, she doesn't know anything about Sanchez."

The drugs must be really working, because Eliza was having a hard time following the conversation.

"What?"

"Here is what I know. The shooter is Michelle Sedgwick. Name mean anything to you, Eliza?"

She shook her head. "Wait, Sedgwick?"

"Yeah. Sedgwick is a rich old guy dating one of your clients." Dean added air quotes around the word *clients*. "Miss Sedgwick is a misguided rich girl, but she isn't a hit man. She told us she was looking for her cell phone in your yard."

"Why was her phone in our yard?" Carter asked.

"She dropped it there last week. Apparently, she and her siblings decided to spy on you after her grandfather started seeing a younger woman. They thought if they could find some way to blackmail you, you'd stop their grandfather from marrying the woman you set him up with."

"Blackmail me? With what?"

"They didn't think that far. And obviously their time at the university was spent drinking instead of going to class for an education. Michelle doesn't know anything about you outside of Alliance."

"Bullshit. I don't believe it. Why did she have a gun?"

"Zod. Apparently, she lost the phone when Zod found her in the bushes. She tossed her shoe at him and ran."

Eliza remembered the week prior when Russell had shown them the tapes of Zod barking in the yard. Eliza didn't question the chewed-up shoe. Carter told her he'd tossed in the trash, and she assumed he'd tossed both of them.

"She told us she had a gun to scare the dog and get her phone and run. I've questioned her, and I think she's telling the truth."

"Why would she risk coming back at all if she knew an attack dog was there? That doesn't make sense."

"She said something about her grandfather announcing his engagement, and how if anyone did anything remotely scandalous, he'd remove them from his will. If her phone was found in your yard…"

Carter growled, "She still shot my wife. Could have killed her."

"That isn't being disputed. She admitted squeezing the trigger. She said she pointed it at the dog. Not that it matters."

"Sedgwick said his kids were clueless, spoiled rotten. I assumed his grandchildren were younger."

"Just out of college, apparently."

How sad. "How bad is she hurt?"

"Zod took a couple bites out of her legs. He doesn't alter his attack for sneakers, apparently."

Eliza felt a smile tug at her lips. "Is Zod OK? He wasn't shot, was he?"

"No. Zod's fine."

"If she's not the hit man, then someone is still out there," Carter pointed out.

Eliza didn't want to think about that.

"Why do you say that?" Dean asked Carter.

Carter told him about the call from his dad, about the hit.

"That's odd."

"Why?"

"Earlier tonight, Mrs. Sanchez talked with me from a station in San Francisco. Apparently, her husband directed her to give orders for a hit. Instead, she went to the cops, asked for their protection, and turned her husband in."

"What? Why?"

"Your statement to the press humbled her, the way you protected her children at your expense. Between Mrs. Sanchez's testimony and the brawl in the prison tonight, Sanchez is going to be in a very dark hole for a very long time. He won't fart without me knowing about it. He's virtually cut off from the world."

"Did she tell anyone else about her husband's request?"

Dean shook his head. "Not that I know of."

"Someone heard something at the prison, spread the news to my father," Carter said.

"Could have been one of the guards listening in, reading between the lines." Dean glanced at the two of them. "Sanchez spoke exclusively with his wife. But you can bet I'll find every person Sanchez has spoken to in the past six months. James is on his way north now. We'll know soon if the threats are behind you."

Maybe it was the drugs, or maybe this was what *hope* felt like. But could it be that hiding and looking over her shoulder was over?

"It's over?"

"Let's wait and see how all the pieces land, but it looks that way to me, Lisa."

Dean's use of her first name made her skin tingle.

Please let it be over.

Two hours later, Carter drove her home at a pace slower than a snail.

It was nearly dawn when he carried her to their room. Once there, he helped her into a pair of clean pajamas and tucked her into bed. "Do you have everything you need?"

"Yes, Nurse Carter," she teased.

He grinned and then bit his lower lip. Moisture gathered behind his eyes in an unexpected wave of emotion.

"Hey." Seeing him tear up made her heart flip in her chest and her eyes well.

"I thought I was going to lose you. I came around the corner, saw the police..." He dropped his head in her lap, and she heard him sniffle. She'd never seen him cry.

She smoothed the back of his head with her hand, calming him. "I'm not dead—nowhere close."

"I love you. I thought you were dead, and I hadn't told you how much I love you."

Tears did start to fall down her cheeks.

When he lifted his head to look at her, she cradled his face in her palm. "I love you too."

He kissed her palm, and she swiped away a tear ready to drip off his jaw.

"Don't ever leave me," he pleaded.

Her heart swelled in her chest as everything she ever wanted to hear spilled from his lips. "Husband and wife forever?"

"Forever might not be long enough." His blue eyes danced with hope.

"Forever is all I have, Hollywood."

Careful with her arm, he kissed her then. She sighed into his touch and knew everything would work out for the two of them. "Forever it is."

Samantha sat beside her father's bed and dozed off. The cold, stale coffee didn't work, and the steady beep of the machines lulled her to sleep. Blake had left the room to call home, and a police escort sat outside the room keeping watch.

She hadn't seen her father in years, not since his incarceration. Her emotions were all over the place. Equal parts hate and love entered her heart when she thought of him—of all he'd done to their family. But seeing him near death did one thing life never could. It brought forgiveness.

If he could wake long enough to hear her forgive him, maybe he could find some peace. According to the guards on duty at the jail, her father and Sanchez had fought. Her father wasn't a violent man, and she couldn't imagine what had provoked it.

Sanchez had a knife—a homemade one, which inmates often assembled inside prison walls.

Her father had suffered a dozen stab wounds to his torso, and one had nicked a major vessel below his heart. He died twice in surgery as the surgeons attempted to repair the damage. Harris survived. And according to the doctors, he might just make it if he could manage through the next twenty-four hours. Well, eighteen at last count.

Something squeezed her hand, and Sam bolted awake. "Dad?"

He squeezed it again, and she bit her lip as new tears welled.

"Dad?"

Harris blinked a few times, and the monitors above him started to speed up.

"Samantha?" he managed to ask.

"Shhh. You had surgery. You're in the hospital." Never mind he hadn't seen her in years. Never mind he wasn't in a jail cell at the moment.

His gaze met hers, and his mouth gaped open. "Sammy."

Samantha brushed tears away with the back of her hand and smiled. "I'm here, Dad."

"I'm sorry, s-so sorry."

"I know."

His eyes drifted closed again. "I love you," he whispered.

She sobbed then and truly prayed he'd make it through. "I love you too, Daddy."

Dean cradled the phone to his ear and cemented his assumptions.

"I can't prove it, and I wouldn't work too hard at this point," Cash told him.

"Family loyalty?" Dean asked.

"I'm not loyal to my brother-in-law. If he was behind the rumors, there won't be anything traceable. He's not sloppy. Besides, the last time I checked the books, telling a bully someone is after him isn't against the law."

Dean had uncovered the truth behind the "hit" on Eliza. Harris had been given a note that Sanchez was after his daughter's friend and that Samantha's life was in danger. Apparently, the father gene hadn't skipped Samantha's father altogether, and he opted to engage Sanchez in a fight. Of course, Harry ended up in the ICU, and Sanchez ended up in solitary—but that had been the goal. Funny how when pushed to a wall, a parent would die to protect, or avenge, his child.

"Who else can reach inside a prison and never be detected?" Dean was sure Max was behind the rumors. His only concern now was what Max would want from Carter and Eliza in return.

"Sanchez is isolated, won't see daylight for years. And Eliza is safe. It's over, Detective."

Perhaps Max wanted to protect his family. Some people did change. Harris Elliot had.

Dean thought of his own daughter. Maybe it was time to fix his own home—long past time to fix his relationships.

Epilogue

Six Months Later

"What shall we toast?"

Eliza stood beside Carter in their living room surrounded by family and friends. Everyone gathered in support of Carter's efforts. "The new governor?"

"I haven't won yet." He kissed her nose.

The election results would be announced within twenty-four hours. The polls had Carter winning by fifteen percent. "Formalities, formalities."

"How about to six months of wedded bliss?"

"Aw, that's sweet, Carter," Gwen cooed from the other side of the room.

Eliza winked at Dean, who stood beside his daughter. They'd been estranged for some time, but Eliza had pushed the man until he called her—and promised to work on his relationship. Life was too short, and regrets cut it shorter.

"How about to family?"

Cash and Abigail lifted their glasses together.

Max stood beside his wife. There was no way the man wasn't going to be a part of Carter's success.

Samantha's father had survived his wounds and was transferred to a penitentiary closer to LA. She and Jordan visited him a few times and were working through their problems.

Sanchez was deep in solitary for the attempted murder of Harris and the hit he'd called out on Eliza. Because of the special circumstances regarding Eliza's case, his connections to the outside were limited to the guards handing him food through the steel door of his cell. Mrs. Sanchez had been relocated deep in Mexico, her testimony the final nail in his coffin.

Michelle Sedgwick's assault with a deadly weapon charge would be considered by a jury. No one believed she was capable of murder, but she would still do some jail time. Needless to say, Stanly had her cut out of his will, and at last check, Aunt Edie had scared away half the family. Some had even taken jobs.

The only unanswered questions were how Cash had known about the hit and how Harris had learned about Sanchez's conversation with his wife.

Eliza had her suspicions about Max. He hadn't been surprised by anything that unfolded after the shooting and never offered a word of concern. It was as if he knew about Sanchez's actions before he'd taken them.

"To family." Eliza lifted her glass and clinked it to Carter's. "To family."

She sipped her sparkling wine and kissed her husband. "I love you."

"I love you too."

Words didn't do the feeling justice. There were days Eliza wanted to pinch herself. Carter's support and love was a gift.

"Oh, by the way," Samantha announced after everyone had toasted, "Blake and I decided that this year we wanted to get married outside of the country. We're going to Aruba."

Eliza nearly groaned out loud. Her gaze shot to Gwen, who happened to be staring at Neil. "I get to pick the bridesmaid dresses."

Carter burst out laughing, nearly spilling his wine.

Neil shook a finger in Gwen's direction. "No honky-tonk bars."

Gwen scowled. "Do not be absurd. Aruba doesn't have honky-tonks."

Blake scowled watching the interaction between his sister and Neil.

Eliza shook her head. Gwen and Neil fought nearly as much as she and Carter had before they married. "Hmmm."

"What?" Carter asked close to her ear.

"I hear wedding bells."

"Sam and Blake are always getting married." He sat his glass down and put an arm over her shoulders.

Eliza peered at Neil over her glass. "I wasn't talking about Sam and Blake."

Carter honed his eyes in the direction of her gaze.

"Seriously?"

Oh, yeah. She knew what love was when she saw it. Eliza saw it every day in the eyes of her husband.

Coming in May 2013
Excerpt from

Fiancé by Friday

Book Three
The Weekday Bride Series

Chapter One

"I think I found you the perfect husband." Gwen Harrison bent her knee and slid her Louboutins from her feet before tossing them to the floor. *You would think shoes that cost nearly a thousand dollars would exempt them from hurting your feet.* Sadly, that wasn't the case.

"You think you found what?" Karen turned down the volume on the television set and twisted around on the sofa.

"A husband for you."

Gwen's words sparked Karen's full attention. The TV went dark and Karen patted the sofa beside her. "Come sit! Tell."

After placing her handbag on the hall table, Gwen turned the lock on the door and set the house alarm. "Let me get out of this dress first. The beading has rubbed my skin raw all night." She turned her back to Karen with a silent plea to unzip the evening gown.

Karen loosened the clasp and lowered the zipper, and then proceeded to follow Gwen up the stairs. "You can't drop the 'H' word and leave the room, Gwen. That's just mean."

Holding the front of the dress up with one hand and lifting the hem with the other, Gwen managed the stairs without tripping.

"The Wilson Charity dinner was filled with people. Lots of couples and plenty of those actor types running about." She stepped into her closet and let the gown slide from her shoulders. After hanging the dress, she grabbed a nightgown from her chest and walked back into her bedroom. "You know, Samantha said I would tire of these dinners, but I'm enjoying them. I've met so many interesting people since I moved here." Gwen had moved to the States six months ago. At thirty-one years old, she had lived a sheltered life on her family estate outside of London. She'd traveled the world, but always with a bodyguard or her mother.

Now that her brother was the duke in the family, the estate belonged to him. Not that Gwen couldn't live there, but his marriage to Samantha was as good as any excuse to move on with her life.

With Samantha taking on the duties of full-time wife, mother, and duchess, she didn't have time to run her business. Gwen had graciously stepped in to help run Alliance. Except Gwen didn't have a business skill to name as her own. However, living a titled life, she did understand how to brush elbows with the rich and famous, the very clients Alliance sought. Where Gwen was lacking, Karen excelled. Together they ran the business flawlessly.

"Getting back to the perfect husband…"

"He's very cute, tall…lovely man." Gwen sat on the edge of her bed and unclasped her garters one at a time.

"You do know that no one wears those anymore." Karen pointed to her lingerie.

"If that were true, finding a place to buy garters and stockings would be impossible."

"Yeah, but you need to go to those sexy bra stores," Karen teased.

"Men love frilly underwear."

"Lotta good that's doing you. Seems I'm the only one who sees it."

Gwen laughed and continued with her news. "His name is Wolfe...Michael Wolfe. You might have heard of him."

"The actor?" Karen asked.

"So you have heard of him."

Karen shook her head. "There is no way Michael Wolfe's looking for a temporary wife through an agency. He's like the hottest thing on the big screen right now."

"So he told me."

"He told you? You mean you didn't know?"

Gwen shrugged, removed her bra, and pulled her nightgown over her head. "When have you seen me go to the cinema? I'd enjoy a good book before watching a movie."

"But Michael Wolfe. He's a big name, Gwen."

Karen followed her into the bathroom, where Gwen ran hot water in the sink and proceeded to remove her makeup. "I don't know who he is. Perhaps if he played in a Bond film I'd know him."

Karen leaned against the frame of the door and watched Gwen through the mirror. "You're serious. Michael Wolfe?"

"Lovely man. Very funny."

"And sexy, and single, and rich...women fall all over him."

And that, Gwen thought, was the problem.

Gwen turned toward the commode and flushed it. While the noise of the toilet filled the room, she leaned into Karen and whispered. "I think he likes men."

Karen's eyes rounded. "Seriously?"

Gwen shushed her. The Tarzana home had undergone an extensive security system, including twenty-four-hour audio and video monitoring. Their friend and former Alliance employee Eliza Billings had lived in the house before she married. Carter, her husband, had insisted on the security measures for multiple reasons. Once Carter had won the gubernatorial race, and they both moved to Sacramento, the security system stayed in place at the insistence of Gwen's brother.

And Neil.

"You think he's gay?"

Gwen hushed her again and pointed toward the hall. There weren't any cameras in the bedrooms or bathrooms, but Gwen knew for a fact the hall was monitored. "Our clients deserve all the privacy they can get."

Karen rolled her eyes. "Good lord, Gwen, we parade around here half naked and you're worried about our *clients'* privacy? You know Neil; he wouldn't allow just anyone to listen to what goes on around here."

Just hearing Neil's name brought warmth to the pit of her stomach. The man was a force of nature with the ability to stand shoulder to shoulder with sixteenth-century Highland warriors. His hard lines and broad physique might threaten others, but for Gwen, all they'd ever done was invite her in.

Too bad Neil never opened the door.

"Privacy is paramount to our clients. Best we keep some details as hidden as possible, don't you agree?"

Karen rolled her eyes and they both descended the stairs.

"So if Michael is…*you know*, why is he talking with you? How did you approach him, anyway?"

Gwen made herself comfortable on the couch and settled in for a long talk. "He came to me. Seems the Alliance name has found its way into a few celebrity circles."

"That's good to know. Lotta deep pockets in Hollywood."

"Actors make the perfect clients. Especially if they want temporary." Alliance helped the elite and rich find life matches, many of whom wanted a temporary bride or groom and were willing to pay heavily for it. Beautiful women like Karen had no problem finding men, but some women weren't looking for love.

For reasons Gwen had yet to discover, Karen wanted a temporary match to set her up financially for years to come. When two people came together with the understanding that their relationship would end on an assigned date, everyone was happy.

"Michael has no problem convincing the world he's in love with every heroine he works with," Karen said. "What makes you think he's..."

"He didn't come right out and say it. Not yet, anyway. He introduced himself and was completely taken aback that I didn't know who he was."

"He's überfamous, Gwen."

"That may be. Anyway, he asked me how my brother's marriage was going. Strange question. I asked him if he knew Blake, to which he promptly said he did not. Michael went on to tell me that he and Blake shared a few acquaintances."

"His subtle way of saying he knew about Alliance."

"That's what I assumed. I asked him if he'd like to meet some of my friends. He winked, said he'd love to, and then handed me his card."

Karen lifted both hands facing up. "So what makes you think g—"

"Ah, just how he presented himself. Sometimes you just know these things." Michael had flirted with the women in the room and appreciated the men. Oh, he'd been subtle, but if there was one skill Gwen had perfected in the past few months, it was reading men and their intentions.

Men searching for someone...anyone...had a certain energy about them. Eliza had schooled Gwen for months about how to approach these men to help them learn about Alliance. There had been social events in which no contacts had been met. And others where Gwen was able to recruit men, and women, into their database.

"Michael Wolfe?" Karen tapped a finger to her chin.

"If he's looking for temporary, I think you'd be the perfect match."

"Oh? Why?"

"First, you're both beautiful people. The cameras would eat you up. Second, Michael's high profile would prove difficult for many women to maneuver without cracking, and you, my dear, never crack. Third, you have no illusions that a temporary marriage might mold into a loving relationship."

"All of our clients say that."

"Yet some keep. If Michael is, *you know*, then that won't be possible."

Karen shrugged and pushed off the couch. "I think I'll turn in early, see if any of his flicks are on pay-per-view."

Gwen wished Karen a good night and made her way into their kitchen. She placed a kettle on the stove and boiled water for tea. She took in the small space with its cottage feel and sighed. When the day came that Alliance did find a groom for Karen, she'd move away and Gwen would once again be living alone.

Acknowledgments

As always, to my critique partner, Sandra; my editor, Maureen; and my amazing cover artist, Crystal. Without you ladies, my job would be so much harder.

Special thanks to Elaine McDonald and the lovely photographs she provided for my cover art.

To Duane, for all the advice on police dogs and their bizarre behavior.

To my Facebook, Goodreads, and Twitter fans and friends—you guys rock! You've been there giving me cyber high fives and kudos along my journey and have kept me going when I was riddled with self-doubt.

About the Author

Photo by Lindsey Meyer, 2012

New York Times bestselling author Catherine Bybee was raised in Washington State, but after graduating high school, she moved to Southern California in hopes of becoming a movie star. After growing bored with waiting tables, she returned to school and became a registered nurse, spending most of her career in urban emergency rooms. She now writes full-time and has penned the novels *Not Quite Dating* and *Wife by Wednesday*. Bybee lives with her husband and two teenage sons in Southern California.